STARTERS

ALSO BY LISSA PRICE

Enders

LISSA PRICE

STARTERS

EMBER

All rights reserved. Published in the United States by Ember, an imprint of Random House Children's Books, a division of Random House, Inc., New York. Originally published in hardcover in the United States by Delacorte Press, an imprint of Random House Children's Books, New York, in 2012.

Ember and the E colophon are registered trademarks of Random House, Inc.

randomhouse.com/teens

Educators and librarians, for a variety of teaching tools, visit us at RHTeachersLibrarians.com

The Library of Congress has cataloged the hardcover edition of this work as follows:
Price, Lissa.
Starters / Lissa Price. — 1st ed.
p. cm.
Summary: To support herself and her younger brother in a future Beverly Hills, sixteen-year-old Callie hires her body out to seniors who want to experience being young again, and she lives a fairy-tale life until she learns that her body will commit murder, unless her mind can stop it.
ISBN 978-0-385-74237-5 (hardcover) — ISBN 978-0-375-99060-1 (glb) —
ISBN 978-0-307-97523-2 (ebook)
[1. Science fiction. 2. Brothers and sisters—Fiction. 3. Orphans—Fiction.] I. Title.
PZ7.P9312St 2012
[Fic]—dc23
2011040820

ISBN 978-0-375-97310-9

RL: 5.0

Printed in the United States of America

10 9 8 7 6 5 4 3 2 1

First Ember Edition 2013

For Dennis,
who always believed

ACKNOWLEDGMENTS

If this were an awards show, the orchestra would probably have to play me offstage because I have so many people to thank.

First and foremost, the person who made it all happen, Barbara Poelle, knew exactly how to sell this book in six days (that included a holiday weekend). Don't be fooled by the fact that she is beautiful, because she is a brilliant agent. I'm grateful fate put us together.

Barbara found me the perfect editor in the wonderful Wendy Loggia. Her notes and support made this a better book, and she did all this with the sweetest demeanor, always keeping it fun. Thank you, Wendy. I am deeply grateful to everyone at Random House from the very top: Chip Gibson, the charming jokester, and Beverly Horowitz, the writers' fairy godmother (if fairies were wise and savvy about publishing); John Adamo, Judith Haut, Noreen Herits, Casey Lloyd, Adrienne Waintraub, and Tracy Lerner; Linda Leonard, Sonia Nash, and Mike Herrod in new media; Joan DeMayo and everyone in the sales group; Melissa Greenberg and the art department; Rachel Feld, who made my BEA visit especially sweet; and Enid Chaban, who first emailed everyone at Random House when the offices were closed due to a move and a holiday and said they had to read this book. And to Ruth Knowles and everyone at Random House UK, as well, especially Bob Lea, the incredibly gifted artist who captured Callie's spirit on the cover.

Thanks to my foreign rights agents, Heather and Danny Baror, who knew how to get the buzz going around the globe. The talented Lorin Oberweger, who runs the Free Expressions workshops, and the on-point Stephanie Mitchell also assisted with this book.

Wait—don't play that music yet!

I was especially encouraged when twelve-year-old Emma in a small village in Nova Scotia loved the manuscript. My dear friend and fellow writer S. L. Card was the liaison, as well as an excellent beta reader and unwavering champion of the project. Thanks to all my other beta readers: Patti, Mari, writer Suzanne Gates, and my dear friends Dawn and Robert, who offered their Oregon home so I could finish the first draft. A special shout-out to my tribe, my wonderful writers' group: Liam Brian Perry and Derek Rogers, both amazing writers.

The support of my friends on the road to publication has meant the world—Lena and Nutschell, Paul and Joan, Luke, Greg, Michael, Marco, Susan, Gene, Paul and Matt, Ray and Marion Sader, Leonard and Alice Maltin, Martin Biro, Gold-diggers, and my author buds Jamie Freveletti, Robert Browne, Brett Battles, Boyd Morrison, Graham Brown, Stephen Jay Schwartz, Sophie Littlefield, James Rollins, and the Apocalypsies. Thank you, ITW, and to Robert Crais, I'm so grateful you were my special writer angel!

As I shout over the music, I'll finish by thanking my husband, who has great story sense, for his constant encouragement and support.

STARTERS

CHAPTER ONE

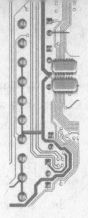

Enders gave me the creeps. The doorman flashed a practiced smile as he let me into the body bank. He wasn't that old, maybe 110, but he still made me shudder. Like most Enders, he sported silver hair, some phony badge of honor of his age. Inside, the ultramodern space with its high ceilings dwarfed me. I walked through the lobby as if gliding through a dream, my feet barely touching the marble floor.

He directed me to the receptionist, who had white hair and matte red lipstick that transferred to her front teeth when she smiled. They had to be nice to me there, in the body bank. But if they saw me on the street, I'd be invisible. Forget that I had been top of my class—back when there was school. I was sixteen. A baby to them.

The receptionist's heels clicked and echoed in this stark space as she took me to a small waiting room, empty except for silver brocade chairs in the corners. They looked like antiques, but the chemical scent in the air belonged to new paint and synthetics. The so-called nature sounds of forest birds were just as fake. I glanced at my frayed sweats and scuffed shoes. I had brushed them as best I could, but the stains would not go away. And because I had tramped all the way to Beverly Hills in the morning drizzle, I was also wet as a lost cat.

My feet hurt. I wanted to collapse into a chair, but I didn't dare leave a damp butt-mark on the brocade. A tall Ender popped into the room, interrupting my little etiquette dilemma.

"Callie Woodland?" He looked at his watch. "You're late."

"Sorry. The rain . . ."

"It's all right. You're here." He extended his hand.

His silver hair seemed whiter in contrast to his artificial tan. As his smile broadened, his eyes widened, making me more nervous than usual with an Ender. They didn't deserve to be called seniors, as they preferred, these greedy old fogies at the end of their lives. I forced myself to shake his wrinkled hand.

"I'm Mr. Tinnenbaum. Welcome to Prime Destinations." He wrapped his other palm over mine.

"I'm just here to see . . ." I looked around at the walls like I'd come to inspect the interior design.

"How it all works? Of course. No charge for that." He grinned and finally released my hand. "Why don't you follow me?"

He extended his arm as if I couldn't find my way out of the room. His teeth were so bright, I flinched a little when he smiled. We walked down a short hallway to his office.

"Go right in, Callie. Have a seat by the desk." He closed the door.

I bit my tongue to keep from gasping at the total extravagance inside. A massive copper fountain flowed with endless water alongside one wall. The way they were letting this clear, clean water fall and splash, you'd think the stuff was free.

A glass desk embedded with LED lights dominated the center of the room, with an airscreen display hovering a foot above it. It showed a picture of a girl my age, with long red hair, wearing gym shorts. Although she was smiling, the photo was straight-on, like some full-length mug shot. Her expression was sweet. Hopeful.

I sat in a modern metal chair as Mr. Tinnenbaum stood behind the desk, pointing at the air display. "One of our newest members. Like you, she heard about us through a friend. The women who rented her body were quite pleased." He touched the corner of the screen, changing the picture to a teen in a racing swimsuit, with major abs. "This fellow, Adam, referred her. He can snowboard, ski, climb. He's a popular rental for outdoorsy men who haven't been able to enjoy these sports for decades."

Hearing his words made it all too real. Creepy old Enders with arthritic limbs taking over this teen's body for a week, living inside his skin. It made my stomach flip. I wanted to bolt, but one thought kept me there.

Tyler.

I gripped the seat of my chair with both hands. My stomach growled. Tinnenbaum extended a pewter dish of Supertruffles in paper cups. My parents had had the same dish, once.

"Would you like one?" he asked.

I took one of the oversized chocolates in silence. Then I remembered my rusty manners. "Thank you."

"Take more." He waved the dish to entice me.

I took a second and a third, since the dish still hovered near my hand. I wrapped them in their paper cups and slipped them into my sweatshirt pocket. He looked disappointed not to see me eat them, like I was to be his entertainment for the day. Behind my chair, the fountain bubbled and splashed, teasing me. If he didn't offer me something to drink soon, he just might get to see me with my head under the fountain, slurping like a dog.

"Could I have a glass of water? Please?"

"Of course." He snapped his fingers and then raised his voice as if speaking to some hidden device. "Glass of water for the young lady."

A moment later, an Ender with the figure of a model came in balancing a glass of water on a tray. It was wrapped in a cloth napkin. I took the glass and saw small cubes glistening like diamonds. Ice. She set the tray beside me and left.

I tilted my head back and downed the sweet water all at once, the cool liquid running down my throat. My eyes closed as I savored the cleanest water I'd had since the war ended. When I finished, I let one of the ice cubes fall into my mouth. I bit into it with a crunch. When I opened my eyes, I saw Tinnenbaum staring at me.

"Would you like more?" he asked.

I would have, but his eyes told me he didn't mean it. I shook my head and finished the cube. My fingernails looked even dirtier against the glass as I set it back on the tray. Seeing the ice melting in the glass reminded me of the last time I had had ice water. It seemed like forever, but it was only a year ago, the last day in our house before the marshals came.

"Would you like to know how it all works?" Tinnenbaum asked. "Here at Prime Destinations?"

I stopped myself from rolling my eyes. Enders. Why else would I be there? I gave him a half smile and nodded.

He tapped a corner of the airscreen to clear it, and then a second time to bring up holo-mations. The first one showed a senior reclining on a lounge chair, the back of her head being fitted with a small cap. Colored wires protruding from the cap led to a computer.

"The renter is connected to a BCI—Body Computer Interface—in a room staffed with experienced nurses," he said. "Then she's put into a twilight sleep."

"Like at the dentist?"

"Yes. All her vital signs are monitored throughout the entire journey." On the other side of the screen, a teen girl reclined in a long padded chair. "You'll be put under, with a kind of anesthesia. Completely painless and harmless. You wake up a week later, a little groggy but a whole lot richer." He flashed those teeth again.

I forced myself not to wince. "What happens during the week?"

"She gets to be you." He spread his palms and rotated them. "Do you know about computer assists that help amputees move fake hands? They just think about it and it moves? It's very much like that."

"So she visualizes that she's me and if she wants something, she just thinks it and my hand grabs it?"

"Just like she was in your body. She uses her mind to walk your body out of here, and gets to be young again." He cradled one elbow in his other hand. "For a little while."

"But how . . . ?"

He nodded to the other side of the screen. "Over here, in another room, the donor—that would be you—is connected to the computer via a wireless BCI."

"Wireless?"

"We insert a tiny neurochip into the back of your head. You won't feel a thing. Totally painless. Allows us to connect you to the computer at all times. We then connect your brain waves to the computer, and the computer connects the two of you."

"Connects." My brow furrowed as I tried to imagine two minds connected that way. BCI. Neurochip. Inserted. This was getting creepier by the minute. That urge to run was coming back hard. But at the same time, I wanted to know more.

"I know, it's all so new." He gave me a condescending smirk. "We make sure you're completely asleep. The renter's mind takes over your body. She answers a series of questions posed by the team to be sure everything is working the way it should. Then she's free to go enjoy her rented body."

The diagram showed graphics of the rented body playing golf, playing tennis, diving.

"The body retains its muscle memory, so whatever sports you've played, she'll be able to play. When the time is over, the renter walks the body back here. The connection is shut down in the proper sequence. The renter is taken off the twilight-sleep drugs. She is checked over and then goes on her merry way. You, the donor, are restored to your full brain functions via the computer. You awake in your body as if you'd slept for several days."

"What if something happens to me while she's in my body? Snowboarding, skydiving? What if I get hurt?"

"Nothing like that has ever happened here. Our renters sign a contract that makes them financially liable. Believe me, everyone wants that deposit back."

He made me sound like a rental car. A chill went through me like someone had run an ice cube up my spine. That reminded me of Tyler, the only thing keeping me in that chair.

"What about the chip?" I asked.

"That's removed after your third rental." He handed me a sheet of paper. "Here. This might put you at ease."

Rules for Renters at Prime Destinations

1. You may not alter the appearance of your rental body in any way, including but not limited to piercings, tattoos, hair cutting or dyeing, cosmetic contact lenses, and any surgical procedures, including augmentation.
2. No changes to the teeth are allowed, including fillings, removal, and imbedded jewelry.
3. You must remain inside a fifty-mile perimeter around Prime Destinations. Maps are available.
4. Any attempt to tamper with the chip will result in immediate cancellation without refund, and fines will be levied.
5. If you have a problem with your rental body, return to Prime Destinations as soon as possible. Please treat your rental with care, remembering at all times that it is an actual young person.

Be advised that each neurochip blocks renters from engaging in illegal activities.

The rules didn't make me feel any better. They brought up more problems I hadn't even considered.

"What about . . . other things?" I asked.

"Like what?"

"I don't know." I wished he wasn't going to make me say it. But he was. "Sex?"

"What about it?"

"There's nothing in the rules," I said.

I sure didn't want my first time to happen when I wasn't there.

He shook his head. "That's made quite clear to the renters. It is forbidden."

Yeah, right. At least pregnancy would be impossible. Everyone knew that was a side effect, hopefully temporary, of the vaccination.

My stomach tightened. I shook the hair back from my eyes and stood.

"Thanks for your time, Mr. Tinnenbaum. And the demonstration."

His lip twitched. He tried to cover it with a half smile. "If you sign today, there's a bonus." He pulled a form out of his drawer and scribbled on it, then slid it across the desk. "That's for three rentals." He capped his pen.

I picked up the contract. That money could buy us a house and food for a year. I sat back down and took a deep breath.

He held out the pen. I grabbed it.

"Three rentals?" I asked.

"Yes. And you'll be paid upon completion."

The paper waved. I realized my hand was shaking.

"It's a very generous offer," he said. "That's with the bonus if you sign today."

I needed that money. Tyler needed it.

As I gripped the pen, the bubbling of the fountain got louder in my head. I was staring at the paper but saw flashes of the matte red lipstick, the eyes of the doorman, Mr. Tinnenbaum's unreal teeth. I pressed the pen to the paper, but before I made a mark, I looked up at him. Maybe I wanted one last reassurance. He nodded and smiled. His suit was perfect, except for a piece of white lint on his lapel. It was shaped like a question mark.

He was so eager. Before I knew it, I put the pen down.

His eyes narrowed. "Something wrong?"

"It's just something my mother always said."

"What was that?"

"She said always sleep on an important decision. I have to think about it."

His eyes went cold. "I can't promise this offer will be good later."

"I'll have to take my chances." I folded the contract into my pocket and rose from the chair. I forced a little smile.

"Can you afford to do that?" He stepped in front of me.

"Probably not. But I have to think about it." I moved around him and walked to the door.

"Call if you have questions," he said a little too loudly.

I rushed past the receptionist, who seemed upset to see me leaving so soon. She followed me with her eyes as she punched what I imagined was a panic button. I kept going. The doorman stared at me through the glass door before opening it.

"Leaving already?" His hollow expression was ghoulish.

I bolted past him.

Once I was outside, the brisk fall air hit my face. I breathed it in as I wove through the crowd of Enders packing the sidewalk. I must have been the only one who had ever turned Tinnenbaum down, who didn't fall for his pitch. But I'd learned not to trust Enders.

I walked through Beverly Hills, shaking my head at the

pockets of wealth that remained, over a year after the war had ended. Here, only every third storefront was vacant. Designer wear, visual electronics, and bot-shops, all for the wealthy Enders' shopping fix. Scrounging was good here. If anything broke, they'd have to throw it away because there was no one to fix it and no way to get parts.

I kept my head down. Even though I wasn't doing anything illegal at the moment, if a marshal stopped me, I couldn't produce the necessary docs that claimed minors had to carry.

As I waited for a traffic light, a truck stopped with a bunch of glum Starters, dirty and battered, sitting cross-legged in the back, picks and shovels piled in the center. One girl with a bandage around her head stared at me with dead eyes.

I saw the flicker of jealousy in them, as if my life were any better. As the truck pulled away, the girl folded her arms, sort of hugging herself. As bad as my life was, hers was worse. There had to be some way out of this insanity. Some way that didn't involve that creepy body bank or legalized slave labor.

I stuck to the side streets, avoiding Wilshire Boulevard, which was a marshal magnet. Two Enders, businessmen in black raincoats, walked toward me. I looked away and slipped my hands inside my pockets. In my left pocket was the contract. In my right, the paper-wrapped chocolates.

Bitter and sweet.

The neighborhoods became rougher the farther I got from Beverly Hills. I sidestepped piles of garbage waiting for pickups that were long overdue. I looked up and realized I was passing a building that was red-tented. Contaminated. The last spore missiles had been over a year ago, but the hazmat teams hadn't gotten around to purging this house. Or didn't want to. I held my sleeve to cover my nose and mouth, as my dad had taught me, and hurried by.

Daylight faded away, and I moved more freely. I pulled out my handlite and strapped it to the back of my left hand but didn't turn it on. We'd broken the streetlights here. We needed the protection of the shadows so the authorities couldn't pick us up with one of their lame excuses. They'd be only too happy to lock us in an institution. I'd never seen the inside of one, but I'd heard about them. One of the worst, Institution 37, was just a few miles away. I'd heard other Starters whisper about it.

By the time I was a couple of blocks from our home, it was as dark as it got. I flicked on my handlite. A minute later, I caught the streaking of two handlites darting at an angle, coming from the other side of the road. Because whoever it was kept their handlites on, I hoped they were friendlies. But then, at the same second, the lights both went dark.

Renegades.

My stomach tightened and my heart leapt up to my throat. I ran. I had no time to think. My instinct took me toward my building. One of them, a tall, long-legged girl with a tattoo on the side of her face, caught up to me. She was right behind, reaching out to grab my sweatshirt.

I pumped my legs harder. The side door to my building was just halfway down the block, waiting for me. She tried again and this time got my hood.

I fell as she yanked me, and I landed hard on the sidewalk. My back hurt and my head stung. She straddled me and went for my pockets. Her friend, a smaller boy, turned his handlite back on and aimed it into my eyes.

"I don't have any money." I squinted and tried to slap her hands away.

She hit the sides of my face with her open palms, smacking my ears hard. A dirty street trick that made your head ring with pain.

"No money for me?" she said. Her muffled words reverberated in my head. "Then you're in it deep."

A rush of adrenaline powered my arm and I punched her across the jaw. She started to fall over but righted herself before I could get out from under her.

"You're dead now, baby."

I squirmed and thrashed, but she locked me down with her steel thighs. She pulled back her fist and put her whole body into it. I rolled my head to the side at the last second and her fist connected with pavement. She screamed.

Her scream propelled me to scramble out from under her while she cradled her hand in pain. My heart was pounding like it wanted to leap out of my chest. The other kid moved in with a rock. My breath came in gulps as I got to my feet.

Something fell from my pocket. Everyone stopped to look.

One of the precious Supertruffles.

"Food!" her friend shouted as he aimed his light on it.

The girl crawled toward it, protecting her crushed hand against her chest. Her friend dove to the ground and snatched it up. She grabbed for his hand, broke off a piece of the truffle, and gobbled it down. He devoured the rest. I ran to the side entrance of my building. I pushed open the door, my door, and ducked inside.

I prayed they wouldn't enter my building. I had to depend on them being too scared of my friendlies and any traps I might have set. I aimed my handlite to check out the stairs. Clear. I climbed to the third floor and peered through a dirty window. Below, the renegade thieves scurried away like vermin. I took a quick inventory. The back of my head hurt from hitting the pavement, but I had made it without any bad gashes or broken bones. I put my hand on my chest and tried to calm my breathing.

I turned my attention to the inside of the building and did my usual scans. I listened as best I could, but my ears were still ringing from the fight. I shook my head to try to clear them.

No new sounds. No new occupants. No danger. The office on the end drew me like a beacon, promising sleep. Our encampment of desks barricaded the corner, sealing off a section of the cavernous, bare room and providing the illusion of comfort. Tyler was probably already asleep. I fingered the remaining Supertruffles in my pockets. Maybe I should just surprise him in the morning.

But I couldn't wait.

"Hey, wake up. Got something for you." When I came around the desks, nothing was there. No blankets, no brother. Nothing. What few belongings we had left were gone.

"Tyler?" I called out.

My throat tightened as I held my breath. I dashed for the door, but just as I got there, a face popped in through the doorway.

"Michael!"

Michael shook back his shaggy blond hair. "Callie." He put his handlite under his chin and aped a scary face. He couldn't hold it and broke into laughter.

If he was laughing, Tyler had to be all right. I gave him a little shove.

"Where's Tyler?" I asked.

"I had to move you guys to my room. Roof started leaking in here." He aimed his lite at a dark blot on the ceiling. "Hope that's okay?"

"Don't know. Depends on your decorating skills."

I followed him to a room across the hall. Inside, in two different corners, the desks formed cozy, protective nooks. As I got closer, I saw he'd re-created the exact arrangement of our belongings. I went inside the nook in the far corner and saw Tyler sitting against the wall, blanket over his legs. He looked too small for his seven years. Maybe it was the momentary thought of losing him, or the fact that I'd been away all day, but it was like I was seeing him anew. He had lost weight since we had been on the streets. His hair needed cutting. Shadows darkened the skin under his eyes.

"Where ya been, Monkey-Face?" Tyler's voice was hoarse.

I made an effort to push away my look of concern. "Out."

"You've been gone a long time."

"But you had Michael here." I knelt beside him. "And it took me a long time to find a special treat for you."

A slight smile formed on his lips. "What'd you get me?"

I pulled out one of the paper cups and unwrapped the vitamin-infused chocolate. It was the size of a cookie. His eyes widened.

"Supertruffle?" He looked at Michael standing near me. "Wow."

"I've got two." I showed him the other. "Both for you."

He shook his head. "You have one."

"You need the vitamins," I said.

"Did you eat today?" he asked.

I stared at him. Could I get away with a lie? No, he knew me too well.

"You guys share it," Tyler said.

Michael shrugged and his hair fell over one eye in that beautiful, effortless way that defined him. "Can't argue with that."

Tyler smiled and held my hand. "Thanks, Callie."

We ate the Supertruffles, sitting around a desk placed in the middle of the room. It served as our dining table, with Michael's handlite in the center, set on candle mode. We cut the chocolates into small pieces and joked about the first bite being the appetizer, the second the entrée, and the third the dessert. They were heaven, the sweet, thick chocolates, a cross between brownies and fudge, rich and smoky on our tongues. They were gone too soon.

Tyler perked up after eating. He sang some song to himself while Michael leaned his chin on one hand and stared at me from across the desk. I knew he was dying to ask me about the body bank. And maybe more. I saw his eyes scan my new scrapes and cuts.

"The truffles made me thirsty," I said.

"Me too," Tyler said.

Michael rose. "I guess I'd better fill up the water bottles." He grabbed our bottles, which hung on straps by the door, along with our washing pail. Then he left.

Tyler put his head on the desk. The excitement of the chocolates was taking its toll. I rubbed his baby-soft hair, his neck. His hoodie had slipped off one shoulder, exposing his vaccination scar. I ran my finger over it, grateful for the little mark. If not for that, we'd all be dead like our parents. Like everyone between twenty and sixty. We, like the elderly Enders, were the most vulnerable, so we had gotten vaccinated first against the genocide spores. Now we were the only ones left. How ironic was that?

After a few minutes, Michael returned with the filled water bottles. I went to the bathroom where he'd left the pail. The first week we had lived there, we had still had running water in the building. I sighed. It used to be so much easier than stealing our water from outside pipes when no one was looking.

The cold water felt refreshing, even though it was November and there was no heat in the building. I splashed water onto the cuts on my arms and face.

When I returned to the room, Tyler was settled back in our corner. Michael was lying in his mirror-image fort in the opposite corner. I felt safer with us all in the same room. If anyone were to break in, one of us would have the intruder from behind. Michael had a metal pipe. I had a mini-ZipTaser that had belonged to my father. It wasn't as strong as a marshal's, but I relied on it. Sad how it had become my new comfort item.

I sat on my sleeping bag and pulled off my shoes. I took off my sweatshirt and slipped into my sleeping bag as if I were going to sleep. I added pajamas to my internal list of things that I missed. Flannel, warm from the dryer. I was tired of always being dressed, ready to run or fight. I ached for fluffy jammies and a deep, forget-the-world sleep.

"Michael moved our stuff over." Tyler shined his lite at our books and treasures on the desks surrounding us.

"I know. That was nice of him."

He aimed his lite at a toy dog. "Just like before."

At first I thought he meant like at our home, but then I realized he meant how we had had it the previous day. Michael had made a point of arranging our possessions exactly as we had had them—he knew how precious they were to us.

Tyler pulled down our holo-frame. He did this every few nights, when he felt particularly sad. He held it in his palm and cycled through the holos—our family at the beach, us playing in the sand, our dad at target practice, our parents at their wedding. My brother paused at the same place he always did—an image of our parents on a cruise, taken three years ago, just before the fighting started in the Pacific Ocean. The sound of their voices was always hard for me. "We miss you, Tyler. We love you, Callie. Take good care of your brother." The first month, I cried whenever I heard their voices. Then I stopped. They sounded hollow now, like nameless actors.

Tyler never cried. He continued to absorb their words over and over. This was Mom and Dad to him now.

"Okay, enough. Time to sleep." I reached for the frame.

"No. I want to remember." His eyes pleaded with me.

"You afraid you'll forget?"

"Maybe."

I tapped the handlite on his wrist. "Remember who invented this?"

Tyler nodded solemnly, his lower lip extended. "Dad."

"That's right. With some other scientists. So whenever you see the light from it, think of it as Daddy watching over you."

"That what you do?"

"Every day." I stroked his head. "Don't worry. I promise. We'll never, ever forget them."

I traded the frame for his favorite toy, his only toy now, a small dogbot. He tucked it under his arm and it went into soft mode, lying just like a real dog. Except for the glowing green eyes.

I put the frame back on the desk above us. Tyler coughed. I pulled his sleeping bag up around his neck. Every time he coughed, I struggled not to hear the clinic doctor's words echo in my mind: "Rare lung disorder . . . Might heal, or not." I watched Tyler's chest rise and fall, and heard the labored breathing of sleep take over. I crawled out of my sleeping bag and peered around the desks.

Michael's handlite glowed against the wall. I threw my sweatshirt over my shoulders and padded over.

"Michael?" I whispered.

"Come on in." He kept his voice hushed.

I entered his little fortress. I liked being there, surrounded by his pencil and charcoal drawings, his art supplies filling every nook. He drew city scenes, interpreting our landscape of empty buildings, friendlies and renegades, complete with handlites and layered, ragged clothes, water bottles slung across thin torsos.

He put down his book and sat up with his back to the wall, motioning for me to sit next to him on his army blanket. "So, what happened to your face?"

I reached up to my cheek. It was burning. "Does it look bad?"

"Tyler didn't notice."

"Only because it's so dark in here." I sat cross-legged facing him.

"Renegades?"

I nodded. "Yeah. But I'm okay."

"How was that place?"

"Weird."

He went silent. His head hung down.

"What?" I asked.

Michael raised his head. "I was worried you weren't coming back."

"I promised, didn't I?"

He nodded. "Yeah. But I was thinking . . . what if you couldn't come back?"

I had no response to that. We sat a moment until he finally broke the silence. "So, what'd you think of it?"

"Did you know they insert a neurochip in here?" I pointed to the back of my head.

"Where? Let me see." He touched my hair.

"I told you, I just went to check it out."

I saw the concern in his face, his eyes soft with kindness. Funny, I hadn't really noticed him much when he lived down the street from us. Strange that it had taken the Spore Wars to bring us together.

I stuffed my hands into my pockets and felt something. A paper. I pulled it out.

"What's that?" he asked.

"The man at the body bank gave it to me. It's a contract."

Michael leaned closer. "That's what they're going to pay?" He snatched the form from my fingers.

"Give it back."

He read the contract. "'. . . for three connections.'"

"I'm not doing it."

"Good." He paused. "But why? I know you. You're not scared."

"They'll never pay that much money. It's unreal. That's what tipped me off."

"How do they get around the law, anyway? Hiring Starters?"

I shrugged. "They must have some loophole."

"It's pretty much off the radar. You never see any ads for it."

He was right. "The only way I knew about it was from that guy who used to live on the first floor."

"He probably makes money for every Starter he brings in."

"He won't be getting any from me." I rested on my side, leaning my head on my hand. "I don't trust that place."

"You must be tired," he said. "That was a long walk."

"I'm beyond tired."

"Tomorrow, let's go to the loading dock and see if we can get some fruit."

His words faded, and my eyes felt heavy. Next thing I knew, I opened my eyes and he was smiling at me.

"Cal," he said gently. "Go to bed."

I nodded. I stuffed the contract back into my pocket and returned to Tyler. My body melted into the sleeping bag.

I set my lite to sleep mode. It glowed softly.

Winter in Southern California wasn't brutal, but it was going to get too cold for Tyler. I needed to get him into some-place warm, a real home. But how? This was my nightly ritual worry. I'd hoped the body bank would be the answer, but it wasn't. As I drifted off to sleep, my lite turned itself off.

My sleep was shattered by the screech of the smoke de-tectors. A bitter stench filled my nostrils. I felt Tyler, near me, sitting up and coughing.

"Michael?" I called out.

"Fire!" he shouted from across the room.

The time on my handband read 5:00 a.m. I felt for my water bottle and opened it. I reached into the drawer above me and pulled out a T-shirt. I splashed water on it.

"Hold this to your nose," I told Tyler.

Michael's lite broke through the smoke. "Let's go!" he shouted.

I locked arms with my little brother. Our handlites partly penetrated the smoke as we all crouched over and made our way to the door.

Michael put his hand on my back, guiding me to the stairs. Smoke clouded the stairway. It seemed to take forever, but we made it down. My legs were rubbery by the time we made it outside.

We stepped away from the building, worried about flames and falling debris. In the darkness of the early morning, we saw other friendlies coming out—two we knew and three others who must have been on the lower floors.

They were staring at the building in shock. I spun around.

"Where're the flames?" I asked.

"Where's the fire?" Michael said.

"Is that everyone?" a man yelled.

"Yeah." I saw an Ender, maybe a hundred years old, approaching. He wore a crisp suit.

"You sure?" The Ender looked at the friendlies, who nodded. "Good." The man raised his hand and three more Enders wearing construction gear walked forward.

One construction man ripped off the tape that covered the lock on the side door. Another used a hand tool to post a notice. The suit gave us a copy of the notice.

Michael read it. "'No trespassing. Premises under new ownership.'"

"They smoked us," one of the friendlies said.

"You must vacate the area now," the suit said in a calm but authoritative voice.

When no one moved, he added, "You have one minute."

"But our stuff . . ." I moved toward the building.

"I can't let you back in there. Insurance liability," the suit said.

"You can't keep our property," Michael said.

"Squatting is trespassing," the Ender said. "I'm warning you for your own good. Thirty seconds."

My heart sank. "All we have left of our things is in there. If we can't go in, please just bring our stuff out."

He shook his head. "There's no time. You have to go. The marshals are on their way."

That made the other friendlies run. I put my arm around Tyler and turned to go, but something made me stop. The man in the suit already had his back to us, but the construction man saw us and nodded to him. He turned.

"Please. Our parents are dead." My eyes burned with tears. "The last pictures we have of them are inside that building. On the third floor, end of the hall. Could someone just give us the frame? Even if they have to throw it out the window?"

He paused for just a moment, as if he was considering it. "I wish I could. But I can't. Sorry." He turned his back. I had never felt so hollow inside. It was hopeless arguing with him. More than a hundred years separated us; he could never understand what we had gone through.

"Callie, it's okay." Tyler pulled my hand. "We can remember them without the pictures. We won't forget."

Sirens blared.

"It's the marshals," Michael said. "Run!"

We had no choice. We ran into the darkness of the early morning, leaving behind the last physical links to our family and to the life we'd lived together just a year ago.

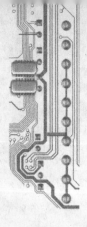

CHAPTER TWO

We raced up the street, away from the marshals' sirens. I glanced back just long enough to see the silver hair and steel-gray uniforms rushing out of their vehicle. Michael scooped Tyler into his arms, and we ran as fast as we could. We ducked down a narrow walkway between our old building and another abandoned office building.

We heard the marshals chasing us, but we were out of the walkway before they made it to the entrance, so they didn't see which way we turned. They had guns and a hundred-plus years of experience, but we had young legs.

We hid in a long row of bushes in the courtyard between the buildings. They were dying and scratchy but still full enough to hide us in the darkness of the hour. Good thing we'd staked out hiding places when we first moved in. I pushed aside branches as Michael put Tyler on the ground, and we huddled together.

The marshals came out of the walkway. I peered at them

through a hole in the bush, watching their movement. One headed left. The other came right toward us.

Tyler made a sound, that wheeze that was always followed by a cough. I felt the hair on my arms rise. Michael slipped his hand over Tyler's mouth.

The marshal was approaching. Had he spotted us? He crouched and edged closer, his gun drawn. My heartbeat echoed in my ears. I gripped Michael's shirt and pressed my cheek to his shoulder.

The marshal's hand groped through the leaves in front of my face. He was so close I could smell the oily scent of his gloves. I held my breath.

"He's over here!" the other marshal's voice called out.

Then the sound that made our spines tingle, that electronic, arcing crackle, broke through the cold night.

ZipTaser.

Excruciating screams followed the crackle. They ripped through us, making our teeth hurt and our souls ache. The leaves shook as our marshal ran off.

I pressed my face to the hole in the bushes to see. A boy lay on the ground, facedown. His screams were giving way to moans.

One of the marshals slapped autocuffs on him and turned him over. I recognized him as one of the newer guys in our building. The side of his neck was burnt black from the ZipTaser. That happened if they held it too close or the gun was turned up too high. They did it on purpose, to brand us.

He started yelling as they ran a strap around his cuffs and across his chest, begging them to leave him. They ignored his pleas, tilting him at an angle and holding a strap over their shoulders to drag him behind them. The boy's heels scraped the ground, and every bump was punctuated with a scream.

It was like they'd snared an animal.

They were cowards, conducting these raids in the dark of night, out of sight of any softhearted Enders who might intervene.

Inside the safety of our leafy cover, we hugged each other in a ball. This kept Tyler warm, kept him from coughing, and kept any of us from making the slightest sound. Every scream made us flinch. If only we'd had a few more friendlies, we could have jumped on the marshals' backs, biting, punching, scratching, until the boy could get away.

The screaming faded as they all entered the walkway. Then we heard their car start. They were leaving, satisfied with one capture. They had bagged their prize, and it filled their daily quota. But they would return tomorrow.

Tyler finally released his cough, which led to wheezing and more coughing. We crawled out of the bushes to get him off the damp ground. Michael removed his sweatshirt and put it over Tyler's so he had a double layer. They huddled together on a low concrete planter while I paced.

"Now what do we do?" Michael asked. "We've lost our sleeping bags."

"And my ZipTaser." I swallowed hard, remembering the marshal's weapon. "And our water bottles," I said. "And anything else we saved, scrounged, or built."

My words hung in the cold night air, the finality of it all too overwhelming. Then Tyler came up with his contribution.

"My dogbot," he said.

His lower lip jutted out, but it quivered as he struggled to pull it back. It wasn't just a toy, or his last toy—it was the last toy given to him by our mom. If I had been a better person, I would have confessed that I understood, that I was devastated over losing our parents' pictures. Those were memory triggers, gone forever. Our old lives, the ones we'd had just a year ago, were history now—undocumented history. The last cord was cut.

But I kept it inside. Falling apart wasn't an option.

"What're we gonna do?" Tyler asked. "Where'll we go?" He went into a fit of hacking coughs.

"We can't stay around here," I said quietly. "They'll come back tomorrow with more men, now that they made a score."

"I know another building," Michael said. "Not far, twenty minutes."

Another building. Another cold, hard floor. Another temporary place to squat. Something inside me broke.

"Draw me a map." I fished in my sweatshirt pocket and pulled out the contract. I ripped off a quarter of it.

"Why?" Michael asked.

"I'll join you guys later." I handed the paper to Michael and he started drawing.

"Where're you going?" Tyler asked, his voice hoarse.

"I'm going to be gone for a day or two." I looked at Michael. "I know where to get some money."

Michael glanced up from his map. His eyes locked with mine. "Cal. You sure?"

I looked at Tyler's tired face, his sunken cheeks, his baggy eyes. The smoke had made his condition worse. If he went downhill and didn't make it, I would never forgive myself.

"No. But I'm going anyway."

By the time I entered Beverly Hills, it was 8:45 a.m. The shops were still closed. I passed a handful of Enders wearing heavy jewelry and too much makeup. Modern medicine could easily extend Enders' life spans to two hundred, but it couldn't teach them to avoid becoming fashion don'ts. The plump Enders opened the door to a restaurant, and the aroma of bacon and eggs teased my nose. My stomach growled.

Those rich Enders acted like they'd forgotten there ever was a war. I wanted to shake them and ask, Don't you remember? No one was winning the Pac Rim sea battles, so they threw their spore-head missiles at us? And we used our EMP weapon, which crashed their computers, their planes, their stock markets?

It was a war, people. Nobody won. Not us, not the Pac Rim countries. In less than a year, the face of America changed to a sprinkling of Starters like me in a sea of silver-haired Enders, well off, well fed, and oblivious.

They weren't all rich, but none of them were as poor as we were, because we weren't allowed to work or vote. That nasty little policy had been in place before the war, with the aging population, but it had become even more of an issue postwar. I shook my head. I hated thinking about the war.

I passed a pizza place. Closed. The hologram in the window looked so real, complete with bubbling cheese. The fake scent blasts taunted me. I remembered the taste, the hot, sticky mozzarella, the tangy tomato sauce. Living on the streets for the past year meant I was always hungry. But I especially missed hot food.

When I reached Prime Destinations, I hesitated. The building was five stories tall, freestanding, covered with silver-mirrored panels. I looked at my reflection in them. Tattered clothes, smudged face. Long hair hanging like tangled rope. Was I still there, somewhere, under all this?

My reflection vanished as the guard opened the door. "Welcome back." He wore a smug grin.

While I waited at the reception desk for Tinnenbaum, I noticed two men arguing in a conference room off the lobby. One of them, facing the open door, was Tinnenbaum. The other man I could see only from the back. He was taller and wore an elegant black wool coat. Only a few inches of his silver hair protruded from his fedora. He slapped his gloves in one hand several times and then hit the table with them, making Tinnenbaum flinch.

Tinnenbaum moved to the left, out of view. The tall man glared at a glass case of electronic equipment. I couldn't make out his face in the reflection, but I got the feeling he was staring at me, as if he had a clearer view than I did. The hair on the back of my neck rose with a prickle. He appeared to be sizing me up.

Why?

At that point Tinnenbaum came out of the room alone, closing the door behind him. He came over to greet me with his trademark freaky grin.

"Callie. I hoped we'd see you again." He shook my hand. "My apologies for making you wait, but that was my boss." He motioned toward the conference room with his head.

"It's okay. He must be important."

"You could say he's Mr. Prime Destinations himself." He spread one arm. "This is all his baby."

I followed him into his office and sat on the other side of his desk while he tapped at his airscreen. To my right was a framed mirror. Observation window, I imagined.

"So who did you say referred you?" he asked.

"Dennis Lynch."

"And you know him from where?"

"He was a classmate. Before the war." Tinnenbaum continued to stare at me, as if I should say more. "After the war ended, I ran into him on the street. He told me about this place."

I didn't want to admit that I'd met Dennis squatting. Tinnenbaum knew I was a squatter, but I wasn't going on record with it.

He seemed satisfied. "And what sports are you good at?"

"Archery. Fencing, swimming, riflery."

He raised one brow. "Riflery?"

"My dad knew about guns. He was in the Science Corps. He trained me."

"He's deceased, I assume."

"Yes. And my mother."

He eyed my clothing. "I assume you have no living relatives?"

Of course, dummy. Would I be living on the street if I had grandparents? "Right."

He nodded and thumped the desk. "Well then, let's see just how good you are."

I didn't move.

"Unless you have any questions?" he asked.

I had to ask. "How do I know I won't get caught? For working?"

He smiled. "Look, we're not hiring you. You're donating services, not working. You couldn't be working when you're asleep." He laughed. "So the generous payment we give is a stipend, not a salary." He pushed his chair back and stood.

"Don't worry. This is a mutually beneficial situation here. We need you as much as you need us. Now let's go see what you can do."

Mr. Tinnenbaum introduced me to an Ender named Doris, who was assigned to be my personal mentor. She had the silver hair of an Ender but the body of a ballerina. She dressed in typical Ender fashion, retro clothing with modern touches. Her suit was classic 1940s, but a power belt cinched her tiny waist. Rib removal, no doubt. She took me to their gym and tested me in fencing and archery, as well as in general strength, stamina, and gymnastics exercises. They weren't going to take my word for it, in case some Ender had her heart set on winning a fencing competition.

We were left with only the target shooting. That was one thing they weren't set up for, so we had to go to a shooting range. Tinnenbaum and I got into the back of a limo and rode for twenty minutes. Trapped in the small space, he coughed and wrinkled his nose, then held his handkerchief to it. I'm sure it was from my eau de street life. We were even, because I couldn't stand the fake scent of his cologne. He didn't even look at me, but instead read his mini-airscreen the whole way.

But I got Tinnenbaum's attention once we were on the shooting range and the Range Master pushed a rifle into my hands. The motion shoved me back, back to three years ago, when I was thirteen, when my dad had done the same thing.

I had protested that the rifle was too big and heavy for me. I didn't want to admit that I was scared and would rather have spent my time with him fishing or hiking.

"Cal Girl, listen carefully," my dad had said.

Whenever he used his special nickname for me in a serious way, it got my attention.

"There's a war going on," he continued. "You must learn how to defend yourself. And Tyler."

"But the war's not here, Dad," I said.

At that time, the war was mostly being played out in the Pacific Ocean. But my father's answer made it clear he knew what was to come.

"Not yet, Cal Girl," he said. "But it will be."

Two years later, the Spore Wars would change us all.

While Tinnenbaum watched with a skeptical gaze, I straightened and brought the rifle into position. I shut one eye and used the other to line up the digital sight on the target, an outline of a man. Then I shut both eyes and quickly opened them. The sight was still dead-on. I breathed in and squeezed the trigger.

The bullet pierced the red circle in the center of the forehead. The Range Master said nothing. He nodded for me to shoot again. My next bullet went through the first hole. Tinnenbaum stood completely still, staring at the target as if it had to be some trick. Other shooters, all Enders, stopped their practice to watch me hit the same spot, every time.

We continued the testing with a variety of guns, so I also impressed them with the number of firearms I could handle. Thanks, Dad.

On the drive back, Tinnenbaum's nose wasn't so wrinkled. He angled his mini's base so I could read the airscreen. It displayed my contract.

I skipped to the important parts: three rentals and the payment. The money would be enough to pay for an apartment for a couple of years. And to bribe an adult to sign the lease for us.

"That amount. It's the same as before you tested me."

"That's right."

"Shouldn't my skill level have bumped me up to a higher stipend?" Why not go for it, I thought.

His smile faded. "You drive a hard bargain. For a minor." He sighed and typed in better numbers. "How's that?"

I remembered something my dad had taught me to ask. "What are the risks?" I said. "What can go wrong?"

"No procedure is without risks. However, we've taken every precaution to protect our valuable assets."

"Meaning me."

He nodded. "You can be assured that in twelve months of operation, we have not had a single problem."

That wasn't a long time. But I needed the money more than I needed a better answer. What would my dad have said about this? I pushed the thought out of my mind.

"The hard part is over," Tinnenbaum said. "The rest is as easy as drifting off to sleep."

My brother could be warm every night. A real home. And we'd have it after only three rentals. I touched the airscreen and my fingerprint appeared on the contract, sealing the deal. Tinnenbaum gazed out the limo window, trying to look casual. But I noticed his leg had an uncontrollable nervous twitch.

When we arrived back at the body bank, I wondered if Mr. Tinnenbaum would introduce me to the tall man from before. But we never saw him. Instead, Tinnenbaum handed me off to Doris.

"Wait till you see what Doris has in store for you." He grinned and then disappeared down the hallway.

"It's time to begin your makeover." Doris flicked her wrist like she was my fairy godmother.

"Makeover?"

Doris eyed me from toe to head. My hand instinctively touched the end of my stringy hair, as if to keep her from chopping it off.

"You don't think we're going to present you like this, do you?"

I pulled my sleeve over my hand and wiped my face. She reached for my arm.

"You're one lucky girl. We're going to give you a free makeover, top to bottom."

She examined my hand. Her nails glowed with a dazzling iridescent polish that reminded me of an abalone shell. Mine looked like I'd dug through tar at the beach.

"We have a lot of work to do." Doris put her hand on my back, guiding me toward a set of double doors. "You're not going to recognize yourself when we're done with you."

"That's what I'm afraid of."

The first station was a human car wash. I stood naked on a raised, revolving platform and held on to a bar hanging above my head. Tiny goggles protected my eyes while bitter-smelling chemicals blasted my entire body. The fish-eye goggles made everything a little more surreal than it already was, including Doris watching me through an observation window. Large foam pads taller than my head pushed out from curved panels, moving closer and closer until I thought I was going to be smothered. But I held my breath as the squishy material conformed to my body and scrubbed it top to bottom. Finally, it stopped and pulled back for the last step, a high-powered water stream that sprayed from every direction and hurt like needles.

I passed through a small chamber lit only by blue lights, and then a hot, dry one. In the last room, which looked like a doctor's exam room, two Enders wearing protective suits scanned me for any bacteria. I was judged to be a clean palette and was whisked off for a series of beauty procedures. First up, laser treatments. This Ender team said it was just to clean up my freckles and teenage skin, but it took a long time. They wouldn't let me see the results, but they assured me I would be pleased. I could see that they had completely healed the cuts on my hands from fighting.

Next up, manicure, pedicure, and, as if I weren't clean enough already, a full-body scrub. It hurt at eleven on a scale of one to ten, like they didn't want any original skin cells left. Then Doris led me to a small room to meet their in-house hairstylist. She was the first Ender I'd ever seen with hair that wasn't all white or silver. Hers had streaks of purple, and it went straight up in spikes.

I tried to pass on the haircut.

"Don't be silly." Doris leaned on a counter, drumming her nails with increasing speed. "She's not going to give you a buzz cut. You'll still have your lovely long hair. It'll just be styled better. Give you some layers."

I let the spiky Ender put a cape over me, but the fact that she refused to let me see a mirror hardly inspired confidence.

When she was done, enough hair lay on the floor to make a cat. I was dying to see the results, but no one seemed to care. The final torturer was a makeup artist named Clara, who spent over two hours brushing and rubbing color into every inch of my face. She lasered my brows and attached new eyelashes. Doris picked out some clothes for me to wear, and I changed in a small room with no mirror. Before I could even look at myself, I was rushed to another room, where I had to stand against a wall and pose for the camera.

I tried to smile like the red-haired girl in the hologram Tinnenbaum had shown me. I don't think I succeeded.

When I left the holo room, I was mush. I didn't feel made over, I felt run over.

"Are we done?" I asked Doris.

"For now."

"What time is it?"

"Late."

She looked as tired as I felt. "I'll show you to your room," she said.

"Here?"

"You can't walk home at eleven p.m. looking like that." She leaned against the wall and drummed her nails.

I put my hand to my face. Was I that different?

"Haven't you heard stories of rich men kidnapping pretty girls?" she said.

I had. "Those are true?"

"Oh, you bet they're true. You'll be safe here. And refreshed for tomorrow."

She turned. I followed her clicking heels down the hallway.

"I don't even know what I look like," I said under my breath.

Moments later, I was lying in a real bed. With sheets. And a cloud-soft comforter. I had forgotten the luxury of a clean bed, how sheets felt slippery against your skin. It was like floating in heaven.

I couldn't keep my hands from touching my face. My new skin was so smooth, it reminded me of when Tyler was a baby and I would pet his big pink cheeks. My mother had said I'd wear them out.

Tyler.

I wondered what he was doing. Was the new place Michael found safe? Did they have blankets to keep them warm?

I felt guilty lying in this plush bed with a trillion pillows. Although the room was just another part of this large facility, it was made to look like someone's guest room, with a full pitcher of water by the bed, next to a vase of daisies. It reminded me of our old guest room, which my mom had decorated with such love.

I looked at the food they'd left beside my bed: potato soup, cheese, and a variety of packaged crackers. I was almost too tired to eat it. Almost. I ate the soup and the cheese but saved all the crackers to bring to Michael and Tyler, later, when I finally got released.

It wasn't until I woke in the morning that I realized that the one thing missing in this imitation guest room was a window. When I parted the pair of calico curtains hanging above my bed, all I saw was wall.

I went to the door and put my ear to it. I could hear only the hum of an office building. I tried to open it to peek outside but it was locked. My heart sped up at the thought of being trapped. I took a couple of deep breaths and told myself the door was locked to protect me.

I was wearing the white pajamas that had been on the bed the previous night. I opened the closet to look for clothes but saw my reflection instead, in a full-length mirror on the inside of the door. I gasped.

I was beautiful.

It was still my face, with my mother's eyes and my father's

jawline, but it was so much better. My skin glowed with a flawless sheen. My cheekbones were more pronounced. This was what money could do. This was what every girl could look like, if she had endless resources. I got closer to the mirror and looked into my eyes, still smoky from yesterday's makeup.

I hadn't had makeup on for a year. What would Michael say when he saw me?

I focused my attention on the closet. One garment hung inside. A hospital gown.

Doris unlocked my door and came in, wearing a belted pantsuit and a too-sunny smile.

"Good morning, Callie." She examined my face. "Sleep well?"

"Great."

"They did such a nice job on you." She scrutinized my skin and then leaned against the wall. She did that drumming thing with her nails, which was beginning to drive me crazy.

"Don't worry about your makeup. We'll have it redone later. Follow me."

My stomach growled. I noticed the dinner tray from last night was gone. When had that happened?

"Doris?"

She stopped. "Yes, dear?"

"Are we going to have breakfast?" I asked.

"Oh, honey, you'll have a feast later. All your favorites." She stroked my hair.

No one had done that to me since my mother died. It hit a trigger point for me, and I felt my eyes getting moist. A lump formed in my throat.

Doris leaned closer and smiled.

"It's just that you can't eat anything before your operation."

I stared at the ceiling as they wheeled me on a gurney down an endless hallway. I had pushed the procedure out of my mind, but now it was here. I hated needles, hated knives, hated being put under and having no control. Maybe they knew that, because they had already started me on some tranquilizer. The pattern on the ceiling began to melt until it was blurry.

Tinnenbaum had made the surgery sound simple. But I had overheard the surgeons when I was in pre-op. It was going to be complicated. I was too woozy to remember the details.

The Ender nurse, trim and handsome, smiled down at me while he rolled my gurney. Was he wearing eyeliner?

This was crazy. I was a wimp who got sweaty palms just waiting for a vaccination. And there I was, volunteering to be operated on.

My brain, no less.

Probably my favorite body part. No one ever complained about a fat brain. No one ever accused their brain of being too short or too tall, too wide or too narrow. Or ugly. It either worked or it didn't, and mine worked just fine.

I prayed it still would after the surgery.

We came to a stop. I was in the operating room, baking under the bright lights. The nurse—his name tag read "Terry"—patted my arm. "Don't worry, kitten. Think of it like the little microchip we put in our pets. Bing, bang, and it's in before you know it."

"Kitten"? Who was this Ender? I already knew it was

beyond microchipping. Arms rustled about me. Someone placed a cone over my mouth and told me to count backward from ten.

"Ten. Nine. Eight."

That was it.

I woke up in a bed in what felt like seconds. Terry, the nurse, stared down at me. "How you doing, kitten?"

My head was like cotton candy, all fuzzy and limitless. "Is it over?"

"Yup. The surgeon said it was a thing of beauty."

"How long was I out?" I felt myself moving slowly as I looked for a clock. All I saw was a white haze.

"Not long." He took my vitals. "Does anything hurt?"

"I can't feel anything."

"That'll wear off. Let me get you upright."

He raised the top half of my bed and I began to feel a little clearer. My eyes focused. I hadn't been in this room before. "Where am I?"

"Your exchange room. Get used to it. It's where you'll make your exits and entries."

It was a small room with one window that looked out on a hallway. To my left, a panel that had to be a one-way mirror. Several silver cameras, one on the ceiling, two on the walls. To my right, a tall Ender with black eyeglass frames and long white hair sat at a computer.

"That's Trax," Terry said. "We're in his domain now, so he's the king."

Trax raised one hand. Big effort. He may have been an Ender, but once a geek, always a geek. "Hi, Callie."

I raised my hand too. I noticed there was a plastic medical bracelet on my wrist. "Hi."

Trax pointed to various icons on his airscreen. "So, Callie, what do you want for lunch?"

It had been a year since someone had asked me that question. I ran through my favorites in my head: lobster, steak—heck, even pizza would have made me happy. Would it have been pushing it to ask for caramel cheesecake?

Before I could say a word, Trax grinned. "So how about we start with lobster bisque and then a steak pizza? With caramel cheesecake for dessert."

My mouth fell open. "But how—"

"Don't worry, we're not mind readers. Food choices are easy. We ran your cerebral input against a small database and scored the hits."

"I don't know if I like that."

"It's okay. What your brain likes doesn't really matter. You're going to be asleep. We just need to make the clear connection between your brain and the renter's. And this proves we have a connection from you to the computer. Your neurochip works. Yay." He twirled his index finger.

"Do they ever fail?" I asked.

"Do computers ever fail?" Trax laughed.

Terry patted my shoulder. I saw he had black nail polish. "Don't worry so much, kitten. Just enjoy the ride."

Back in my little guest room, I sat at a table, wearing a robe. I ate the lunch they had ordered for me. It killed me not to be able to share this feast with Michael and Tyler. I was finishing the cheesecake when Doris came in.

"See? I told you we'd feed you. Get enough to eat?"

"I'm ready to explode."

"Can't send out a rental without a full tank."

I wondered if I saw a bit of sadness in her eyes. If so, she

41

shook it off. She opened the closet and pointed to a hanger with a casual pink top and white jeans. Underwear was also on the hanger, a modest polka-dotted bra and panties cut larger than I usually wore.

"You can put this on when you're done eating. Remove everything, including that." She pointed to my handlite.

"Will it be safe?" I wrapped my other hand around it.

"Your belongings will be locked up securely."

"Who picked the clothes?" I kept my voice even in case Doris had.

"The renter always dictates the wardrobe. Clara will come in here to do your makeup and brush out your hair, and you'll be ready for your first rental."

"Now?"

She nodded. "It'll just be for a day. We always do it that way, sort of a dry run. To make sure it all goes as planned."

"Who is it?"

She folded her arms and looked as if she were reaching back for a speech she'd given before. "We maintain complete confidentiality. Better for them, you, and us. It's cleaner this way. We do screen our renters very carefully, so rest assured, this is a lovely woman."

"If she's so lovely, introduce us."

"Don't worry. They sign a contract too. They can't do anything with your body that's off-limits. No sports that are not on the accepted list, no car racing, skydiving, none of that stuff." She put her arm around me. "We do have your best interests at heart. All you have to do is relax and collect your money at the end. You'll see how easy it is. I've had some very happy girls go through here. Some of them come back to see me. And you'll be one of them."

"One last question. I saw a man talking to Mr. Tinnen-baum who I haven't met."

"When?"

"The day I got tested. Tall, a long coat and a hat."

She nodded and lowered her voice. "He's the big boss. The CEO of Prime."

"What's his name?" I asked.

"We affectionately call him the Old Man. But don't ever repeat that. Now stop thinking so much and be happy."

Easy for her to say. It had been a long time since I'd been happy. A long time since life was just lip gloss and music and silly girlfriends. A long time since my biggest concerns were whether there would be a test or if I'd forgotten my home-work. I was aiming for more like safe, free, and alive.

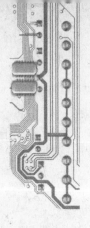

CHAPTER THREE

The mood in the exchange room crackled with tension. Trax sat at the computer console while Doris and Terry hovered over me. I was betting that Tinnenbaum was watching through one of the cameras.

I was all ready to go, sitting in the chair with perfect makeup and hair. Doris put a charm bracelet on my wrist. It was silver with little sports charms.

"Just a little something I give all my girls," Doris said.

The charms sparkled: a tennis racket, air skis, ice blades.

"Touch it," she said.

She reached over me and, with her index finger, lightly touched the blades, setting off a holo-projection of blades spinning on ice.

"Wow." I touched the tennis racket and a tennis ball sailed through the air. "I love it. Thank you."

She seemed a bit flustered.

"She's nothing if not thoughtful." Terry sort of sang this out.

He put a smock over me to protect my clothing. Was he afraid I would drool?

"It's okay, you can lean back," he said in a hushed voice.

"It won't muss your hair." Doris patted the pillow. "It's silk."

My chair was in its upright position. If all went well, I—my body, that is—wouldn't be in this place very long.

Somewhere in this building was my renter. She was sitting in a chair like mine. Soon, she was going to be controlling my body, as if she were me.

The thought gave me a shiver.

"Are you cold?" Doris asked.

Terry became alert, ready to get me a blanket.

"She's fine," Trax said. Our eyes met. No hiding anything from him.

Terry wheeled over the anesthesiology cart with the cone. Soon, I would be out cold. Soon, my body would belong to someone else.

I was dreaming. And I knew I was dreaming. They hadn't told me this could happen. But there I was, dreaming. I saw Tyler, running out of a house by a lake. He had a huge smile on his face. He ran through the grass and picked up a fishing pole.

He looked healthy. I wanted to tell Michael, but I couldn't find him. I ran into the house, a large, woodsy cabin. He wasn't in any of the rooms. Finally, I found him on the deck overlooking the lake. But when I ran to him, he turned and it wasn't Michael.

I heard voices far away. Mumbling.

I recognized them. A woman's voice. My mother?

45

"Her eyes fluttered," the woman said.

Mom?

"Callie? Kitten?" a male voice said.

"Don't call her that."

I opened my eyes.

"How do you feel?" It was a woman, but not my mother. It was an Ender.

"Callie?" A man wearing eyeliner bent over me. "How you doing, girl?"

"Where am I?"

The woman looked concerned. "You're at Prime Destinations. You just had your first rental."

I remembered this woman. "Doris?"

A relieved smile softened her face. "Yes, Callie."

"How did it go?"

She patted my shoulder. "You were a big success."

I was dying to know where my body had been. What sports did I play? My arms weren't particularly sore. Same with my legs. So weird being unaware for a whole day where your body went and what it did. Who you met, who you liked, or didn't like. What if my renter had made someone mad? Would I have a new enemy?

I looked at my body. All parts in working order. One down, two to go. I was one-third of the way to my goal.

Trax asked me a list of questions, a kind of debriefing. There wasn't too much to say; I couldn't remember anything other than my dream. He was interested in that and recorded it. Evidently, it wasn't unusual to dream. He wanted to know if I felt rested and refreshed, and I had to admit that I did.

Terry checked my blood pressure and my temperature and nodded to Trax.

"It's all good, little lady," he said. "You're good to go on your next rental."

"I don't get a break?"

"What for? Your renter ate and took care of all your bodily needs," Trax said.

"Not that kind of break," I said. "I need to go somewhere."

His eyes widened. He leaned forward and called out, "Doris."

Within moments, Doris came clicking into the room. "What's wrong, Callie?"

"Can I go now, before the next rental?"

"Leave? Why?"

I looked down. Maybe it was better not to press this.

She put her hand on my back. "Why not just carry on? It will be over before you know it. So much work has been invested in you. Why risk your payout? You could get an injury out there." She fluttered her hand and grimaced as if the outside world was hell.

She was partly right. But it was where I lived, after all.

"If you don't fulfill your contract—providing a healthy, fit body—you won't get paid."

"Do you have another renter waiting?" I asked.

"Yes. And she's a . . ."

". . . lovely woman?" I rolled my eyes. "Okay, let's do it."

"Wonderful. This one will be three days."

The second rental flew by, like the first. One thing I learned: when you're out cold, time sails. I had strange dreams again but couldn't remember them. There was one odd thing

I noticed when I came to. I had a four-inch gash on my right forearm. It didn't hurt—they must have used some numbing spray—but it was hideous. Doris got me into the laser room. They healed it so there were no scars, but I wanted to know how it had happened. They wouldn't tell me. Maybe they didn't know.

Doris took me back to her office. It was decorated in whites and golds, sort of neo-Baroque. She had me sit and informed me that my third and last rental would be for an entire month.

"A month?" I gripped the chair. "I can't be away for a whole month."

"This is normal. We start with shorter terms to make sure everything's fine before we move to a longer rental."

"Nobody told me this would be for that long. I have to see my little brother."

"Your brother?" She pushed back a lock of hair from her eye. "You never said you had a brother."

"What's wrong with that?"

"You were expressly asked whether you had any living relatives when you signed with us."

"I thought you meant parents, grandparents. He's only seven."

Her shoulders relaxed. "Seven." She stared at the wall. "I see. Well, they're still not going to let you go. They can't take that risk."

"What can happen to me? I might cut myself?" I stood and gestured to the arm where the gash had been. "I take better care of myself than your lovely renters do."

She shook her head. "Sorry, Callie, it just isn't done."

"I want to talk to Mr. Tinnenbaum."

"You sure you want to do that?"

"Positive."

Doris spoke to the unseen microphone in the room. "Mr. Tinnenbaum, please."

She straightened her suit and smoothed her hair. Then she started that awful nail drumming on a counter. After a few moments, Mr. Tinnenbaum marched into the room.

"Callie is requesting a leave to see . . . her brother." Doris put emphasis on the word "brother."

Tinnenbaum shook his head. "Impossible."

"No one ever told me I'd be gone for an entire month," I said. "Shouldn't that have been clear before I started?"

"You never asked. And you didn't tell us you had a brother," he said. He shifted his weight. "As for the scheduling, we often don't know the schedule until we've already begun the process. That was the case this time."

"But you knew that might happen. I didn't even know a month was possible."

"It's in the contract," he said.

"In the fine print?" I turned to Doris. "Something that important should have been said."

"Just like you should have told us you had a brother," Tinnenbaum said.

Doris looked at the floor.

"I really need to see him before I go, to let him know how long this will be. He's only seven and I'm all he's got."

"Perhaps we could have someone check up on him?" Doris looked at Mr. Tinnenbaum.

Tinnenbaum's head gave the most imperceptible shake.

"I don't want to be difficult." I made a point of standing as tall as I could. "I'm guessing the process goes a lot smoother

49

if you have a cooperative donor. But I won't be feeling very cooperative if I can't speak to my brother first."

Tinnenbaum nervously tapped his toe, as if it helped him think. "What time is her exchange tomorrow?" he asked Doris.

"Eight a.m.," she said.

He chuffed like a horse. "I will give you three hours and a bodyguard who will watch you every second. Don't do anything foolish, because we can monitor you via that chip in your head." He pointed at me. "Keep this body exactly as it is. Because right now, it still belongs to us."

I never once saw his teeth. Guess he was all out of smiles.

I followed Doris back down the hallway. "I'll have to get you some fresh clothes," she said. "I'll meet you in your guest room."

She ducked into another doorway, and I continued on to what I remembered as my guest room. But when I opened the door, there was another girl standing there. She was about my age but had short black hair. She was changing her clothes, already in a pair of flowered pants, but held a top to her chest to cover her bra.

"Sorry," I said. "I must have the wrong room."

I realized her room was decorated exactly like mine, only in shades of green. I closed the door. The next door was my room. In pink.

Doris came a minute later, holding some white pants and a top. "You'll want to shower. And here's a change of clothes. You've been wearing those too long."

"Where are my own clothes?"

"Honey, we disposed of those the minute they came off you. You can keep these."

"What about my handlite?"

Doris opened a drawer. She took out the handlite and held it with as few fingers as possible. "Rodney will escort you home. No need to stop for food. You won't be hungry for hours."

"I won't? Why?"

"You've already eaten."

It was so weird having people know more about your body than you did.

Doris walked me to an underground parking structure that connected to the back of Prime Destinations. Rodney stood by a town car. He had a short fuzz of silver hair, and his biceps were so massive that his suit looked ready to burst.

He noticed I was carrying the handlite. "You won't need that," he said. "I've got a mega-torch."

I put the handlite on anyway. It felt good and solid to have it on my wrist again.

"She's your responsibility," Doris said to him. "Get her back here no later than twenty-two hundred."

"Yes, ma'am." He opened the back door for me, and I climbed in.

Rodney got into the driver's seat. Doris watched us go.

I noticed a food container on the seat next to me.

"That's for your brother." Rodney gestured to the container. "From Doris."

It smelled good. "Yum."

He pulled out into the Beverly Hills traffic. "She's a sweetheart. Known her for over sixty years. We used to work in the travel industry together, back when you could travel. Now nobody can leave the U.S. with the other countries paranoid about the damn spores. And no one will come here. Mexico, can you believe they built that wall so Americans couldn't cross over?"

I let Rodney babble on. My mind wasn't on Ender stories. They always went on forever because they had so many decades to cover. All I could think about was getting to see the two people I cared about the most in the whole world.

I pulled Michael's map out of my handlite pocket and used it to navigate to the new home. When we got to the right street, I saw several abandoned buildings. The first one had been stopped midconstruction. A skeleton that had never seen life. The building Michael and Tyler were in was the fourth one down. Rodney parked the town car in front.

He led the way, carrying his mega-torch. I had never had a bodyguard before. It kind of made me feel like I was the president's daughter. Rodney held open the large glass door for me.

"What floor?" He arced his flashlight around the lobby.

"Third."

"You like climbing stairs, huh?"

"Third floor equals safer. More getaway time." I flicked on my handlite. "If we hear screams downstairs, we've got some time. Maybe run for the fire escape."

We took the large open stairway to the third floor. Rodney led the way, shining his light into each abandoned office we passed. A figure came out and stood at the end of the hallway, holding a large pipe like a weapon. It was Michael.

"Stop!" Michael said.

I pointed my handlite to my face. "Michael, it's me."

Rodney put out his arm to restrain me. "Stay back."

I ducked under his arm. "He's my friend." I ran down the hall. Michael held his defensive position until I got closer.

"Callie?" The pipe fell out of his hands and clanged to the floor.

I threw myself into his arms and hugged him. Rodney came up and stopped a few feet away.

"This is Rodney," I said. "He works for Prime Destinations."

Rodney nodded as Michael eyed him suspiciously.

"So you're not done?" Michael asked.

I shook my head. "I can only stay a couple of hours. How's Tyler?"

"He misses you a lot." Michael aimed his lite at my hair. He reached out and rubbed a lock. "I didn't recognize you. You look so different."

"Bad different? Or good different?" I asked as we walked.

"You kidding? You look fantastic," he said.

He led us into a room at the end of the hall, a space with carpeting, which helped make up for the fact that we no longer had sleeping bags. Tyler sat in the corner, a dark green blanket over his legs.

"I'll stay here," Rodney said quietly, nodding at a chair by the door. He set up his light so it illuminated his part of the room.

I went over and knelt beside Tyler. I reached out to give him a hug, but he pushed me away.

"What happened to your hair?" Tyler aimed his lite at me and scrunched his face.

"Don't you like it?"

His eyes scanned my features. "What'd they do to your

face?" He tugged at my new dangling earrings. "Those are dangerous."

"This place, where I work, they made me pretty and dressed me up. Don't you like it?"

"You're just going to get dirty." He looked at me like I was stupid. "And who's that?" He pointed across the room at Rodney.

"Someone I work with. He gave me a ride." I showed Tyler the box. "He also gave me this yummy food for you. It's still warm. Smell."

"It stinks." He turned away.

I moved to his other side. "Tyler, I know you're mad I've been gone."

"You've been gone a week." His face was flushed. He was on the verge of tears.

"I know, I'm really sorry."

"Seven whole days." A week with no dogbot, no images of our parents, no familiar surroundings, and no sister.

"But hasn't Michael been good to you? Didn't he get you this blanket? And that water bottle? Looks like you guys have been eating okay."

I glanced up at Michael, leaning against a filing cabinet that was part of the new fort. He shoved his hands in his jeans pockets and nodded.

"In fact, I'll go get us all some water now." He winked.

After he left, Tyler turned to me. "Callie?"

"What?"

"I'm glad you're back," he said in a soft voice. He reached out and I put my hand in his. "Even if your hair's funny."

"Thanks." I leaned in until our heads touched. I wanted so much to stay with this moment, this hard-won truce, but I had to tell him the truth. "I wish I could stay. But I'm just here for a couple of hours. I have to go back to work."

He let go of my hand. "Why?" His eyes welled up.

"Because I'm not done." I put my arms around him and held him tight. "I need you to be brave for me. Because once we get through this, we're going to have a home again."

He held on to me. "Really?" he whispered, his voice cracking. "Promise?"

It broke my heart.

"I promise."

We sat on the floor around a crate that served as a table. Michael's handlite flickered in candle mode as Michael and Tyler finished eating the box lunch of fried chicken and potato salad from Doris. Rodney had moved his chair to the hall, but within sight. He had ear buds in his ears and moved his head to some beat.

"Is it good?" I pointed to the chicken.

"'S'okay," Tyler said as he sucked on a bone. "We've been eating pudding and fruit cups."

"Church south of the old airport gave them out," Michael said. "Twelve-hour walk, round trip."

"Where're you getting the water?" I asked.

"Houses around here. I just never go to the same one twice."

"Just think," I said to Tyler. "Soon we'll have a kitchen and water out of a faucet."

"Where are we going to live?" Tyler asked. "After you get paid all that money?"

"Anywhere we want," I said.

Tyler tossed up his arms. "The mountains."

"Why there?" Michael asked.

"So we can fish," Tyler said.

Michael laughed. "Fish? Why?"

"Our dad promised he'd take Tyler fishing," I said. "Then the war started."

Michael patted Tyler's shoulder. Talk of the war always dampened the mood.

"So what about you, Cal?" Michael asked. "You a fisher-woman?"

"Not really." I thought about the time I was eight. Dad helped me catch my first fish. Catfish. But I couldn't stomach cleaning it. Instead of getting mad or frustrated, Dad just smiled and did it for me.

"I've never been to the mountains," Michael said. "What's it like?"

"Clean. Crisp."

"And there's fish," Tyler said.

"That aren't contaminated, like in the ocean," I said.

"True," Michael said. "But you have to be brave to fish. You know why?"

"Why?" Tyler asked.

"Because you have to handle slimy, gooey worms." He tickled Tyler's stomach. "Oops, I think one got loose now. He's crawling down your shirt."

Tyler giggled like he was five again.

After the laughter died away, Tyler started to crash from his big day. It wasn't long before he fell asleep, his head on my lap.

"So, tell me. What was it like?" Michael looked at me.

"Unbelievably easy. It's just like sleeping."

"Really?"

"Yeah." We kept our voices low, so as not to wake Tyler. "And I'm getting paid for this. Hello, house money."

"A real home again. He'll love it." Michael looked down at Tyler.

"You too," I said.

He shook his head. "I can't mooch off you."

I wanted to protest, but I held back. Maybe for him, this was too much, too soon.

He dipped his head and caught my eyes with his. "Maybe, if I did the body bank too, we could put our money together. Maybe buy some little place outright."

I smiled. The thought warmed me. No more running. After three years, we'd be of legal age and could do anything we wanted. Get real jobs.

Michael came over and sat next to me. He put his arm around my shoulder and sniffed my hair.

"Smells like . . . cherries," he said.

"Is that good?"

"What do you think?" He smiled. "It's like you were a car, a nice car, that hadn't been washed for a year," he said. "And then you got a wash and wax and all the trimmings." He flicked my dangling earring. "You're sparkling, but you're still the same great car."

I turned to him and leaned in closer. His eyes searched my face as if asking permission. I nodded slightly and, without thinking, licked my lower lip. He leaned down to me, but just then Rodney knocked on the wall.

"Callie? Sorry. We've got to get you back."

Michael closed his eyes. Bad timing, we both knew it.

"Okay, Rodney. Be there in a minute."

We heard him walk back into the hallway. Tyler woke, sat up, and rubbed his face. I touched his arm.

"Tyler, I'm going to have to go. So listen to me, please. You and Michael are a team now, okay?"

"A team," he said, his voice slowed by sleep.

"I'll be thinking about you. I'll be gone a long time, a whole month, but then I'll be back for good. No more leaving. And everything will be better. Okay?"

He nodded. He looked so solemn, it made my heart ache.

"You're the man of the family."

He beamed sleepily.

"Be brave," I said. I held his hand, then pulled him into a hug.

"Hurry back," he whispered. I felt his breath hot on my shoulder.

When I let go, his eyes were filled with tears.

"Be strong," I said.

"Be quick," he answered.

Michael walked me down the hallway. Rodney led the way.

As we got to the top of the stairway, a tall girl was climbing up. Rodney aimed his high-powered light on her and she raised her hand to shield her eyes.

"Do you mind?" she said.

"It's okay," Michael said to Rodney. "She's a friendlie."

Rodney lowered his light so it would be out of her eyes but illuminate her body. She wore a handlite and had short dark hair. She was skinny, like all of us, but still had curves going on.

"Hey, Michael. I was just going to give you something." She reached into a cloth bag and pulled out two oranges. "Got them from an Ender gardener."

"Thanks." Michael took the oranges, which were probably stolen.

She gave a half smile and a half curtsy. "Gotta go. See you later."

"Who's she?" I asked.

Michael looked at me as the girl vanished into the darkness. "Just a friend."

"What's her name?"

"Florina."

"Pretty."

I was glad to have one more friendlie in the building. Rodney, no doubt sensing we needed a moment, walked down a half flight and waited with his back to us.

Michael folded me into a hug. A long, tight one. Our bodies felt the same, more bone than flesh. But the contact felt good.

"I'll miss you," he whispered into my hair.

"Me too." I could have stayed there forever, but I had to pull away. "See you in a month."

He handed me a folded piece of paper.

"What's this?" I asked.

"Look at it later."

I wanted to know more, but there was no time. I slipped it inside my bra, my best hiding place. Then I gave him a smile I hoped he'd remember. "Be good."

"Be careful," he said.

On the ride back, Rodney left me alone with my thoughts. The car rocked me like a baby as the city night flew by my window. Between the boarded-up buildings, life went on, making the landscape look more like a third world country, with makeshift food carts and smoke from barrel-cookers. I thought about how hard the last couple of years had been for Tyler and me.

A light from the street flashed in my eyes for a moment, just like the marshal's lights had when they'd come to capture us.

"Run to your backpack," I'd whispered to Tyler.

We'd scurried to the kitchen in the dark while the marshals banged on the front door. Tyler grabbed his backpack and water bottle; I took mine. Mine had the gun in it.

We ran into the night before the marshals made it to the backyard.

I helped Tyler crawl under fences and run through vacant yards. I was grateful our dad had mapped out the escape plan for us, before he was taken away to the quarantine facility. Tyler and I stayed in our house as long as we could, like the other kids without relatives. We were doing okay, but we knew that eventually the government would come and condemn our house, the way they had the rest of the block. It had been a nice middle-class area, but it was becoming a ghost town. Whatever healthy adults were left served as neighborhood den mothers—until the disease took them too.

Just the other week, the kids across the street had been taken—screaming—by the marshals. We were luckier. We knew when it was time for us to leave because my dad sent us a Zing. I knew that meant the worst.

Before he had left for the quarantine facility, Dad had made me promise that if this day ever came, I was not to think about him, not to grieve. Just be strong and protect my brother, because I would be all he'd have left.

It was the hardest thing I'd ever had to do.

Dad. Gone. Images flashed by me. Steadying hands, guidance, support. Hugs.

I bit my tongue to keep from crying. Don't think about him. Take care of Tyler.

Be strong.

We'd made it to the old library building, next to the park.

It was pitch-black, but our handlites lit our way. We climbed in through a broken basement window in the back.

The scent of musty books filled my nostrils. And the odor of some dirty bodies. A group of kids huddled in the dark behind the stacks, asleep. One of them recognized me.

"She's okay."

I found a space for us against the wall and put our packs beside us.

"Are we safe yet?" Tyler asked between hitched breaths.

"Shhh. It'll be okay," I whispered.

In the morning, some idiot had started a cooking fire, and the smoke brought the marshals. We grabbed our bags and ran. It wasn't until we got to the next stopping point on Dad's map that I reached into my pack and realized my gun had been stolen. Nothing else was missing. All that training and no gun. My insides turned hollow.

No gun. My father would have been so upset. But he didn't have to know. He was dead.

Now, as Rodney sped along the silent streets, I leaned my head against the car window and thought about all the places we had run from in the last year. I let my eyes zone out on the city lights until they became fuzzy pom-poms of color.

The body bank would be the end of running.

Back at Prime Destinations, there was a lot of excitement. It turned out my renter wanted to go tonight. I stood in Doris's office while she ran her fingers through her hair.

"It's all right," she said. "I always pad in extra time. But now we're really pushing it. Go put those on." She pointed to a set of black clothes on a hanger behind me. "You can use my restroom."

I did as she instructed and came out wearing a black turtleneck and pants.

"Excellent. Let's send you off."

"No meal this time?" I asked. "I'm kinda hungry."

Doris put her hand on my back. "This renter prefers you that way." She shrugged. "Maybe she's got reservations at a four-star restaurant."

We hurried to the exchange room, the same one as for the two previous trips. Trax and Terry were waiting for me.

"You look good in black." Terry patted my shoulder as I sat in the chair. "Almost as good as *moi*."

After a few computer checks, Trax looked over at me.

"So everything's the same as before. Just relax," he said. "See you in a month, Callie, right back here."

The cone came toward my face. I waved goodbye to my little team.

My dreams this time were very strange. Tyler had the head of a baby bird. I didn't think anything of that; it just was what it was. I was searching for birdseed—I was going to feed it to Tyler—but I couldn't find any. I called for Michael, but he wasn't around. We were living on some abandoned farm. I ran out to the barn to look for him, climbed a ladder to the hayloft. When I got to the top, I found Michael with a girl. It was Florina. The two of them were lying in the hay, surrounded by hundreds of oranges.

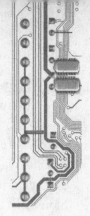

CHAPTER FOUR

Boom, boom, boom. Percussion coursed through my body and my head pounded in sync. A sickly sweet smell assaulted my nose.

Where am I?

I opened my eyes. The world slanted at an angle in a dimly lit place. I was on my side, on the floor. I pressed my palm against it to push myself up and felt a disgusting stickiness. I smelled my hand—pineapple.

Flashes of lasers cut the dark space. In the moments of light, I saw glimpses of people trying to escape, their hands waving in the air. But they kept being pulled back. Then I realized they were just dancing to music.

A pair of shiny patent-leather stiletto heels approached. My ear felt the vibration through the floor of every step.

The owner of the heels knelt beside me. "You okay?" she shouted.

"I don't know." I hadn't had time to take inventory beyond my throbbing head.

"What?"

"I'm not sure!" I shouted back. The yelling made my head hurt.

She crooked her arm in mine. "Upsy-daisy."

She was my age, with a geometric blond bob that covered one eye. Her glittery dress was so short it should have been a blouse. Maybe it was. She guided me over to the side of the room, to a spot where the music wasn't as loud.

"Where am I?" I asked her, touching my temple. I was so confused.

"Club Rune." She gave me a puzzled look. "Don't you remember?"

I shook my head. "How did I get here?"

She giggled. "Oh, you *are* drunk. I'd better get you some caffeine."

"No, don't leave." Was I drunk, or was it something else? Panic rose in my throat and I gripped her arm like a life preserver. "Please, I'm—"

"Let's get you to a chair."

She supported me as I hobbled across the room in my heels. I looked down and saw that I was also wearing a dress, a short metallic sheath. It felt cool against my skin. An evening bag hung from a strap on my shoulder. And my shoes, also stilettos, were like something I'd only seen on stars in the Pages.

She stopped at a velvet love seat by the wall and eased me down onto it. Soft. I hadn't sat on something that comfortable in so long, I'd forgotten what it felt like.

The music stopped. I'd seen nightclubs in holos, back when my parents were alive, but I had never been in one. I didn't even know they existed anymore, especially ones just for teens. Was this what the privileged Starters got to do?

"You're looking better already." She smiled at me.

The blue neon light from the bar spilled over onto the love seat. Even under the unflattering light she was stunning.

"You're new at this, aren't you?" she asked.

"What?"

"Sorry, I didn't introduce myself. I'm Madison."

"Callie."

"Cute name. Do you like it?"

I shrugged. "I guess so."

"I like mine too. Pleased to meet you, Callie." She extended her hand. Weird, but I shook it. "So, as I was saying, this is your first time, isn't it?"

I nodded. "My first time here."

The last thing I remembered was being put under at the body bank. I should have woken up there. What could have happened? I was on the edge of panic, but I had enough sense to remember I wasn't supposed to talk about the body bank. I had to act like I belonged here.

"Darling frock," Madison said, feeling the fabric of my dress. "It's such fun to be able to wear little things like this again, isn't it? And come to places like this? Sure beats sitting in a rocking chair, crocheting in front of reruns on a Saturday night." She winked and elbowed me. "Maybe with you it's mahjong? Or bridge?"

"Yeah." I put on a smile while I looked around. I had no idea what she was talking about.

"Callie, dear, you don't have to pretend with me."

I blinked.

"It takes one to know one, missy. You passed all the tests."

Madison used her fingers to count. "No tattoos, no piercings, no neon hair colors . . ." She then used me to illustrate the rest of her points. "Expensive clothes, fine jewelry, good manners, and flawlessly beautiful."

Me? She was talking about me?

"Oh, and of course, we know so much." She patted my arm. "Because we've lived it."

My brain was fuzzy, but I was beginning to get it.

"Come on, Callie, you're a PD client. You're a renter. Like me." She leaned in close and I smelled gardenia.

"You . . . ?"

"Don't I fit the list to a tee?" She waved her hand down her own body. "It is flawlessly beautiful, this little body, don't you think?"

I didn't know what to say. She was a renter. She might report me if she knew I was a donor who had somehow malfunctioned. I might be fired and never get the money to help Tyler.

"It's great."

"Okay, I confess, this is Club Rune, after all." She gestured to the room. "Lots of us come here, so you were easy to spot."

"There are more of . . . us? Where?"

Madison scanned the room. "There. That guy over there, the one who looks like a star? Renter. And there, that redhead?"

"Renter?"

"Look at her." She put on an exaggerated accent. "Could she be any more perfect?"

"But the others are real teens?"

"For sure."

"What about him?" I nodded to a guy across the room who had caught my eye. He was holding a soda and talking to two other guys. There was definitely something special about him. "The one in the blue shirt and black jacket? He's got to be a renter."

"Him?" Madison folded her arms. "Oh, he's cute, all right. But I talked to him earlier. All teen, inside and out."

I wasn't very good at guessing. To me, he looked every bit as hot as the renters she'd pointed out. Maybe more so. He turned his head and stared right at us. I glanced away.

"Plenty of regular, filthy rich teens here," Madison went on. "You can tell because their provincial grandparents won't let them get any work done."

"Work?"

"Surgery. So they're not as beautiful as we are. And you can always test them by asking about life before the war. They barely know anything." She laughed. "Guess they don't teach history in their private Zype Schools."

I felt my heart racing. It was all so upside down. I had to keep reminding myself that the stunning Madison was really a hundred-and-something-year-old woman.

And the fact that she thought the same about me was really messed up.

"If you're feeling better, Callie, I really need to go get a drink. Something with a long, naughty name."

"They'll serve you?"

"Honey, this club is all private. Totally hush-hush, just like the body bank." She patted my arm. "Don't worry, sweet pea, I'll be just steps away."

She slinked off the love seat. I leaned my elbows on my knees and put my forehead in my palms. I wanted the world to stop spinning. But the more I tried to figure it all out, the worse it got. My head throbbed. Why had I woken up in a club instead of the body bank? What had happened?

Everything had been going so well before. I was going to get paid, going to get Tyler a warm place to sleep, a real home. And now this.

Then I heard a voice.

Hello?

I raised my head. It wasn't Madison. She was halfway across the room, standing at the bar. I looked behind me. No one was standing near me.

Had I imagined it?

Can . . . hear me?

No, it was real, the voice was . . .

Inside. My. Head.

Was I hallucinating? My heart raced. Maybe Madison was right and I was drunk. Or maybe I had hit my head when I fell. Something was very wrong. I started to hyperventilate.

The voice sounded female. I held my breath to try to calm down and also to hear better.

The club noise muffled my perception. I put my fingers in my ears and tried to listen, but all I heard was the pounding, of my own heartbeat. I couldn't shake off the shock of hearing a voice this way.

Where was the exit? I wanted out. I needed air.

The next voice I heard was young, very male, and coming from right there in front of me.

"Are you okay?" It was him. The guy in the blue shirt, "all teen," as Madison had put it. He looked concerned.

What did he just say? He was asking if I was okay. I fought to control myself, not to appear panicked.

"Yeah. Good." I tugged on my dress in a lame effort to cover my legs.

He was even better-looking up close, complete with dimples. But I had no time for this distraction. I needed to see if that voice was going to come back again. He just stared at me while I listened.

It was silent in my head. Could it have been my imagination? Because I was so disoriented, suddenly being thrown back into my body this way? Or maybe this guy had just scared the Voice away.

Dimples wore an expensive-looking black jacket. I thought about Madison's verdict on him. I stood up and ran through the checklist.

No tats, piercings, or strange hair color: check. Expensive clothes and jewelry—what brand of watch was on his wrist?—check. Good manners, flawlessly handsome, check. Renter.

Then he turned his face toward the light from the bar, and I was close enough to spot an inch-long scar near his chin. No way Doris would've let that go.

"I saw you fall." He held out a hand towel. "I went to get this from the restroom."

"Thanks." I put it to my forehead and saw a smile creep over his face. "What's so funny?"

"It's not for your head." He gently took it back from me and wiped my arm, dirty from the floor.

"I slipped," I said. "Someone spilled a drink. And with these heels . . ."

"Great heels." He glanced at them and smiled, sparking those dimples.

Being the focus of his attention was too much. I had to look away. A guy like this, rich and good-looking, interested in me, the street kid? Then I caught my reflection in a mirrored column and was jolted back to the new reality. I had forgotten I looked like a megastar.

As I turned back, I noticed Madison was still at the bar, struggling to get the attention of the Ender bartender, who seemed hard of hearing.

Dimples twisted to look in the direction I was looking and then dropped the towel on a small table.

"She your friend?" he asked.

"Sort of."

He held up a finger, like he was trying to remember. "Her name's Madison, right?"

I nodded.

"We talked earlier," he said. "She's kind of funny."

"How?"

"Asked me a lot of questions."

"What kind of questions?"

"History, if you can believe it. Things from like twenty or thirty years ago. I mean, would you know what holo won ten Oscars a decade ago?"

I squinted and tried to remember if my dad had ever mentioned that. He would have known. I shrugged.

"See, you don't know either," he said. "I obviously failed Madison's test. When I didn't know the answers, she just turned and left. I came to dance, not to audition for a game show." He looked at his feet and then at me. "Would you like to . . . ?"

"Me?" I realized the music had restarted, but quieter, slower. "No. I can't."

"Sure you can."

I thought about Michael, back there, taking care of Tyler

for me. It didn't seem right. I had no business dancing. I still had no idea what had happened, or where I was, or how I had gotten there, and I really wasn't myself.

"I'm just too woozy."

"Maybe later?" he said, sounding hopeful. He raised his brows.

"Sorry. I'm gonna be leaving soon." I knew it was blunt, but there was no sense giving him false hope.

He hid it well, but his eyes reflected the disappointment I felt. He looked like he was about to make some other move, but just then Madison returned, a cup in one hand, a cocktail in the other.

"Here, the java is for you. I hope black is okay." She handed me the cup and then noticed the guy. "Oh, Blake, right? Hi again."

Blake nodded but didn't take his eyes off me. We shared a smile, a secret moment, at Madison's expense. One of those "she doesn't know we talked about her" bonding experiences. She didn't seem to notice, too busy freeing a piece of pineapple impaled on a tiny sword from her drink.

"Better get back to my friends," he said.

Madison swallowed the fruit and gave a polite smile. "So nice to see you again, Blake."

"Night, Madison." Then he smiled at me. "See you later, Callie." He cocked his head and turned on his heel in a kind of dance spin.

I had never told him my name. Somehow, he had found out.

I watched him walk away, hands in his pockets. I was feeling a little better.

Listen . . . please . . .

A chill went up my spine. No. That Voice again. In my head. If I was imagining it, I was doing a great job, because it sounded so very real. This was all wrong. I had to get out of here.

Wherever the Voice was coming from—from my mind or from someone else—the next words stabbed at me like needles.

Listen . . . important . . . Callie . . . do not return to . . . Prime Destinations.

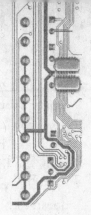

CHAPTER FIVE

I stood in the club, frozen. Was this some reaction to the drug Prime had given me? Or maybe it had to do with the chip.

I turned to Madison.

Don't say anything to her. . . .

She gripped my arm. "Don't. Forget. The. Rules. About. Boys." She punctuated each word with a wag of her finger.

Madison brought me back to the physical world. She looked like a pop star but acted like a granny.

"Pay attention," she said, her slant-cut bangs falling over one eye. "This is important."

"Which rule are we talking about?" I asked neutrally.

"You know." She lowered her voice. "No s-e-x." She raised her brows. "Especially with real teens."

"What do you mean 'especially'? If it's a rule, then there's no 'especially' clause."

"You know what I mean." She rolled her eyes. "Just forget about that boy."

With voices in my head, I had much bigger things to worry about. "What boy?" I asked.

That made her laugh.

Blake hung with his male friends at the far end of the club. "So he doesn't know we're renters?" I asked.

"Did you not read your contract, missy? Of course he doesn't know! We're not supposed to tell any outsiders."

"Who reads contracts anymore?" I shrugged. Blake looked back at me from across the room, pulling me with his eyes.

Madison folded her arms, sparkling from glitter dust. "You better finish that coffee."

I drained my cup, wincing from the bitterness. Maybe it would clear my head. Maybe it would make the Voice go away completely.

"What's the matter, you don't take it black?" she asked.

My mouth felt itchy. "No. Never." The only coffee I'd had was in lattes with lots of sugar and whipped cream, before the war.

"Consider it necessary medicine." Madison looked at her watch. "Heavens, it's late. I must go." She opened her tiny purse and pulled something out. "Here, Callie dear. My card."

She handed it to me. Before I could look at it, she asked, "Where's yours?"

I opened my purse and didn't see one. There was a valet ticket, a universal ID, a phone, and a wad of cash. I tried not to gasp at the sight of all that money.

"I must've run out," I said.

"That's okay, just send me a Zing. Well, I'm going. Big day tomorrow. How about walking me out?"

She linked her arm with mine. As we passed Blake, I felt his eyes on me. I didn't look back. I kept my focus on Madison, noting how she walked with long, confident strides, how she let stares from admirers bounce off her as if she were surrounded by a force field.

Two Ender doormen opened the tall metallic doors for us. We stepped out into the chilly night air, where a cluster of teens waited for their cars. Madison handed her ticket to the valet and then turned to me.

"From the voice of experience." She wrapped her arms around herself and rocked on her heels. "Take it easy your first time out. Nothing too wild. Don't let anything happen to that body, because the fines are simply atrocious."

She didn't need to tell me to protect this body. I kept quiet, knowing we'd soon say goodbye and I'd never see her again.

She tilted her head. Her hoop earrings dangled. "I remember my first rental. It was nine months ago."

"How many have you done?"

"Sweet pea, who's counting?" She smiled. "So many different bodies to try. I spend more time young than old now."

The Ender valet pulled up in a flashy red convertible, all curves and grooves. He looked over at Madison and waved.

"That's yours?"

"It's just my 'teen' car." She winked.

I walked with her to her car and admired the glossy, dimensional paint. The illusion of layers was so real, you felt like you were looking into a canyon.

"To the edge." I nodded to her car.

Madison's brows furrowed. "Callie, are you sure it's your first time?"

I tensed. "Why?"

"Because you sound like the real deal. I still have to think about what I say, when I'm trying to pass."

Trying to pass—that was exactly what I was trying to do, only the other way around. I wanted to leave her convinced I was a renter, like her. What could I do? Of course. Go the other way.

Leaning in, I touched her arm, the way she had touched mine earlier. I deepened my voice slightly and spoke slowly, deliberately. "I made the greatest effort to study voices before I began my rental. Besides, I am truly young—only ninety-five!" I winked.

"I hate you." She tipped the valet. "Just kidding. You'll have to teach me your tricks sometime."

Another car pulled up behind hers. "Must go. Pleasure meeting you, Callie. Tomorrow, I go parasailing!" She threw her arms in the air. "Have fun with your new body."

Madison got in her car, revved the engine, and roared off. Nothing old about her driving.

"Miss." The valet held out his hand. "Your ticket?"

I pulled it out of my purse. I'd waited until Madison left in case I had trouble driving. How was I going to do this? My palms felt clammy. The last time I'd driven had been two years ago, when Dad had me practice in a school parking lot. What was it he had said? Hold the wheel at ten and two o'clock. Slow down before braking. Never Zing while driving.

Some guys exited the club and undressed me with their eyes. Total teens, from the look of their zits. I turned away. I didn't want them discovering who I really was. I just wanted to get out of here.

I realized the Voice hadn't returned. No one was talking to me and the Voice hadn't come back. That was good.

I needed to recall everything I knew about driving, but the more I tried to remember, the faster my heart beat. Please let the car be something easy to drive, I thought.

Then the valet drove up in a yellow mega–sports car that looked like a spaceship.

No. Not that one.

Sure enough, the valet stopped in front of me. The car was twice the machine Madison's was. The top was down. Even here, with all the spoiled, rich teens, murmurs rippled through the waiting crowd.

I felt every eye on me as I walked to the driver's side. I tipped the valet like Madison had, slid into the plush leather seat, and faced more gauges and buttons than a jet pilot. The valet shut my door and I held up my hand so he wouldn't leave.

"Wait," I whispered. "Where are we?"

"Where?" He looked puzzled.

"What city?" I kept my voice low.

"Downtown. You're in downtown L.A." He pointed to something on my dashboard before running off to the next car.

I realized he was pointing to the navigation system. I pressed the button to turn it on. The airscreen lit up in the space between my face and the windshield. I saw the word "home" floating there and I touched it.

Home. That was what I wanted. The car knew where I lived, even if I didn't.

I put the car in drive and released the brake. Unlike Madison's, my grand exit was in total turtle mode. As I inched away, I heard a guy saying goodbye.

I looked in the rearview mirror and saw Blake standing there, one hand in his pocket, the other waving at me.

Once I was out of sight, a few blocks from the club, I pulled over to the curb by an office building. My heart raced, my legs shook. But at least I hadn't crashed the car . . . yet. I hadn't been drunk tonight, just disoriented, because my head was getting clearer by the minute. I had to figure out what was going on. How could I hear voices inside my head?

At this late hour, the streets were empty and quiet. If that Voice was going to return, this would be the time. I listened, holding my breath, afraid of what I might hear.

Silence. Thankfully. The mystery voice was gone.

What had Prime done to my head? Maybe when they inserted the chip, something had happened to my brain. Could it have been the chip itself? I never should have trusted them with my body.

I needed to pull myself together. I stared at the car controls. The engine purred like a tiger while I reached for the purse on the passenger's seat and pulled out the universal ID. It had my holo on it, which rotated to show my profile. I recognized the pictures—they were the ones they'd taken at the body bank. But the name on the ID was Callie Winterhill, not Callie Woodland. The address matched the one on the GPS airscreen navigator.

The body bank probably printed up IDs for all the renters. My stats would be encoded in the card—my DNA, fingerprints. "Winterhill" was probably the renter's last name. That way, she could pretend to be a relative if stopped by any authorities. She could pose as her own grandniece or grand-daughter.

So I had this great car to take me anywhere. I really wanted to go see my brother. But I remembered how Tinnenbaum said they could track me via my chip. They knew where Tyler lived; Rodney had driven me there. If they saw my chip go there, they'd know it wasn't my renter inside, but me. And they might accuse me of breaking the contract.

I could return to the body bank—wasn't that what they'd want me to do? But the Voice—*Don't return to Prime*—had sounded so ominous. I shivered. What would happen to me if I did?

The club had been so loud that I couldn't hear the Voice clearly. But the more I thought about it, the more the Voice seemed like it was an Ender. Could it have been somebody at the body bank, speaking to me via the chip somehow? Doris, maybe? But why would she tell me not to return to Prime? Did she want me out in the field because this would be fixed soon? Or maybe there was some other reason not to go back.

If I let the car take me to the home of my renter, I might be able to find some answers. If my rental had ended early for some reason, maybe she would be there. I glanced at my watch—well, Winterhill's super-fancy diamond-studded timepiece. It was past midnight.

I also saw that it was November 14. It had been a week since my rental started. I still had three whole weeks to go.

What had happened?

Just then, movement flashed across my rearview mirror. Soft footsteps rushed closer, athletic shoes pounding pavement.

Renegades, running at my car from behind.

Five of them, with chains and pipes and angry eyes.

My blood froze. I scanned the buttons. Drive. Where's drive?

One of the creeps leapt onto the back of the convertible. Shaved head covered with tats.

I found drive and slammed the car into gear hard. Floored it. The renegade flew back and fell off.

The view in the mirror showed him getting up. His pals were giving me the finger. I shuddered.

This was a whole new game. Just because I had a car didn't mean I could let my guard down. In fact, now that I looked rich, I needed to be more alert than ever.

I took a deep breath and exhaled.

From then on, the navigator was my only company. He had an Australian accent and a voice so relaxed that it helped calm me. I followed his instructions to the freeway. It was much easier driving on the straight highway, and this late, there were few cars in my way. I passed a couple of work corps crews, about twenty Starters doing road construction. A wave of guilt washed over me as I whooshed past them in that expensive car, with my designer clothes and diamond watch. I wanted to shout out that none of this was mine.

But they were already white dots in my rearview mirror.

After a half hour heading west, the nav took me to the community of Bel Air. I remembered how, before the war, lots of celebrities had lived there. I passed a private security guard who stared at me as he drove by. I passed dream mansions, some with guards. Then the nav said I had arrived home.

He hadn't warned me it was going to be a mega-mansion.

There was no guard that I could see, but there were big iron gates. I drove up to them and stopped, braking so hard I lurched. I sat back and looked for the opener. A tiny black disc sat in the cup holder. I pressed it, and the gates opened like they must in heaven.

I drove up the cobblestone driveway. To the left, the driveway curved around to the front of the mansion. To the right, it led to a five-car attached garage. The garage doors had opened when the gates did, revealing three parked cars: an SUV, a limo, and a small blue sports car. I pulled into one of the two empty spots and turned off the engine.

I went limp. I hadn't hit anything. I had gotten Mrs. Winterhill's priceless car safely back where it belonged. I sure hoped she appreciated that.

Now what? I realized there were some strange possibilities here. I hoped Mrs. Winterhill would be home so she could explain what had happened. Maybe everything would get straightened out and we could start over. If I was lucky, I'd get credit for my days so far.

A door inside the garage served as a side entrance to the house. I knocked on it. No one answered. It was close to one a.m. I looked at the touchpad by the door but had no idea what the code was.

I walked through the garage and went out a door at the back. My stilettos tapped on the cobblestones as I walked toward the front of the house past super-lush landscaping—

rolling lawns, flowering bushes, stately trees. Winterhill's water bill had to be humongous.

I climbed two slate steps to the massive front doors. My presence set off the bell sensor, and I heard chimes from inside the house.

After a minute, I heard footsteps. The door opened.

A thin, sleepy Ender gripped her robe and stepped aside to let me in. "So you finally decided to come home."

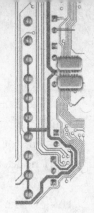

CHAPTER SIX

My mouth went dry as I entered the impressive foyer of Winterhill's mansion. It was like something from an old-time movie. Antique furnishings, a ceiling that reached to the clouds, and a grand staircase to take you there.

The Ender shut the door.

She glared at me for an awkward moment. If she was waiting for me to go first, she was going to wait forever.

Finally, she spoke.

"I trust you enjoyed yourself, Mrs. Winterhill?" She tightened her robe's sash as if it were a noose.

With that question, I knew there was zero hope of finding the real Mrs. Winterhill at home. If I told this stern Ender the truth, I'd either be thrown out or taken back to the body bank. Maybe I'd get in trouble. Maybe they'd fire me and I'd never get our house money.

I was not in any shape to make a quick decision. I needed sleep.

"Yes," I said. "It was fabulous."

She examined my face. Or maybe I was just being paranoid.

"Forgot your key again?"

I nodded.

"You'll find it in the car, I'm sure. Would you care for anything?" she asked. "I made some of your favorite cookies."

I wanted to avoid any interaction with her. My brain was fried from having had to lie all night.

"You must be as tired as I am," I said. "Don't worry about me. Go to bed."

"All right. Good night, Mrs. Winterhill."

She turned toward the corridor to the right. Then she stopped.

"I almost forgot," she said. "Redmond called."

"Thank you." Whoever.

I watched as she continued down the hallway to her room. I glanced around the grand foyer. My old house, our family home, had been nice enough, a modest ranch in the Valley. Winterhill's mansion had me awestruck. It was like stepping back in time or being in some museum. An antique marble table dominated the center of the foyer and served as a base for a massive display of white flowers that would have thrilled my mother. Their fragrance added to my floaty sense of intoxication.

I looked up at the grand mahogany staircase that led to the second floor. Her bedroom had to be up there. I held on to the buttery-smooth banister and climbed the stairs.

I turned to the left at the half level, passing various portraits. They were all of the same woman—Mrs. Winterhill, no doubt—at different stages of her life. She was always beautiful, with high cheekbones and a strong nose and jaw line. Her eyes followed me.

I reached the second-floor hallway, which was dimly lit by wall sconces. I turned to my right. There were several doors on either side of the hallway, and all of them were closed. Did anyone else live here? I figured I was about to find out.

I opened the first door on the right. I waved my hand where the light pad should be and the lights came on.

This first room looked like a guest room—no personal items in sight. I shut off the light and went to the next door, which proved to be a sewing room. The next room was a bedroom decorated for a teen girl. I wasn't sure if it was Mrs. Winterhill's fantasy teen room or whether an actual teen lived there. I was relieved to see that it was empty.

I went across the hallway. The first door I tried was locked. I continued to the next door, where I found what I was looking for—Winterhill's master bedroom. An ebony four-poster bed sat in the center of the room. The posts twisted like taffy, each one ending with a claw clutching a ball. Over the bed hung a gold-colored canopy with precise pleats gathered in the center. The green-and-gold striped spread had generous tassels dangling at each corner. A mountain of pillows crowned the head of the bed.

The best thing about the bed was that it was empty of any Mr. Winterhill.

As inviting as the bed looked to me, what drew my attention was the area to the left of it. There was a separate sitting area with a chaise lounge and a small antique desk. On the desk was a flat, inlaid wooden box.

I opened the box. Inside was a computer.

I hurried to bolt the door, rushed back to the computer,

sat down, and kicked off my heels. I noticed a yellow light on the panel and I waved my hand over it. The airscreen appeared above.

If a power or cell outage had hit Beverly Hills, maybe that would explain why I had lost my connection to my renter. I searched the Pages.

Nothing came up. I continued to read, but the news wasn't anything new.

I searched for my mom and dad, hoping some pictures of them still existed somewhere. I found one of them at a party. I stared at it, soaking up every detail of their faces.

I sank low in the chair and felt my eyelids getting heavy. It was two a.m.

Next to the computer was a holo-frame with an image of Mrs. Winterhill. Her name was etched into the edge: *Helena Winterhill*. Her features were the same as in the wall portraits, but this was a more recent image of her. Although she appeared to be around a hundred, she still had a great figure, as well as an elegance and a strength about her.

"Helena Winterhill, where are you?"

She just smiled back at me.

I rose, slipped off the party dress, draped it over the chair, and crawled into bed in my underwear. I pictured Tyler and Michael in their little fortresses, already sound asleep.

In the morning, I opened my eyes to a gold canopy above me. Beneath me, silky smooth sheets. My head floated on the world's softest pillow, while the delicate scent of cedar blended with honeysuckle, making the room incredibly relaxing. I was in definite princess territory.

I climbed out of bed and picked up my renter's cell phone.

No call from Prime. Was I being too optimistic to hope I could somehow salvage this?

It was nine o'clock. Michael would be getting washing water for Tyler about now.

I walked over to Helena's bathroom. A large, open marble area defined the shower. As soon as I stepped close enough, a waterfall began to flow from the ceiling. There were two pads for adjusting the temperature. I waved my hand in front of the red one to make the water warmer. I slipped out of my silk bra and panties and stepped under the waterfall.

I felt a second of guilt about the waste of so much water. Just a second. It was so refreshing to close my eyes and feel water flowing over my head. I was renewed.

I wrapped myself in a thick heated towel and wiggled my toes on the fluffy rug as warm air jets blew my skin dry. When I bent down to pick up the bra, I remembered the paper Michael had handed me when we'd said goodbye. I'd stuck it inside my bra.

Only that had been a week ago. A different bra.

I went to the dresser in Helena's bedroom. I was going to check the underwear drawer, but a piece of paper on top of the dresser stopped me.

The paper had crease marks from having been folded. It was a drawing of me. My face. I didn't remember posing for it, but it was definitely Michael's style. This had to be the paper he handed me before I left with Rodney.

Helena must have found it hidden in my—our—bra.

I stared at the drawing, mesmerized. It was beautiful. Ethereal. And a little bit haunting.

It wasn't an exact likeness. He took artistic liberties, like giving me two different-colored eyes. But I saw it as a perceptive interpretation of my spirit. It made me wonder, was it because Michael was such a gifted artist? Or were we that connected?

I wasn't sure of the answer, but I was touched. I put it back on top of the dresser.

The dark wooden paneling of the bedroom concealed two closets. I opened the first one and sorted through the Enderwear: dark suits and dresses, all in a size way too big for me. I tried the next closet and found clothing for me. Just my size.

I picked out some jeans and a knit top and put them on. Perfect. On the dresser was a locket on a chain that went well with my outfit, so I put it on. As I fastened it, I felt my hair was still damp. I guessed I hadn't stood in front of the jets as long as I should have. When I patted the back of my head, I touched something odd—the incision where Prime had inserted the chip. It was an oval shape. It was tender.

Also on the dresser was the watch I had been wearing last night. I could only guess how much it must have cost. It could probably feed a family for a year. I opened a drawer and put it away. I didn't want to be responsible for that if it got stolen or damaged.

I held up the evening bag from last night. Too dressy. I found a cool leather shoulder bag in the closet—just right—and transferred the driver's license and the cell phone into it. I took out the wad of cash and fanned it. It wasn't really mine. But I needed it now, for gas and food, while I tried to figure out what was going on.

I decided I would keep track and pay Mrs. Winterhill back out of my paycheck. After counting the bills, I transferred the cash to the shoulder bag.

There was one more thing in the evening bag. Madison's card. It read "Rhiannon Huffington." The holo showed Madison as she really was, a plump 125-year-old woman in a silk caftan, with a toothy grin. She was blowing a sassy kiss and winking. This was the big woman inside little teen Madison. Rhiannon might be ditzy, but she sure knew how to enjoy herself. I had to hand it to her.

I slipped her card into the shoulder bag.

I put away last night's clothes and made the bed. Then I realized that Mrs. Winterhill probably didn't ever make her own bed. She had that housekeeper. So I messed it up. I was about to leave when I noticed I'd left the computer out.

I sat down and closed the box that held the computer. Maybe there was something else here that might tell me more about Mrs. Winterhill. I opened the desk's side drawer and saw only pens and notepads. But in the middle drawer was a silver case sized for business cards.

"Helena Winterhill" was the name on the cards. The hologram picture was the same as the one on the desk. I took out a couple of cards and slipped them into my purse.

Helena's cell buzzed. I looked at it. Someone had sent a Zing.

It read: *I know what you're going to do. DON'T. Don't do it.*

I stopped. Who was this? Some friend of Helena's who had discovered her little renting excursion? Enders could be so judgmental.

Or did this have something to do with the Voice?

I dropped the phone into my purse. I wanted to get out of there, and I wanted to do it without running into the housekeeper. I unbolted the bedroom door and peeked out into the hallway. No one was there, not in either direction. I closed the bedroom door behind me as quietly as I could and went down the stairs.

When I turned at the half-level landing, I saw the

housekeeper waiting for me at the bottom. She had a watering can in her hand. She set it down on the floor near the table with the flowers.

"Good morning, Mrs. Winterhill." She wiped her hands on her apron. She wore simple black pants and a black shirt.

"Good morning."

I tried to determine which room would lead to the garage entrance. I wasn't sure.

"Breakfast is waiting," she said.

"I'm not hungry. I'm going out."

"Not hungry?" She pulled her head back as if this was something Mrs. Winterhill never said. "Are you ill? Should I phone the doctor?"

"No, no. I'm all right."

"Then you must at least have your coffee and juice. To wash your vitamins down."

She turned and walked down the hallway, leading me to the gourmet kitchen. Like the bathrooms, it wasn't true to the period of the rest of the house but instead was filled with the latest modern conveniences.

The smell of cinnamon filled the kitchen and made my heart ache. It reminded me of happy weekend brunches Mom, Dad, Tyler, and I used to have when we were a family. The housekeeper had set a place for me at the large center island. A massive silver bowl was filled with cut fruit, including my favorite: papaya. I could feel my mouth watering.

I sat and put my napkin on my lap. The housekeeper had her back to me as she fussed at the stove. I looked to the right and saw a short hallway that led to a door. Was that the way to the garage? She came over carrying a pan and put a piece of French toast on my plate. It had been so long since I'd seen

French toast. She brought over a sifter and sprinkled powdered sugar on top, just like my mother used to do.

I was starving. I had no idea when Mrs. Winterhill had last eaten, but it felt like it had been days. The housekeeper had mentioned vitamins. Interesting that my renter was so keen on taking good care of a temporary body.

Everything tasted so good, so fresh. The juice was like ambrosia, a mix of several tropical flavors. I was happy to see a pitcher there because I was so thirsty. I stared at the cornucopia of fruit and wondered if there was any way I could get some to Tyler and Michael.

After I had finished my meal, the housekeeper brought me a small bowl of vitamins. The pills were all different colors, so I assumed she wanted me to take all of them.

"Have to take care of that body," she said. "Even if it isn't yours."

I nodded, my mouth full of vitamins, and drank some juice. I put my napkin on the counter and stood. "Thank you. It was delicious."

The housekeeper shot me a funny look. I wondered if that was the wrong thing to say. I walked to the door that I hoped would be my exit.

I put my hand on the knob and pulled it. I was facing the pantry.

"What are you looking for?" the housekeeper asked.

I scanned the shelves and grabbed a Supertruffle. "Found it."

I came out and saw another door through a small side foyer. That had to be it. I was about to walk that way when a sound startled me.

It was the front doorbell.

The housekeeper left to answer it. I went to the side foyer and opened the door. I smiled when I saw the yellow rocket ship and the other cars waiting like my trusty steeds.

I heard the housekeeper calling to me as she rushed back to the kitchen.

"What is it?" I asked.

"There's a . . . boy here to see you," she whispered, her face pale.

"A boy?"

She brought her wrinkled hand to her mouth and nodded. Her features were twisted, as if she had the worst possible news in the world to relay. She let her hand fall to her apron and clenched it.

"He says you have a date."

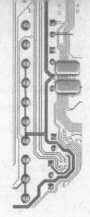

CHAPTER SEVEN

I hurried to the front foyer with the housekeeper on my heels.

It was that guy from the club, Blake, wearing jeans and a leather jacket. What was he doing here?

"Hey, Callie."

"Blake." I walked to the marble table to anchor myself. In the daylight, his eyes were actually more piercing.

"You feeling better?" he asked.

"Yeah, thanks." Had he come all this way just to check on me?

"As I told Eugenia"—he nodded to the housekeeper, who stood behind me—"we had a date for noon." He looked from her to me. "You didn't forget, did you?"

How did he know where I lived? I stammered something incoherent.

"You did," he said, sighing.

I looked back at Eugenia. At least now I knew her name. "Could you . . . please?"

She headed toward the kitchen. I turned back to Blake.

"When did you ask me out?" My mind was racing. Images of the evening blurred together. "And when did I say yes?"

He stepped closer. "When I met you last night, sitting at the bar in Club Rune. Don't you remember? You couldn't get the bartender's attention. I ordered for you."

"The bar?"

"We talked, had some laughs. You said you like horses," he said.

I had been in Club Rune, but I hadn't sat at the bar. He must have talked to Helena, before I reclaimed my body. That was how he'd known my name. His gaze was so intense, I thought it would melt me. I ran my fingers over the cool marble table. The overwhelming perfume of the flowers was not helping.

"I wasn't feeling like myself last night," I said.

He lowered his head to catch my gaze. "You want a rain check?"

I was about to turn him down, because theoretically, I was working. But the body bank hadn't contacted me yet. They knew how to find me via my chip. And they could call Helena's house if they wanted to reach me. So far, I hadn't done anything wrong. I was just waiting for them.

And the memory of that voice in my head convinced me I should not go to them.

"No," I said.

He looked at me with a question on his face. "No, meaning no?" he asked. "As in go away, don't ever bother me again?"

I smiled. "No." It was fun teasing him. "No as in no rain check needed. Just give me one minute, okay?"

I dashed upstairs to Helena's bedroom. I told myself the

real reason I could justify this date was because I needed a big favor from him. This was my chance to make friends with an actual teen, not just some Ender claiming to be one. A teen with a car and the freedom and ability to go anywhere. He could deliver a favor and Tyler and Michael would benefit. I'd wait for the right moment and ask him.

I took the drawing of me off the dresser, folded it up, and slipped it in my purse.

Blake and I walked outside together. His car, a sporty red bullet, waited in the curved driveway. It had a brushed metal finish with smooth lines and no useless extras. He opened the door for me and then got in on the driver's side. The restraints whirred as they hugged us to the seats.

I noticed the gate was open. Maybe it hadn't closed last night?

As Blake pulled away, I saw the housekeeper, Eugenia, standing at a window on the second floor. Disapproval clung to her face like an extra layer of powder. And in case I wasn't getting the message, she shook her head from side to side.

We drove through the gate and onto the street, and suddenly my stomach tightened.

What was I doing?

"You okay? Comfortable?" Blake asked.

I nodded.

I was a sham. He was rich and I wasn't, yet there I was, pretending, wearing pricey designer clothes and acting like I lived in a mansion, with a servant, even. I knew I should tell him the truth about me, but how would it sound? Blake, guess what, I'm really a street orphan who sleeps on the floor of abandoned buildings and is only alive because of food salvaged from restaurant garbage bins. I have no home, no clothes, no relatives. Nothing. And worse, I sold my body to this place called Prime Destinations. Two weeks ago, I didn't look like this. They lasered and bleached and plucked and buffed me. And technically, this body now belongs to an Ender named Helena Winterhill, because she paid for it. You could be dating her right now, some hundred-plus-year-old woman, and not even know it. What do you think of that?

I looked over at him. He was blissfully unaware, driving with ease. He caught me staring and smiled, then focused his attention on the road.

I leaned back in my seat and inhaled the scent of new leather.

Did Cinderella ever consider fessing up to the prince, that night she was enjoying herself in the fancy ball gown? Did she even think of telling him, oh, by the way, Prince, the coach isn't mine, I'm really a filthy little barefoot servant on borrowed time? No. She took her moment.

And then went quietly away after midnight.

As we drove, I did the math in my head. I was thirteen when the war broke out and had been living the street life since I was fifteen. That was a pretty good excuse for this to be my first date. What I knew about dating came from watching holos with my dad, who loved them so. I remembered going out to the local Xperience for the total immersion of sight, sound, and weather. I missed how the seats would rumble and shift, making it feel like you were really in the cockpit of a spaceship or gliding along, flying with fairies. I loved it so much, I used to dream of doing it for a living, working with the creation of Xperiences when I grew up.

For me, dates were something out of musicals, where

everything went perfectly, or comedies, where everything was zany and wacky. Which was it going to be?

Blake took me to a private horse ranch in the hills north of Malibu. The one time my dad had taken us riding at a public stable had been nothing like this. Those horses had been dull and tired, and we had mostly walked on flat, dry trails surrounded by skeletal shrubs. I'd thought it was the greatest—what did I know? But Blake and I rode through lush meadows on spirited Arabians with glossy chestnut coats. We trotted on a path through a pine forest and crossed bubbling streams. It was just the two of us, no other riders—no other people at all—as far as I could see. Blake was the better rider, but he paced his horse to match mine. I didn't want to go beyond a trot. I didn't dare risk falling and hurting myself.

After a couple of hours, Blake stopped his horse and dismounted. "Ready for lunch?"

We were in the middle of nowhere. "Sure. But no flash food drive-thrus here."

He smiled. "Just follow me."

He took the reins and walked his horse around a bend. Under the shade of a large oak tree was a table covered with food: several kinds of sandwiches, grapes, fruit kebabs, brownies. He saw my expression and laughed.

"I just asked for peanut butter and some chips." He shrugged.

He helped me dismount and we tied our reins to a tree. There were buckets of water and some hay for the horses.

He pulled out his phone. "Come here."

A quirky smile formed on his lips. I hesitated a second, then stepped forward.

He turned me around so my back was to him. Then he

wrapped his arm around my neck and pulled me close. His skin was warm from the sun and smelled of sunscreen. I held on to his arm with both hands, feeling his strength. He held out the phone with his other hand, aiming the camera at us.

"So we'll remember," he said.

Click.

Without looking at it, he slipped his phone back in his pocket.

"Aren't you starving?" he asked.

We sat at the table and filled our plates. I noticed a large picnic basket on the ground.

"Who did all this?" I asked between bites.

"The fairies." He handed me a soda.

"They're artistic little folk. They even put out flowers." I touched a small vase of tiny orchids.

Blake pulled one out and handed it to me. "For you."

I took the flower and admired it. The petals were yellow with dark purple leopardlike spots.

"I've never, ever seen an orchid with spots like this," I said, touching the end to my nose.

"I know. They're rare. Kinda like you."

I felt my cheeks flush. I suddenly got very involved sipping my soda.

"So who are you really, Callie, girl of mystery?" he asked. "How come I've never met you before?"

"Then I wouldn't be a mystery."

"What's your favorite food? Don't think, just answer."

"Cheesecake."

"What's your favorite flower?"

"This one." I twirled the stem of the spotted orchid.

"Holo this year?"

"Too many to choose from." Didn't want to say I hadn't seen any.

"Animal."

"Whale."

"That came out fast." He shook his head and we both laughed.

"What about you?" I asked. "Let's do you."

"Color: blue. Food: potato chips. Instrument: guitar." He shot these out. "Cause: endangered species."

"That's a good one," I said. "Can I share that one?"

He squinted, pretending to be seriously pondering it. "Okay."

We sat in the sun for a long time, chatting and getting to know each other. I could have stayed there with him forever. But it was getting cold. I rubbed my arms.

"What do you think, should we go?" he asked.

I nodded and started to pick up the plates.

"Don't." He put his hand on my arm. "Someone will get it."

"Who, the fairies? It's kind of mean to make them work so hard, don't you think? Hurt their soft little fairy hands?"

"They like to work. They like the fairy salary."

"This is your ranch, isn't it?"

He pursed his lips. It seemed to me that he didn't want to boast. "My grandmother's."

I sensed something else, some sadness. It must have belonged to his parents at some point, but then they'd died, like every Starter's parents. I nodded. "Then we'll definitely leave it for the fairy hands."

We untied the horses and rode back as the sun was setting over the mountains. It had been a long time since I'd had a day when I didn't have to fight just to survive. My throat tightened at the thought of it ending. As if he could read my mind, he stopped and we watched the sunset together, our horses side by side.

"Did you have fun?" he asked.

I wanted to gush, but I stopped myself. "It was okay."

I glanced over at him sitting on his horse and flashed him a smile. He returned it with one of his own. Then he just stared at me, one side of his face red from the sunset. I felt an invisible warmth radiate from him. If it had been an airscreen game, there'd have been tacky heart icons floating between us.

Suddenly a flash of guilt came over me about Michael. Even though we weren't really boyfriend and girlfriend, there was something special between us. And there were other reasons I had to stop thinking about Blake. Where could this go? Nowhere. Nowhere. Nowhere.

I took a deep breath. Gave myself a mental slap. Stop analyzing and enjoy whatever time you have left with him, I thought as the last sliver of the sun slipped away.

In the car, I was thinking about how to ask him for that favor I needed. But he wanted to stop at his grandfather's mother's home. She needed help with her airscreen.

She lived in a tall condo building in Westwood. In the elevator, he explained that his great-grandmother's name was Marion, but he called her Nani. She never liked to reveal her age, but she was probably two hundred, he guessed.

When she opened the door, she wasn't what I'd expected to see. She was tiny, and her hair wasn't silver or bright white, but a soft off-white. She was wearing gray cashmere sweats.

But the biggest surprise was that she wore her wrinkles with pride, skipping surgery and treatments.

She held my hand as she walked me to a chair. She smelled like lavender.

"Blakey, the airscreen won't turn on." She sat on a love seat near me. "He told me he might bring a friend over. I'm so happy to meet you."

Blake sat next to Marion and worked with her mini-airscreen in his palm.

She patted his hand. "He's such a good boy. I don't believe all this negative talk about the young people. You know, the ones who don't have good homes like you two. Everyone says all they do is fight, steal, and vandalize. That's not all they do, that's just what we hear about. I don't believe in putting them in institutions. It's wrong. How will they ever become contributing members of society if we don't integrate them?"

All I could do was nod. If only she knew my real story.

Marion leaned toward Blake and pointed at the air display. "You got it working already?"

"The cell was loose," he said.

"Have you met my son? Blake's grandfather?" Marion pointed to a painting on the wall.

I shook my head.

"He's a senator, you know." She beamed. "Senator Clifford C. Harrison."

"Really?" I looked at the portrait of a serious Ender. "You look like him," I said to Blake.

"He does, doesn't he?" Marion said.

"Nani . . . ," Blake said.

"Why shouldn't I be proud of my own son? And my great-grandson?" She pinched his cheek. "He's so good to me, calls me all the time. And comes whenever I need him. How many grandchildren can you say that about?"

He blushed. Cute.

In the elevator on the way to the ground level, I looked at Blake with even more envy.

"You didn't tell me your grandfather was a senator."

He slipped his hands in his pockets and shrugged. "Now you know."

I liked that he didn't feel he had to brag.

"She's great," I said, nodding back to his great-grandmother's condo.

"Nani's a gem. I only wish my grandmother was like her."

The elevator stopped, and we walked out to the front of the condo. Blake gave his ticket to the valet.

"She doesn't see things the way Marion does?"

He shook his head. "As long as she can shop at Tiffany's, everything's right with the world. What about you? What's your grandmother like?"

I looked down at my feet while we waited for the valet. "Kind of like yours."

"Too bad."

I purposely didn't ask him about his grandfather. He didn't seem comfortable with the fact that he was this big senator.

It was dark by the time we made it back to Bel Air. He parked the car on the street, just outside the gate, and shut off the engine. The interior of Mrs. Winterhill's house glowed with dim golden lights.

"I had a really good time," he said.

"Me too." I had to ask him, but I didn't know how to say it. So I just blurted it out. "I need you to do a favor for me."

He looked at me for a second. "Whatever you need."

"Do you have some paper? And a pen?"

He opened the glove compartment, pulled out a pen and pad, and handed them to me. I drew the map as best I could from memory.

"I need you to go here." I pointed to the building.

He peered at my drawing. "What kind of place is this?"

"It's an abandoned office building."

"Are you kidding?"

"Please. I have a friend who's had some trouble. He needs this money." I emptied my purse of cash. "When you get there, park on the side street. Don't get out of the car if you see anyone. If it's clear, go in this door and go right to the third floor. As soon as you're on the floor, call out his name— Michael—and say 'Callie has a message for you.' Wait for him to come out, don't go into any rooms."

I held out the cash but Blake didn't take it.

"You're joking, right?" He gave a nervous laugh.

"I'm serious." He reminded me of Michael. Apparently I was doomed to deal with stubborn guys. I pushed the cash so it touched his hand. He still wouldn't take it. "Once he comes out, give him the money. And this." I handed him the folded drawing. "He'll believe you once he sees this. Ask him if everyone is okay, he'll know what that means. If he won't take the money, call me and I'll talk to him."

"Don't you want to come too?"

"I really wish I could." It would have been great to see Tyler. "But I can't." Not without Prime knowing I went there.

"Sounds kind of iffy."

"It's not exactly safe there. So leave as soon as you can."

He took the money with reluctant fingers. "Don't worry, I will."

"Thanks, Blake. For doing this."

"Hey, it's important to you." He looked into my eyes. "So it's important to me."

He was doing so much for me. I was used to going to places like that, but he wasn't. They'd know instantly that he was an outsider.

But that money could buy food and vitamins for Tyler.

"And thanks for not asking any questions." I got out of the car. Before I closed my door, he leaned over.

"But I don't guarantee I won't ask them in the future," he said. "Questions."

I smiled. It felt good to hear that word . . . "future." Then I felt guilty because poor Blake didn't know that we had no future, the prince and the poor peasant. But all that shifted to the background as something very real started happening to me.

My hands went icy cold.

Numb.

Dizziness washed through me, as if someone had spun me around ten times. Like Alice chasing the rabbit, I was falling into a deep, black hole.

CHAPTER EIGHT

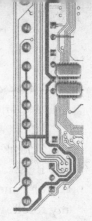

When I came to, I had a gun in my hands.

What?

A gun?

Why?

Was I defending myself? Sweat beaded on my forehead. My heart pounded so hard, I swore I could hear it.

Who was after me? I gripped the gun with both hands, my finger on the trigger.

My ragged breathing echoed in my ears. I was ready to shoot.

But no one was there.

I was alone, standing in the middle of someone's bedroom. Large, plush. Looked like a museum. I recognized it.

Helena. It was Helena's bedroom.

What had happened?

Images ricocheted in my head. Faces, cars, smiles, flashing like leaping fish. The minute I tried to focus on one, it was already gone.

I looked down at the gun in my hands. It was a Glock 85. I'd used one before, but this one was modified.

It had a silencer.

I checked to see if the gun was loaded. It wasn't. I went to the dresser and placed it on top. As soon as I did, a searing pain hit me and I doubled over. Pressure rose up my neck to my forehead, as if my skull would explode like a volcano.

Trying to stop the throbbing, I pressed my temples. I fell to my knees, rocking from side to side. The pain kept coming in waves. Just when it subsided and I thought it was over— *bam*—there it was again.

After what felt like forever but was probably just minutes, it went away. I waited, afraid this was just a longer pause between waves, but it was over. It was as if a switch had been turned off. I was bent over on the floor, hands clammy, body drenched in sweat.

The quiet in the room overwhelmed me. All my senses were heightened.

I got to my feet and leaned on the dresser, my brain racing.

What was Helena doing with a Glock in her bedroom? Protection? But it was heavier and larger than the usual nightstand security gun. It would be difficult for an Ender woman to handle.

And why the silencer? This was not a good sign.

I noticed that one of the doors to Helena's closet was open. A case lay open on the carpet in front of it. I walked closer and confirmed it was a gun case. I brought the gun over and placed it in the indentation that held it perfectly.

Inside the closet, the carpet had been pulled back, revealing a secret compartment under the floor. It was just big enough to hold the gun case. I closed the case, put it in the compartment, and replaced the carpet.

Just getting the gun out of sight made me feel better.

Then I tried to get my bearings. What had I been doing before the lights went out?

Blake. I'd been saying goodnight to Blake. I'd given him the money for Tyler and gotten out of his car. It had been late. Now there was sunlight blazing through the windows. The clock read 3:00.

Where was the leather purse I'd been using? I swung around and saw it on the desk. I opened the bag and pulled out the cell phone to check the date.

It was . . . tomorrow. So I had blacked out for eighteen hours. And then, for some reason, I came to.

I figured that whatever had caused me to snap into consciousness before, when I was in the nightclub, was what had caused me to return now. Questions flew through my brain. Was someone controlling this, or was it totally random? Maybe something was wrong with my neurochip? Did this happen to other donors, or was I special?

As easy as falling asleep. Sure.

Odds were, it was my renter who had regained control of my body. Helena had already owned that gun; that was clear from the hidden compartment in her bedroom. And when I came to, I was in that bedroom, holding that gun. If my theory was correct, that meant Helena had gained control of my body after I said goodnight to Blake. Had she said anything to him or just gone into the house? Had she said anything to Eugenia?

I wasn't sure how I should act. What to say, what not to.

It was scary when you didn't know what your body had been doing without you.

And what about Tyler? Had Blake found him? I gripped the phone and sent Blake a Zing. He didn't answer.

A gun. Not just any gun. A Glock with a silencer. This wasn't just target practice, this was way more than I'd bargained for.

I had to return to Prime.

In the garage, I bypassed Helena's yellow rocket and went to the small blue sports car at the end of the row. It didn't scream "notice me" the way the rocket did. From the outside, I saw a fuzzy green alien hanging from the rearview mirror. Not exactly Helena's style. Probably a granddaughter's car.

The key hung from a rack on the wall, on a chain dangling another little alien, this one much smaller. I got in the car and started up the navigator. She spoke with the voice of an old cartoon character.

"Where to?" the navigator asked in that chirpy voice.

"Prime Destinations, Beverly Hills."

A couple of seconds passed and then it said, "Cannot find that location."

Of course. Prime wouldn't be listed.

"New address," I said, setting it up for a manual entry.

I started to read out their address when the Voice came back.

Callie . . . don't . . . don't go back . . . Prime. Can you hear? You cannot return. . . . It's dangerous. . . . Extremely dangerous. . . .

Goose pimples rose on my arms. "Dangerous," the Voice had said, just like the first time. She was consistent. She was very clearly warning me about returning to Prime Destinations.

"Why?" I asked the Voice. "Can you tell me why?"

Silence.

"Who is this?" I asked. "Helena?"

No answer.

Guns. Warnings. Danger. I didn't like waking up with a gun in my hand—but at least I could handle a gun. I didn't know what waited for me at Prime.

I shut off the engine and went back into the house.

I got on Helena's computer to find out more about her. If that was her taking over my body whenever I blacked out, I needed to know everything I could. Why the gun? Maybe someone was after her, and I was now the target of that anger.

How many of her friends knew she was renting? Other than the Zing sender who didn't approve. If that was a friend.

I looked through Helena's computer files. Over a hundred years of memories, work, letters, and photos. I sifted through it and found out that her son and his wife had been killed in the war, like most people their age. They had a daughter named Emma, my age. That would be Helena's granddaughter.

I went to the CamPages, the portals to the parts of people's lives they wanted to share. The truly self-absorbed recorded their entire day and played it in straight airscreen or in holo mode. The really crazy kids never shut them off.

Helena didn't have a Page, but that wasn't unusual. A lot of Enders erased their Pages once they passed a hundred. Guess they thought they were too mature for that kind of nonsense.

What was strange was that Emma's Page came up as deleted. I ran a search on her name and found an announcement of her funeral. Two months ago. No mention of cause of death.

I remembered the teen bedroom I had seen the first night I was exploring. I got up and crossed the hallway, then entered Emma's room.

The sadness came over me like a fog. Sunlight filtered in through brittle-thin white curtains, frozen in the still air. Less a bedroom than a memorial. Something flickered in my peripheral vision. I turned to the nightstand. A holo-frame cycling through memories, displaying them 24/7 to no one.

I sat on the edge of the bed to get a closer look. I felt a pang inside as I remembered our holo-frame, now gone forever. The inscription on the base of this one read "Emma." She bore a resemblance to her grandmother, the same strong jawline, same willful expression. She had the confident, relaxed air of a rich girl, although she was not rental beautiful. Her skin was vibrant, but her proud nose was just a bit too long. The images boasted of a lush, privileged life—playing tennis, attending opening night at the opera, vacationing in Greece with her arms around her parents.

My eyes scanned her room. It had only been a couple of months since her death. Looked like Helena kept everything the way it had been. I would have done the same for my parents, if I'd had the luxury of staying in our house.

One thing was missing, though: no computer.

I went to the closet to look for secrets. That was where people usually hid them. I saw a high shelf filled with hats and acrylic storage boxes. I pulled over a chair to stand on and began my search through Emma's memories.

I looked through everything on that shelf, as well as under the bed and in every drawer, spreading everything out. I came up empty. I sat at her desk, chin in hand. My vision settled on one thing I hadn't examined: the jewelry box on her dresser. I didn't expect to find any clues there, but it was the only thing left to inspect, other than her makeup.

Inside the box, I found gold, silver, a mix of precious and costume jewelry appropriate for an impossibly wealthy sixteen-year-old.

And one thing that I never would have expected to find: a charm bracelet.

Not just any charm bracelet, a silver one with little sports charms. A digi-tennis racket, air skis, ice blades. . . . I touched them and saw the familiar holo of the spinning ice blades.

I put it next to the bracelet on my wrist, the one Doris at Prime had given me.

It was exactly the same.

How could Emma have this? There was only one answer, and it made my face burn.

Emma had been so stinking rich, living in this palace, she could have had anything she wanted. Why would she sell her body to the body bank?

That night I arrived at Club Rune in the small blue sports car, Emma's car. I stepped out wearing a designer microdress I had found in Emma's closet, my accessories—heels, necklace, and designer bag—also thanks to Emma. I had styled my hair the way she had in her photos, pulling back the top and securing it with one of her diamond clips. No one would mistake me for her from the front, but in a dark nightclub, and certainly from the back, I figured it couldn't hurt. Maybe I would draw out someone who had known her.

It was early, and the music was at a level where you could

still hear people talking. I felt more in control this time around. I walked slowly, letting my eyes adjust to the darkness. I tried to re-create Madison's stride as I paraded across the room, doing the Madison real-or-renter test on each person I passed.

I glanced at the astrotech bar area and saw that all the stools were taken. So were the antigrav chairs in the nearby lounge area. I stood by a mirrored column for a moment before a girl came up to me. Time for the Madison test. She was amazing, with long, straight red hair, green eyes, and porcelain skin that looked like it was lit from within. Renter.

"Well." She looked me over. "That's quite a body."

"Thanks," I said. "I like it."

"Hello, Helena, guess who?" She leaned closer, her voice low.

She held up her cell phone. The hearts at the top of the screen were flashing. Helena's name was next to them.

"You can't hide from my Sync," she said.

I took out my/Helena's phone. The hearts were also flashing. The name beside them read "Lauren."

"You sent the Zing," I said. "The other day."

"Of course I did, who else?" She sounded annoyed.

So not only was this Ender a close friend of Helena's, but she might be the only person who knew Helena was renting, other than the housekeeper. It seemed odd that Lauren had tried to talk Helena out of renting when she was also renting.

"Well, I had made up my mind," I said, winging it. "And you know how I am."

"More stubborn than Kate in *Taming of the Shrew*."

I decided to return her earlier compliment. "You look great. Good choice."

"How can you say that?" She put her hand on her perfect cheek. "May heaven strike us both down. I feel horrible doing this, using this poor little girl's body this way." She looked down at the torso that she had on borrowed time. Her red locks shimmered in the bar's neon lights as she raised her head. "But as you always said, if they're going to victimize thousands of hapless teens, then we may have to use a few of them ourselves to stop them."

It sounded like Helena had a plan and Lauren knew about it. "You always had a good memory, Lauren."

"Don't call me that." She leaned in closer. "I'm Reece now." She raised her brows to make sure I got that. "We shouldn't risk talking too long. Someone might see us and figure it out." She glanced around. "You must not have done anything rash yet, or I would have read about it online."

"No. I didn't."

"Don't." She touched my arm. "I beg of you. You and I are coming from the same place, but this is not the way to solve anything. It will only make it worse."

She was talking all around it but not saying what "my" plan was.

She let go of me. Her eyes scanned the room. "I should go. I have a lead to follow up on."

I put my hand on her shoulder. "Can we get together tomorrow? Someplace quieter?"

She moved back a step, leaving my hand in the air. "On one condition: that you listen to reason."

"I might surprise you." I might surprise myself, I thought.

She tilted her head as if intrigued. She took another step back and then stopped, looking me up and down.

"Isn't that Emma's dress?" she asked.

Since she thought I was Emma's grandmother, this must have seemed really tacky. But there was no hiding it. "Yes."

"And her necklace?"

"And the shoes." My stomach tightened. I was about to lose this Ender and I needed her, needed her answers. "I thought I might attract them this way."

She nodded. "Clever."

She left me alone in the crowd. I scanned the others, wondering if Blake was there. There was one empty seat in the lounge section. It was the last of four deeply cushioned chairs surrounding a caffeine table. The others were taken by two guys and a girl. The girl saw me staring and casually motioned to me.

"No one's sitting here." The girl moved her purse off the chair and patted it, the way you would for a poodle.

I joined them because they were clearly renters. They looked like a fashion spread. Two handsome guys—one dark and sporting a European-cut suit, the other a smoldering Asian in black leather—and a girl with lustrous ebony skin and long, straight hair. Their faces and bodies were 100 percent perfect.

Maybe they could tell me something about Emma. But I had to be careful not to slip and give away my secret.

"Would you like a drink?" the suit asked me. He had the lilting accent and smoky eyes of stars I'd seen in old Bollywood musicals.

"No, thank you." I tried to sound older and sophisticated.

"My name's Raj. At least, it is here." He glanced sideways at the other guy and they both laughed.

They all looked at me, waiting for my introduction. "Call me Callie." I rolled my eyes. "Still can't get used to using that name."

"I can't get used to this accent," Raj said, gesturing to his throat. That started another round of laughter between the guys.

The girl nodded at me. Her name was Briona, and she looked like a model, her long limbs shimmering from Glo-Dust. The Asian guy with high cheekbones was called Lee. I had to remind myself that they were really creepy old Enders.

"So, this your first time, Callie?" Raj asked.

"It's that obvious?" I said.

They all chuckled.

"We've never seen this body before," Briona said. "It's nice."

"Yeah, it's great," Lee said.

"How are you doing so far?" Raj asked.

I shrugged. "Good."

"What have you done?" he asked. He had a little smirk. "Or is this your first night?"

"Not much. I went horseback riding."

They smiled. "That's fun," Lee said. "Where?"

"Someone's private ranch."

"A renter?" Raj asked.

"No."

They exchanged looks.

"A real teen?" Raj asked.

My eyes flicked from Briona to Raj to Lee. They looked concerned. "Is something wrong?" I asked.

"It's just that, well, that sort of thing is frowned upon," Raj said.

Briona reached over and touched my arm. "Never mind that. You paid to have a good time. Haven't we all earned it?"

"Speaking of which, let's blow this joint and go have some real fun," Lee said.

He leaned forward, a wicked grin on his face.

Raj finished his bottled water and slammed it on the table. "Great idea."

Everyone stood. Briona hooked her arm in mine. "Come. We can have a girl gabfest. I love helping first-timers. Do you crochet? Knit?"

Maybe it was just because I was the odd man out and they were all friends, but I kept getting the feeling that they knew something I didn't.

Maybe if I tagged along, they would fill me in.

The wind whipped my hair as we rode in Lee's convertible. I sat in the back with Briona; Raj was up front with Lee.

"Where are we going?" I asked.

"Who knows?" Briona said. "I'm sure it's something dangerous and quite stupid."

"Joyriding," Lee said.

"This isn't your car?" I asked.

Raj stifled a chuckle. "A different kind of joyriding."

Lee drove the streets with abandon. "We're almost there."

He whipped around a sharp corner and I saw an arroyo with a bridge crossing it. Several cars were parked there. I caught a flash of something moving away from the bridge.

"There they go." Lee pointed.

"No." Raj shook his head. "Not on your life."

"You mean not on *his* life." Lee pointed to Raj's belly and then poked it.

Both guys laughed.

"That's where we're going?" I asked.

"This isn't funny," Briona said.

"It's not funny, it's fun," Lee said.

Soon we were parked on the bridge with the other cars.

The guys ran out of the car to a crowd of people in the middle of the bridge. I grabbed Briona's arm.

"What is this?" I asked, confused.

"Band-bounce. Idiots jump off a bridge and the only thing that keeps them from turning into pancakes is a thin tech strap. Supposedly, it's intelligent enough to adjust for your weight and velocity." She paused. "Supposedly."

"Sounds dangerous," I said.

She shrugged. "Well, at least it's not your body."

We held on to the railing separating us from a long fall into a canyon below. The wind blew our hair as we watched some guy throw himself over the side, plunging into the arroyo. I gasped and closed my eyes.

"No, watch," Briona urged, peering downward.

He fell and fell, coming dangerously close to kissing the dirt, but his tech strap stopped him at the last moment, just as Briona had said it would. He bounced back just the right distance for the guys on the bridge to pull him in.

Raj and Lee were several yards away, against the railing, having an argument.

"Briona..." I turned to her. "I need to ask you something."

"Yes, honey, anything."

"Did you ever meet a donor body named Emma?"

Briona stared back at me. Maybe she was trying to remember.

"She was tall, blond curls, strong features," I said.

"Doesn't sound familiar. Did she do something to you?"

"No. I'd just like to find someone who knew her."

"Sorry. Wish I could be more help. After a while, most of these donors begin to look the same, you know?"

"What about your friends? Could they have known her?"

"Doubt it. In spite of all their bravado, they really haven't rented much." She looked over at Lee and Raj. Lee was getting ready to jump. "I don't believe it."

In a second, Lee's body became a black bullet arcing into the air and falling in slo-mo.

So much for contracts and rules.

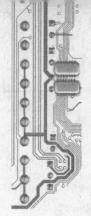

CHAPTER NINE

After Lee survived his crazy techno bounce, he drove us back to Club Rune. Raj stayed in the car while Lee kept the engine running. Briona got out with me to say goodbye. I smoothed my windswept hair.

"Definitely keep in touch, Callie. We could have so much fun together. Do you play bridge? Listen to me, only thinking of spinster games. Never mind that. We could go shopping. Or dancing. Or z-blading."

She gave me a long hug. When we pulled apart, I opened my wallet to look for a card for her. Instead, I was surprised to see a wad of cash. I had emptied my purse yesterday, so Blake could give it all to Michael.

"What are you doing?" Briona asked.

"Getting a card to give you."

"You don't need that, silly. That's just for ol' Enders." She winked.

I'd never heard an Ender call themselves that, but then, she was in her pretend-teen mode.

She held up her cell phone. "I grabbed your number. Gave you mine. If you're about to do something fun—"

"Or dangerous," Lee interrupted, his hand resting on the back of the car seat.

"—call me," Briona continued. "Call me for any reason. I do want to see more of you. I feel like we're old friends already."

Old is right, I thought.

She got back in the car and waved her lovely jeweled hand as they drove away.

All I could think about was the cash in my purse. Once I was in my car with the doors locked, and before I pulled away from the safety of the valet zone, I counted the bills in my purse. It was exactly the amount I had given to Blake.

The next morning, I drove a few blocks away from the house and pulled over to the curb. I called Blake but got his voiceZing.

"Hey, it's Blake. You know what to do."

"Hi, Blake. It's Callie. Can you call me, please?"

After I disconnected, I wished I had said more. But I wasn't about to call him back. He hadn't called me since our date.

I wouldn't have called at all if it weren't for my brother.

I met Lauren at a Thai restaurant she chose. It was in the Valley, tucked deep in the corner of a minimall with way too many signs. Not really a hangout for a rich Ender like Lauren. But I knew she had picked it because the chances of running into anyone who would know us were next to zero. Not that we were recognizable, but we didn't want someone to hear us talking.

We sat at a booth in the back. The Ender bus boy brought us water and checked us out. The working Enders had no idea that the exclusive body bank even existed. They didn't know that the hot young "Reece" was really the hundred-plus-year-old Lauren, or that my drop-dead looks were not thanks to Mother Nature but to state-of-the-art technology. It wasn't part of their world. They were just happy to have jobs to carry them into their older old age.

And it made the chaotic transition after the Spore Wars somewhat easier that the Enders were already back in the workforce, due to their extended lifetimes.

After we ordered, Lauren glanced around, her glossy red hair swinging. The closest party was two booths over, and the recorded Thai music covered whatever they were saying. She seemed satisfied that no one could hear us.

"Helena, are you still going to go through with it?" She stared at me with those mesmerizing green eyes.

I sipped my water. I needed to say something that didn't give away the fact that I had no clue what Helena's plan was.

Finally, I settled on "I don't know."

She straightened and her eyes brightened. My words gave her hope.

"It's wrong," she said. "You know it's wrong."

"I suppose so."

"Of course it is." She lowered her voice to a whisper. "Murder is always wrong."

Murder?

I did my best not to show the shock that hit my gut like an unfriendlie's fist. I placed my elbows at the edge of the table and dropped my forehead into my hands, trying to cover my surprise as Ender angst.

Inside, I was reeling.

I had to know more. But I couldn't ask her straight out. I bit the inside of my cheek. Then I remembered what Lauren had said yesterday.

"But victimizing Starters"—I caught myself—"teens . . . is wrong too. Don't you think?" I asked.

"Of course it's wrong. Every day, I wake up thinking about my Kevin. With my daughter and son-in-law gone, he was all I had left."

"Like me."

"But you've given up. I still have hope that my grandson's alive out there somewhere. That's the great difference between us."

If she only knew.

It was strange hearing such refined words coming from those pouty teen lips.

"This is a horrible puzzle . . . tracking down people who saw him, clawing for bits and scraps of information."

"Did you find out anything last night?"

She shook her head. "It was a dead end. They never even saw Kevin."

The food arrived, but neither of us was very interested in it.

"He was always a cute boy." She contemplated her plate of pad thai. "He didn't need that makeover."

I looked at her, my mind racing to catch up in this crazy guessing game. She put her hand to her mouth.

"Oh, Helena. I'm truly sorry. You know I didn't mean that Emma needed . . ."

I didn't have the whole picture, but I was beginning to get a corner of it. "Emma was never conventionally pretty," I said, taking a risk. "I know that."

"Until she got her makeover," Lauren said softly.

Was that why she did it? To get the makeover?

"I guess . . . I guess she really wanted it," I said, looking for confirmation.

Lauren reached across the table and patted my hand.

"It's not your fault. How many things have our grandkids asked for that we had to say no to? Just like our children? Guardians have to be able to say no."

I leaned my chin on my palm and nodded, encouraging her to say more.

"We both thought we were doing the right thing," she said. "Titanium plastic surgery, green laser sculpting at sixteen? How could we possibly condone that?"

"But Emma found her way to get it."

"As did my Kevin." She pulled her hand away and sat back. "Who knew boys could be as vain as girls?" She shrugged.

So I was wrong. Emma—and Kevin—might have lived in luxury, but they didn't have everything they wanted. They wanted physical perfection. And the only way they could get it was through the body bank.

"So they must have lied," I said.

"Of course. Prime wouldn't have taken them if they'd known they had relatives. They want the unattached, unencumbered, disenfranchised. The kids with no families to investigate if they don't come home. Prime releases some of the kids to enlist more bodies, but ours weren't the lucky ones."

I could have sworn I saw a hint of her weary age behind those green eyes.

So the puzzle picture formed. Some rich, spoiled teens lied to the body bank, using fake last names so they could pretend to be poor orphans. They didn't want the bucks.

They wanted the free laser makeovers their grandparents wouldn't allow. Then they never came home.

"Lauren—"

She interrupted. "Practice calling me Reece, will you?"

"Reece, about killing. It does concern me." I looked down. I didn't have to fake the angst anymore. "I've been thinking. . . . It is wrong."

"Really?"

"But Prime Destinations . . ." I had to get her to tell me who I was going to kill. Somebody at the body bank was my best guess. "I do blame them. . . ."

"You're not alone."

"Yes, you, me . . ." I let my voice trail off, hoping she'd pick up the slack.

". . . and the Colemans, the Messians, the Posts," she ticked off on her fingers. "The other grandparents we found blame Prime. But none of them are talking about shooting anyone."

Now it was my turn to look around. I caught the waitress two tables over staring at us.

"Don't worry, I've kept my word," Lauren said. "Haven't told anyone. Yet."

"The head of Prime Destinations . . ." It must be him.

"Don't start that again. The Old Man's impossible to find."

"He's tall. And wears a hat," I said, remembering seeing him from the back that day at Prime. "And a long coat . . ."

"So we've heard. But I've never seen him."

I had. Arguing with Tinnenbaum at Prime. But Lauren seemed certain he was not Helena's target. If the head of Prime wasn't the man she planned to assassinate, then who?

Lauren leaned closer, looking me straight in the eye. "Just tell me, Helena, who is it? Who do you want to kill?"

She didn't know.

"I can't say." I looked away. It might have been the only true thing I'd said.

"This target of yours isn't the only one who'll die. This poor girl you're inside, that lovely young body?" Lauren reached over and gave my hair a flick. "She'll be shot dead on the spot."

The world went silent.

That's me! I wanted to shout. My body! Me! But any words were stuck somewhere deep inside my throat. The pungent smell of lemongrass and fish sauce was making me queasy. All I could do was look down at my bowl of yellow curry, the first food in a year that I had no stomach to eat.

What a great appetite suppressant, finding out your renter is an assassin. And that you'll probably be killed too.

I drove the freeway as fast as I could without pulling a ticket. So Helena didn't want to go surfing or jump off bridges, she was going to use me to murder someone. Kill and be killed. That must have been why target shooting was one of her requirements.

I saw my phone flashing. Blake had Zinged me while I was in the restaurant.

The message read: What's left to say?

That was weird. I pressed the call button in the car and got him on the line.

"Blake, meet me at Beverly Glen Park in thirty minutes. I'll explain everything."

"Thirty minutes," he said. His voice was dry.

I walked through the park, past Enders lounging on lawn chairs and sunbaked benches. Two sat on the swings, gently rocking. Children were scarce outdoors ever since the war. Many Enders who didn't have grandchildren didn't want to be around small kids, maybe because they'd all lost their grown-up children. And people were paranoid about residual spores in the air, vaccinations or no.

A private armed guard wearing sunglasses stood watch, hands on hips. I flinched when I noticed her gun, thinking of the Glock. I noticed another Ender couple, both with shoulder-length white hair, arguing under a tree. The woman poked her finger into the man's chest repeatedly.

It reminded me of my parents, a year and a half ago. It was summer. We'd just finished dinner, and Tyler and I were watching the airscreen. News coverage of the war broke in. The grim-faced announcer said the war had escalated to the spore-head missile attacks that had been rumored. They were focused on the northwest. I ran back to the kitchen to tell my parents, but it sounded like they already knew. I paused just outside the door when I heard them arguing.

My mother stood by the sink, a dishcloth in her hand. "Why can't you get it for us? With all your government connections?"

My father wiped his face with his palm. "You know why. The protocols."

"We need that vaccine, Ray. This is your family. Your children."

He leaned on the counter. "Those protocols are for everyone's protection."

"Celebrities are getting it. Politicians are getting it."

"That doesn't make it right."

She flung the dishcloth to the counter with a snap that made him flinch. "What's right about abandoning our children to be orphans with no one to protect them? Condemning them to starvation or murder or worse?"

She poked her finger into his chest several times to punctuate her questions. Angry tears welled in her eyes.

My father grabbed her by the shoulders and held her a moment to calm her. Then he pulled her into an embrace. She melted into him and rested her head on his shoulder. At that moment she saw me.

She had looked so scared.

I pushed the image of her frightened face out of my mind and scanned the park for the Ender couple. They were walking away.

Where was Blake? Then I spotted him sitting on top of a concrete picnic table. I walked over and sat next to him.

Like the guard, he wore sunglasses, a barrier between us.

"What's up?" His tone was icy.

"Did you see my friend?" I felt awkward asking him about Michael, but I needed to know.

"No," he said with an exasperated tone, like I should already know. "You told me not to."

My skin prickled. "I did?"

"Yeah. Remember? When you got really mad and demanded your money back?"

I'd been afraid of that. Helena. "What else?"

He shook his head. "Don't make me go through all this. You know what you said."

"Actually, I don't. I know that sounds weird. Please tell me."

He shoved his hands in his pockets. "Not to call, not to Zing. You never wanted to see me again."

I sighed. Helena had said that.

"I'm so sorry." I touched his arm. It was warm. "It was a mistake. Really."

"I thought . . . I thought we had a good time." He didn't respond to my touch, but he didn't move away either.

"It was a wonderful day." I ached inside. "One of the best ever."

He looked out at the Enders swinging. "So then why . . . ?"

"I wasn't myself. I get like that sometimes." I reached into my purse and pulled out the cash. "Haven't you ever had a bad day you wish you could do over? Can I have a redo? Please?"

I extended the cash. He hesitated. "You're sure you want me to give this to your friend this time?"

"Yes. I couldn't be more sure."

"And you really don't want to do it yourself? Or come with me?"

And have the body bank see me go back home? "I wish I could, but I really can't go there. And he needs this now." I pushed the money closer, touching his shirt with it. "Please, Blake," I said.

He took the cash and curled it in his fist. Finally, he looked me in the eye. "I guess everyone has bad days sometimes."

Then I remembered the drawing. It wasn't back in my purse, the way the cash was.

"You know that piece of paper I gave you?" I asked.

"You mean this one?" He pulled it out of his pocket, still folded.

I hoped he wouldn't unfold it now. I didn't want any questions. "Yes. Just give it to him. With the money."

He slipped the cash and the paper into his wallet. I tried not to show my relief.

"He's really talented," he said. "Your friend."

So he had looked at it. I detected the faintest note of jealousy in the way he said "friend." And I had to admit, it gave me a little thrill.

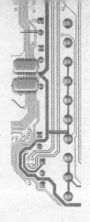

CHAPTER TEN

I drove away, making a U-turn that started Emma's fuzzy green alien bouncing from the rearview mirror. As it swung back and forth, I thought about my choices. If I hadn't needed this money so much, I might have been tempted to give up. But it wasn't that easy. I had a chip in my head. I couldn't just walk away. If I returned to Prime, what were the chances that the Enders there would believe me over a wealthy renter? I could see myself getting into an argument that ended with me being sent to an institution. My year on the streets had taught me how to survive day by day. That was how I was going to deal with this.

Back in Bel Air, I parked the car and slipped into the house without Eugenia spotting me. I went into Helena's bedroom and shut the door.

I went to the closet and pulled back the carpet, exposing the hidden compartment. I removed the case and looked at the Glock.

Where to dump this? As much as I would have liked to have a weapon again, I couldn't keep it. I had to get rid of it so Helena wouldn't have it the next time she took over my body. Hiding it someplace in the mansion wasn't good enough, because Eugenia might see me and tell Helena when questioned. Helena could try to get another gun, but any delay might help prevent a murder. She'd have to sit out the weeklong waiting period—a new law since the war—or spend the time and money shopping on the black market. Helena didn't strike me as a black market type, although she had proven to be a goody bag of surprises.

Where did people toss guns, I wondered? The shoreline was still war-ravaged and blocked to the public. If I gave it to anyone, there would be questions I couldn't answer. I would have liked to have gotten it to Michael, but I couldn't ask Blake to do that. And really, I didn't want it to be anywhere Helena might track it, once she was back in my body.

I went into the bathroom and poured makeup remover on a towel. I used that to wipe the Glock and silencer for any DNA residue, just like I'd seen in the holos. Then I put the gun back into the case and slipped it into a Bloomingdale's brown paper bag from Helena's closet.

I drove to a megamarket and cruised through the large parking lot. The store's armed guard was patrolling the front entrance. I passed all the parking spots up front, choosing one midway down the lane. I picked up the bag and folded over the top to form a seal. Act normal, I told myself.

I got out of the car. An Ender eating air yogurt on a bench in front of the store stared at me as I passed.

There were two large garbage bins. I picked the one on the right and lifted the corner of the lid. It was heavier than

I'd expected. I had to use both hands, and before I knew it, the bag slipped out and fell to the ground.

The case slid out halfway.

I snatched up the bag, opened the lid, and threw the bag into the bin. It made a loud clunk that echoed as it hit the metal bottom. Just my luck, the bin had recently been emptied.

I turned around and headed for the car. The Ender stared as if she knew I was doing something wrong. They always had that attitude toward Starters, whether we were rich or poor. She got up and waved to the guard, who was on the other side of the building.

By the time they connected, I was exiting the parking lot.

With the gun taken care of, I could focus on finding out who Helena was planning to kill. I parked the car in front of a convenience store and went through her cell phone. Her z-mails didn't offer up any clues. Nothing stood out, no references to point me to the assassination target.

Her phone calendar. The entries were filled for every day until she'd gone into the body bank. The date of the transfer was marked "P.D.," with various entries after that.

Before I could go any further, a noise interrupted me. I looked up and saw a small gang of street kids, renegades, running toward my car. At least I wasn't in a convertible this time. I floored it and sped away, leaving them standing in the street, tossing rocks that probably made a few dents on the back of the car.

I grinned. Last time this had happened, I had been terrified. But finding out you're supposed to be an assassin puts everything else in perspective.

About ten blocks away, I stopped at a red light. I glanced back at the phone calendar while I waited for the green. November 19, 8:00 p.m., was marked with a check. All the dates after that were blank.

The assassination day.

If that was true, I had two days to figure this out. Less than two days, really. I had the what and the when. Now I needed the who and the where. And a way to stop it.

The light changed, and I turned onto the freeway. I merged and wasn't afraid to speed up. I was getting more confident with my driving. I gripped the wheel as I crossed over to the fast lane. My hands felt tingly. I wiggled my fingers, but it didn't help.

Then I felt dizzy.

No.

That sinking feeling was coming over me. And it was winning.

I was going seventy miles per hour, and I was blacking out.

When I came to, my head was throbbing, but nothing as bad as that first headache I'd had. I leaned my back against a wall. I was in the lobby of an occupied office building. Black marble walls, silver trim. I didn't recognize it.

The Ender guard at the desk at the other end of the lobby was staring at an airscreen car zine. The colors were reflected on his features.

I looked up at a wall clock and saw that it was almost four-thirty. I was wearing the same clothes as before I'd blacked out. Only an hour had passed.

My cell phone rang. I pulled it out of my purse. The caller ID said *Memo Return*. I pressed the memo button and listened. A mechanical voice, a woman's, read the announcement.

"You have a memo to yourself, set for four-thirty p.m."

The voice that followed wasn't mine. It was an Ender. A woman.

"Callie, this is Helena Winterhill. Your renter."

My heart pounded. I recognized her. She was the Voice. I turned up the volume.

"There's so much to say, but I have no idea how long I have before I'm back into my own body. As you may have guessed, we don't have a consistent connection. There is a glitch in the system. I hope it will soon be repaired. Until then, do not contact Prime under any circumstances. I hope that is clear."

I put my hand over my other ear so I wouldn't miss a word. There was a nervous tone behind her strength.

"In the meantime, I ask that you not wear my granddaughter's clothes. It breaks my heart when I am suddenly back in your body and find I have them on." Her voice cracked. "But that's not the reason I am leaving you this message. I want to assure you that if you continue as planned with our contract, no matter what happens, you will receive a bonus when this is over. A most generous bonus, as long as you cooperate fully."

The message ended.

I was stunned. She obviously had no clue that I knew about her assassination plot. Of course, she only knew what she learned in those brief periods when inhabiting my body. She was in the dark about my conversation with Lauren.

A generous bonus, she had said. But I'd likely end up dead. Pretty easy to promise bonuses to dead girls.

Since I had only been out for an hour, Helena wouldn't have had time to go home. She didn't know that I had thrown away her gun. That was good. What was bad was that I was trapped in her plan.

I looked up and saw the guard watching me. I'd been standing there too long. I turned around to face the directory. The wheels of his chair squeaked as he pushed it back to get up.

So who was Helena there to see? She had just walked in, because I was facing the lobby when I came to.

I scanned the alphabetized names on the directory list. There were mostly lawyers, some accountants. About a third of the way down the list, I found a name that stood out.

SENATOR CLIFFORD C. HARRISON.

Blake's grandfather.

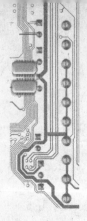

CHAPTER ELEVEN

I stared at the directory listing as the guard approached. Did Helena know Blake's grandfather? It had to be more than a coincidence. Blake must not have been aware of the connection; otherwise, wouldn't he have said his grandfather knew "my" grandmother?

"Can I help you, miss?" the guard asked.

From the tone of his voice, it was clear he was one step away from kicking me out. I scanned the rest of the directory. No other name rang a bell.

"I'm speaking to you." His voice was last-straw stern. "Minor."

He'd used the dreaded M-card that was ten seconds from the final M-card: marshals. I turned to him.

"I'm going up to the sixteenth floor. To Senator Harrison's office."

"Do you have an appointment?"

"No. I'm just going to speak with his assistant."

Maybe it was the defiance in my voice, or maybe it was Prime Destination's drop-dead makeover magic, but he nodded. Then he pointed to the electronic logbook built into the counter. "Sign there. And print."

I signed and pressed my thumb next to it. The elevator dinged open and I rode it up to the sixteenth floor. I hoped to learn what the relationship was between my renter and Blake's grandfather. Something wasn't right here.

When I got out, I was greeted by a set of double doors labeled with laser-cut metal letters: DISTRICT OFFICE, SENATOR HARRISON.

Inside, an Ender male receptionist looked up with a smile on his lips and condescension in his eyes.

"Is Senator Harrison in?"

"Sorry, he's at a fund-raiser. Anything I can help you with?"

I glanced around. There was a hallway that led to several offices. Harrison's was probably at the end.

"When will he be back in the office?"

"He sees constituents only by appointment." He looked me over. "You're a bit young to vote, aren't you?"

He grinned as if his joke were funny. They could do all kinds of medical improvements on Enders, but they couldn't fix their lame sense of humor.

"Maybe I'm older than you think," I said.

His grin faded to puzzlement. But he recovered. "Here's what you can do." He handed me a card. "That's his website. You can contact him through that."

I took the card, knowing no one but a bot would ever read my z-mail. "Actually, I should have explained. I'm doing a story for my private tutor and I was hoping to get a quote from the senator. Could I get a short appointment? I only need a few minutes."

He softened. "The senator is a pretty busy man," he said. "He's up for re-election, you know."

A severe Ender woman stormed out of the first office and stood behind him.

"It's you." She glared at me. "Didn't I tell you never to come back here again?"

"Me?" I said. "I've never been here before."

"I didn't realize . . . ," the man said to her, palms up.

"You were out sick that day," she said to him. She kept her eyes on me but spoke to him. "Call security. This time we're holding her for the marshals."

He picked up the phone.

This wasn't the first time Helena had been to this building. My body had been here, with Helena inside. "When was I here?"

"Don't insult my intelligence." The Ender marched toward me as I backed away.

I backed into the office door. I turned, opened it, and ran down the hall. I waved my hand over the elevator pad but the elevator was on another floor. I turned to the stairway door, pushed it open and ran down the stairs. Cobwebs got tangled in my face, my hair, my mouth. I cursed the Enders who wouldn't use stairs. I wondered if I could outrun the security guard in the lobby. I pictured him waiting for me with autocuffs.

When I got to the first floor, I stopped to catch my breath. Then I peeked out the door. The guard was facing the elevator, waiting for me to come out. I made a dash for the main doors. By the time he turned around, it was too late for him to catch up; his old legs were no match for mine. I was half-way down the block before he even made it to the door.

"Helena, what have you done with my life?"

But if we had a connection, she wasn't answering.

I sat at the computer in Helena's bedroom suite, frantically searching the Pages for any information on Senator Harrison. This was my life we were talking about. What had Helena said to the senator? Since she'd said it in my body, it must have been just days ago. It would help to know as much as I could, in case the senator's people had called the marshals.

I worked as fast as possible. As a senator, Harrison was involved in a lot of programs involving Starters, but his pet project seemed to be something called the Youth League. Could that have anything to do with Helena's granddaughter? Had Helena tried to enlist his help regarding Emma's disappearance?

Maybe he had refused to get involved. Helena could have gone to the senator for help, maybe looking to stop the body bank, and been rejected. And then maybe she'd ended up blaming him for her granddaughter's death.

Enough to kill him?

I was doubting my theory until I found a key date on the Pages. Harrison was going to be a guest of honor at the Youth League Awards on the nineteenth, the same date as the last entry on Helena's calendar. That was just a couple of nights away. And the time was the same as Helena's notation—8:00 p.m.

I knew the person who could give me the best insight into the senator. I phoned Blake.

When I got to the lookout point on Mulholland Drive, it was dusk. Blake's red sports car was the only one parked in the turnout. I pulled in and parked next to it.

Blake sat on a guardrail fence, watching the sun sink behind the mountains. "Hi."

He gave me a hand and pulled me up to sit beside him. I locked my feet into the lower railing and held on to the top one. The hill below was steep.

"I saw your friend." He looked out at the view. "I gave him the money."

I felt my shoulders relax. "What'd he say?"

"He wanted to know who I was. I told him I was a friend of yours."

"Did you see anyone else?"

He shook his head. "Then he wanted to know why he hadn't met me before."

"What did you tell him?"

"The truth. That we just met a few days ago." He looked down. "Can you believe that? Feels like longer. Anyway, the truth usually works best. You know?"

I swallowed. I searched his face. How much did he know? "What did he say when you asked about everyone?"

"He said everyone was good." He stared at the canyon. "So what's the story on this guy?" he asked.

My throat tightened as if an unfriendlie had his dirty hands around it. "He's just had some bad luck. His parents were killed in the war. His grandparents are dead."

I looked down. The fence felt wobbly. I was dizzy.

Trees and rocks and dirt swirled in my vision as I tilted forward. Blake caught me, one hand on my belly, the other on my back.

"Careful," he said. "You okay?"

My heart pounded. His touch felt caring. Protective.

"I'm not sure."

"We'd better get you down." He held my shoulder as he dismounted, making sure I was steady. Then he took me by the waist and helped me down.

"Want to sit in my car?" he asked.

I nodded. As we walked to his car, a couple of Enders parked and got out to see the view. Blake put his arm lightly around my shoulder to steady me. It felt good.

Once inside Blake's car, I felt better. Safe. The world stopped spinning.

I was torn as to whether I should tell him about his grandfather. How would it help? To explain my theory about how the senator might be in danger, I'd have to explain the body bank, since it wasn't common knowledge. And to explain that, I'd have to admit who I really was. There was a good chance he wouldn't believe me and would just think I was crazy. I'd started with a lie, and now it was just about impossible to untangle it without breaking something.

Blake looked into the distance, toward the city below. "I think you've been hiding something, Callie." He turned to me. "Something important."

I felt my mouth open, but nothing came out.

"That's true, isn't it?" His eyes searched me. "I can see it in your face."

My heart was like a hummingbird trapped in my chest.

"You're sick, aren't you?"

I blinked. "What?"

"It's okay, you don't have to tell me everything. It's obvious you have some condition. Getting dizzy, then blacking out. And then you're like an entirely different person." He was quiet for a moment. "But don't worry, I won't push. Just do me one favor?"

"What's that?"

"Promise me you'll say something the next time you start to feel bad. We can keep you from falling off cliffs and stuff."

He smoothed the hair away from my face; then he ran his hand down the back of my head. I flinched.

"What's wrong?"

"It's okay." I had to keep him away from my chip wound. I took his hand and held it. It was warm and strong and smooth. There he was, so concerned for me, and then happy because I held his hand. And there I was, totally lying to him.

I took a breath. "Blake?"

"What?"

"You said you weren't very close to your grandmother."

"That's right."

"What about your grandfather?"

He squinted and stared into space. "He's all right. He's busy. Away a lot." He looked at me. "But I think he's trying. He never really got over losing my dad, so he tries to be close to me. I don't always make it easy for him."

I looked down at our hands. They were still clasped. Neither of us made a move to release.

"What's it like for him, being a senator? Does he have a lot of enemies?"

"Oh yeah. Hate mail. Hate packages. Anything we didn't order goes right to the marshals. There're some freaky seniors out there with weird ideas."

"I'll bet." I rolled my eyes. Then I turned to him. "I'd really like to meet him."

He pulled his head back. "You would?"

I nodded.

"I don't know if we can find a break in his schedule. He's crammed in a ton of appearances before he heads off to Washington to see the president."

"The president?"

"Yeah, he wants me to go with him," Blake said. "Says it's an opportunity to build character."

I pushed my hair back with my free hand. "Is your grand-father doing something special on the nineteenth?"

Blake cocked his head. "How'd you know? That's his last appearance before he takes off. The Youth League Awards at the Dorothy Chandler Pavilion, the Music Center."

"Downtown L.A." The last date Helena had marked on her calendar. Everything was pointing to the senator being her target. "Let me guess, it starts at eight o'clock?"

"Yeah. I have to be there to present an award. How did you know about it?"

I needed to figure out what I could do to prevent this. "Sorry, I gotta go now."

"Wait." He used the hand holding mine and pulled me to him until our faces were so close I could feel his breath on my cheek. "I've been wanting to tell you something."

That close, his eyes made the world disappear. He smelled clean. Like summers before the war. Like sanctuary.

"What?" I asked.

"Callie." His eyes examined my face, traveling over my cheeks, my eyes, my lips. "I don't know why, I can't explain it, but I feel connected to you."

"I know. Me too."

"But do you know why?" he asked.

I didn't know. I just felt it inside. "I guess sometimes there isn't a reason for everything."

"It just is."

"It just is." My heart was beating so hard, he must have been able to hear it.

He held my face with his hand. It was warm and smooth.

"You are really something special," he said. Then he leaned in and kissed my lips.

Tentative.

Gentle.

He pulled away with a boyish smile, like a five-year-old at the fair who had just won a goldfish bot.

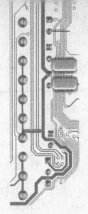

CHAPTER TWELVE

I went back home and slipped into Helena's bedroom. I knew it was a luxury and a distraction to think about Blake. But I was drawn to him. He had the manners and easy ways of someone who had never had to scrounge on the streets. Maybe that was what I liked about him, that he brought me back to the civilized life I used to have. Not that we were ever wealthy, but we had structure. Stability.

But I refused to think of myself as being that shallow. I liked Blake because he was kind and thoughtful, good to me and to his great-grandmother Nani. My mother always said, look to how a boy treats his mother to see how he'll treat you one day. I guess how he treated his great-grandma worked just as well.

I really wished Blake's grandfather hadn't been mixed up in this, but at least it wasn't my fault. Helena must have gone to him in her own body first, to appeal for help when Emma went missing several months ago.

I went to Helena's desk to try to find some evidence that she knew Senator Harrison would be at the awards event at the Music Center. Nothing in her computer about it, but I found a folder in a drawer. Inside was an envelope. I pulled out two tickets for the Youth League Awards, 8:00 p.m., Dorothy Chandler Pavilion at the Music Center.

That confirmed it. I gripped the tickets with both hands. If I was still in control of my body, then no problem. But if I blacked out, Helena would try to go through with her plan to kill the senator.

Blake's grandfather.

I tore the tickets into two pieces, then four. I ran to the bathroom, shredding them in my hands, and dumped them into the toilet.

With one touch, I flushed away Helena's opportunity to kill the senator.

I didn't want to be sitting around the house when the awards were going on in two days. That would make it too easy for Helena in case she was able to get inside my body. I needed a plan.

I went to the closet and pulled out the dressy purse I'd had at the nightclub. Inside was the card from Madison, or rather, Rhiannon. The hot, funny girl who was really a frumpy, funny Ender.

I was glad Rhiannon was still using her Madison body rental, because it made it easy to spot her the next morning. I showed up at our arranged meeting place, a super-blading rink.

It was freezing inside, with all that ice. Only the wealthiest of teens and a few courageous Enders were skating, all in state-of-the-art skating suits designed for maximum speed and body safety. Not that they needed any help. Super blades, the sign explained, had tiny lasers mounted right above the ice, controlled by buttons in the gloves. These melted the ice slightly so the skater could get better speed. But the real fun was in the jet-stream buttons, which drove a blast of air that made you slightly airborne. They could only be used for a few seconds at a time, and only raised you a couple of inches, but the sensation was compared to flying.

The things you could do if you were rich. The cost of one day here could feed ten friendlies for a week.

I spotted Madison doing spins in the center. She stopped, and I waved to her. She waved back and glided over to the side of the rink.

"Callie, this is so much fun. I feel so limber. Put on some skates and try it."

"Some other time. Madison, I need to ask a favor."

"Anything." She leaned forward. "We renters have to stick together." She pulled back and laughed. "What can I do for you?"

"You live alone, right?"

"Sweet pea, who'd want to live with me?" She laughed. "My housekeeper has her own place."

"Could I come over tomorrow? And stay overnight?"

"At my place?"

I nodded.

She clapped. "Girly slumber party!"

"That's great, thank you."

She grinned. "So, are we, like, best friends, then?" She extended her pinky.

I felt like a child, but I put mine out too, and we shook on it.

I sat in my car at a drive-thru, third in line to pick up my flash meal. Madison was the perfect choice to keep my body out of trouble on the slim chance that Helena regained control the night of the awards. She was ditzy enough not to figure out that something was wrong with my rental. I did like her, but making friends with a 150-year-old wasn't at the top of my list of priorities. I just wanted to finish up the two weeks left on my contract without any snags, like assassinations.

The car in front drove away with its order, and I moved up in the line. I eased my car forward, reached in my purse to get money. Then I felt it.

The dizziness. The fainting.

It was happening again.

When I came to, I had an assault rifle pressed against my cheek, my eye aiming down the scope. My finger started to squeeze the trigger, pulling it in slow motion. I was leaning against a wall, by an open window, aiming at a crowd of people below.

No. No, no, no!

My breath stopped. I carefully eased my finger off the trigger, letting it slowly move back to a neutral position. The world—and all its sounds—stopped for a frozen moment. Then I noticed a noise, like some demon hammering. It was my pounding heart.

A single bead of sweat escaped from my forehead and stopped at my eyebrow.

My mind was racing a million miles an hour, wondering what had happened. Was I too late?

I stood inside a hotel room. Outside, about ten stories

below, a crowd was gathered in a square, facing a stage with an empty podium.

My heart beat even faster. Was the senator already dead? Please, no.

I examined the rifle. It was loaded. Fully. The barrel was cool to the touch. Below, the crowd was calm.

I breathed out. I hadn't shot anyone.

Where was I? The tall buildings looked like downtown L.A. The park below, Pershing Square.

On the desk, there was a leather folder embossed with *The Millennium Biltmore Hotel* in gold foil. Nice place Helena had picked to kill someone. I lifted the rifle to remove the cartridge.

Callie. Please don't.

Her voice came in more clearly than ever.

Don't unload.

"Helena?"

Yes.

"You can hear me?" I asked.

Now I can. We have a better connection.

"How's this possible?" I shivered, as if to shake her out of me. "What have you gotten me into?"

I took the cartridge out of the rifle and put it on the desk.

Could you reload the rifle, please? We don't have much time.

"No, I'm not going to reload!" I shouted. "You shouldn't have a weapon in the first place." I threw it on the bed. "Where did you get it?"

If you destroy it, the way you did my gun, I'll just get another.

"I didn't destroy it. I threw it away." I went to the window and looked down.

Senator Harrison was arriving. He climbed to the podium area and began addressing the crowd.

"I'm not going to shoot anyone for you, and I'm not going

to let you use my body to kill." I reached up and slammed the window shut.

Listen to me, Callie. I want to prevent a crime. One that will affect tens of thousands of people your age.

I shook my head. "You've got a bad track record for telling me the truth."

I decided it would be smart to get far away from the rifle and such a dangerous vantage point, just in case. I stormed to the door.

Callie, stop.

I slammed the door behind me and ran down the hallway. "What kind of person plans something like this?"

Don't run. You just had surgery.

My feet slowed to a walk. Was she making this up? To control me?

Your chip.

I touched the back of my head. It was sore. More sore than when Blake had touched it.

"What'd you do to me?" I screamed.

An Ender couple came out of their room and stared at me. I was a crazy girl in the hallway, shouting to no one. I rushed ahead to the elevators and slipped into an open one. As the brass-plated doors closed, I saw my reflection in them. I was wearing a black jumpsuit and my hair was pulled back in a tight ponytail. What look was Helena going for, ninja chic?

We altered the chip.

I gripped the railing inside the elevator. "You had someone operate on me?"

He's a biochip expert. And a surgeon. We had to alter the stop-kill switch.

"The what?" The elevator stopped and an Ender joined me. I had no choice but to shut up and listen to Helena.

The chip's design prevents renters from killing. My friend disabled it when I began the rental. But there were the problems, the sporadic blackouts, me getting pushed out of the—your—body, the bouncing back and forth. At that point I asked him to try to fix it. The best he could do was make it so we could communicate like this.

I glanced at the Ender in the elevator with me. He seemed to like the way I was dressed. Great. When the elevator stopped at the lobby level, I let him go ahead of me, until he was out of earshot.

"Well, I don't want you messing with my head. And I don't want you *in* my head," I said to Helena. "That wasn't part of the deal." I felt my cheeks on fire.

The lobby was swarming with people pressing against the windows to get a glimpse of the senator speaking in the park across the street.

"Where's the car?" I asked Helena.

Please, don't go.

I reached in my pockets and found a valet ticket. As I exited the hotel, I handed it to the doorman.

A microphone amplified the senator's voice so I could hear him from where I stood. I watched as he addressed the crowd from the podium.

"Our youth could have a productive role in our society," he said.

He is such a liar.

"All politicians lie," I said. "It's a requirement for the job."

His lies are big. The kind that kill children.

On the drive Helena insisted on telling me her thoughts about the senator. At first, she had thought his platform was to improve the standards for youth, promote better living conditions and health care, particularly for the institutionalized.

But lately, in the last six months, she had discovered that he had a secret plan.

He's involved with Prime Destinations.

"How?" I drove past other drivers also talking to voices in their heads. But at least theirs were at the end of an earpiece.

He's got a financial stake in the company. He's going to Washington to persuade the president to use Prime before the next election. To press them into service for the government.

"Doing what, exactly?" I had no patience for Helena's wild theories.

I can only guess. The main point is that these teens will not be volunteers. My sources say they'll be conscripted at best, kidnapped at worst.

It was all coming at me too fast. I didn't know what she was talking about. It seemed like her anger over losing Emma was blinding her. What if there wasn't some big conspiracy? Who was to say Emma hadn't just run away? And that Lauren's son, Kevin, hadn't run with her?

But I had to ask. "So what do you think they'd be doing?"

Anything for which it would be beneficial to have an Ender with over a hundred years of experience and wisdom in the strong, youthful body of a teen. Spying comes to mind. But that's probably just the beginning.

"And you uncovered all this because your granddaughter went missing?"

They killed her. The body bank killed her.

The anger in her voice chilled my blood. "You've got proof? You never saw the body."

I have considerable proof. You think I reached this decision lightly? I have spent the last six months working on this. And there are other victims, other grandparents.

"They don't all agree with your conclusions."

Helena was quiet for a moment. *So you've been talking to Lauren. She's naïve. She can't believe any company would kill young people.*

"Just like the way you were going to get me killed? Shot by marshals after I'd killed Senator Harrison?"

Her long silence said a lot. Finally, she broke it.

You're fast. Strong. You'd get away.

"I'm not faster than a bullet."

The tone of her voice changed. It became almost childlike. *Where are we going?*

"Not we. Me! It's my body. You're just along for the ride." I pictured her back at Prime, strapped in that chair.

Not Prime Destinations, you can't.

"That's exactly where I'm heading."

Why would you want to go there? You won't get paid if you don't fulfill your contract.

"I think the odds that I'll get paid are getting slimmer by the minute. Your plan would've gotten me killed first." I exited the freeway. "Maybe I'll bargain for half."

What do you think you can say to Prime Destinations that they'll understand? You're breaking your contract, that's all they'll care about.

"I'll tell them about you. About altering my chip. Then they can fix it."

If you let on that you know about any of this—the donors who were killed, or Senator Harrison's plan—they'll kill you.

"You're missing one little thing, Helena. I don't believe you. I'm not buying anything you say."

But you have to. The altered chip. The blackouts. The very fact that I can talk to you like this proves what I'm saying.

I gripped the wheel. What she said about the chip had to

be true. But did that mean everything else was? My temples started to pound. I pulled over.

We were four blocks from Prime Destinations.

"I want you out of my head. Now."

Don't go back there. Please. I'm begging you.

I cringed. She sounded so scared. "Give me one good reason."

If you go back, we're both dead.

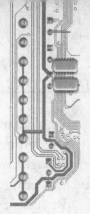

CHAPTER THIRTEEN

I was idling near a coffeehouse, keeping an eye out for renegades.

"Helena. I'm going to need more proof."

She believed the body bank would kill us both if I returned there.

To help keep me from going to Prime Destinations, she had offered to tell me where to go to get the chip removed. Probably to the geek friend who had altered it in the first place. How could I trust him? He was the guy who had nullified the stop-kill switch, turning me into Helena's own personal killing machine.

She was silent.

"Helena?"

She'd had moments of quiet before, but this was different. Empty. Like when someone was no longer at the end of a phone line. I pressed at the chip beneath the stitches in the back of my head in a lame effort to get Helena's "signal" back. But all I got was a sharp pain.

"Ow."

She didn't even respond to that. It was clear she had left, whether intentionally or not.

Before Helena's voice had shown up in my head, I had thought the assassination attempt would happen at the Music Center. But then Helena had surprised me by trying it at Pershing Square. She had moved it up, seeing that I was getting to be too much of a problem, taking away her gun and all. Assassins hate that.

I decided to go ahead with my original plan, because it was likely Helena was going to as well.

The next day, I showed up at Madison's house, aching to confide in her. I wanted to tell her everything I'd learned, how Helena's voice could come into my head while I was in control of my body.

But that would freak Madison out. If she knew that inside I wasn't an Ender like her, like I'd been pretending to be, she wouldn't trust me anymore. She could turn me in to Prime. She really wasn't my audience for sympathy at this point.

Madison's house was stuck in a décor that had been stylish maybe twenty years ago: alien chic. Shimmery green chairs floating in the air, strange hologram chandeliers, and 3-D alien landscapes on the walls.

As she led me down the hall, she explained how she liked to use certain rooms when she was "in character," meaning renting. Her place was big, so she had a lot of rooms to choose from.

We went to the game room, a dream hangout that made me forget my troubles. She showed me to the buffet table by the wall and handed me a bowl. Rows of the best snacks in plexi-tubes called to us, and we filled our dishes with candy and chocolates and pretzels. The last station was an amazing soda fountain she could program so that the syrup made funny colored designs in the glasses.

We took our stash to a humongous velvety sectional, where we spread out. The centerpiece in the middle of the room was a floating Invisascreen, 200 by 350 inches, that could project holos. I'd never seen one like this in someone's home. Besides holos and shows, it also had games that let us play super soccer, or air tennis, or golf, with the sports' biggest stars.

We could be cast members of shows seen only by subscribers she'd friended. This was way out of my family's league. But for the rich like Madison, there was almost no end to the possibilities for starstruck fans.

"I used to be a production manager, so I got an industry discount," she explained with a wink.

I guessed even the rich liked bargains.

Madison ordered the latest sequel to a popular holo. The characters were projected in space, life-sized. Seeing them this close and at this scale was different from seeing an Xperience. After a few minutes, Madison got up and stepped into the space. There were two actors in the scene, and the taller one turned to her.

"Hello, Madison," he said. "Glad you could join us."

"Wow. How'd you make that happen?" I asked, fascinated.

"You have to stand here"—Madison pointed to the rectangle of space in the center of the room—"or it doesn't work."

As soon as I entered the space, the other actor, the shorter one with fierce eyes, turned to me.

"Hello, Callie," he said. And I thought I would melt.

He stepped closer. I could smell him, kind of a woodsy scent, like cedar. He didn't look exactly like real life. It was more like the way a good hologram fooled you at first, but on closer inspection you saw the giveaway, a slight shimmer around the edges. But it was still pretty amazing.

"How do they do this?" I didn't want to take my eyes off him, but I turned to Madison. She was deep in a conversation with her actor.

My actor touched my arm, drawing my attention back.

"Don't worry about how. Just worry about who." He smiled at me.

I could feel his touch. It wasn't like in real life; it was subtler, like a breeze across my skin. It made the hair on my arm rise.

A phone rang.

Everyone stopped and folded their arms, waiting for me to go silence it.

"Callie." Madison put one hand on her forehead. "That just ruins the illusion."

"Sorry."

I stepped out of the space and went to the sectional. The caller ID displayed the last name I wanted to see at that moment.

"Blake?" I said into the phone.

"Callie. How's it going?"

I turned back to see Madison smiling at her actor while he played with her hair. My actor stood there with his hands in his pockets.

"Look, Callie, I know this is last-minute, but I just got the okay from my grandfather. Would you like to come to the Youth League Awards with me?"

"Tonight, you mean?"

"Yeah."

"I—I—really can't."

"It's important. I'd like you there. And you said you wanted to meet my grandfather."

"He'll probably be too busy anyway," I said.

"There's a reception afterward. Everyone who's anyone will be there, even the mayor. It'll be fun."

It was the last place in the world I should be. I bit my lower lip to keep from saying yes. I wanted to be with Blake, but this was exactly what I was trying to avoid—being in the same place as the senator. What if I blacked out and Helena took over?

"I want to, Blake. Really. But I promised Madison I'd spend the night here. It just wouldn't be right."

We said goodbye and hung up, and I could feel his disappointment. It matched mine.

Madison looked over at me as I put my phone back in my purse. "Everything okay?"

"Yeah, fine." I slumped on the sectional.

"Come and join us." She waved me over. Both actors were now talking to her.

I shook my head. "I'll just watch from here."

Madison shrugged and held hands with both actors as she turned away and the three of them walked off into a jungle. I thought about how Helena hadn't taken control of my body for a while now. And she hadn't spoken to me for the longest time. . . .

I gasped. What if she had left the body bank? Could she have cut the rental short because our connection had been compromised? If she had decided I wasn't going to cooperate with her, maybe she'd left the body bank and was on her way to assassinate the senator herself. At the awards, as planned. Doing it herself hadn't been her original plan, but she might have jumped to something that desperate since I had made it clear I would never shoot him.

If I went to the awards, I'd get to speak to Blake's grandfather. I could try to explain, warn him. And I no longer had a weapon. Helena would have to use up precious time finding another one, if she took over my body again.

I'd been stupid to turn Blake down. I excused myself and took my phone into Madison's guest bathroom to call him.

Blake drove me to the underground parking lot of a downtown building. He was thrilled that I'd changed my mind. I reminded him how much I was looking forward to meeting his grandfather. Maybe even having a chance for a moment alone with him. Blake said he'd try to make that happen. He didn't even question it. If only all guys were this nice.

Blake flashed a special key, and the underground doorman led us to a private elevator with black and gold carpeting. The doorman put his own key in a slot and tipped his hat as the doors closed between us.

"This isn't the Music Center," I said.

"It isn't?" Blake said. "Oh no, I made a wrong turn."

I gave him a sneer that he answered with a grin. The elevator stopped at the top level, marked "Penthouse."

The doors opened to a very short hallway that led to another door. Blake inserted his key and unlocked it. Inside were dark wood and low lights. On the right was a curved bar, complete with an Ender bartender wiping a glass.

"Welcome, Blake."

"Hey, Henry."

Blake didn't pause but continued walking through the room, past leather chairs, to a sliding glass door. He waved his palm over a pad on the wall and the door slid open. We stepped out onto a large terrace.

A modern square fountain dominated the center, making a calming bubbling sound that covered the bustling downtown noise. I walked to the edge of the terrace and peeked through the potted palms bordering the railing. It was clear why the trees were there. Boarded-up, crumbling buildings surrounded this oasis. Some were completely demolished, as if smashed by a giant monster.

I turned my back to the sight.

"So this belongs to your family."

He nodded. "Yeah. We use it before the opera or receptions at the concert hall. The staff doesn't really like having to wait on me when my grandfather's not here, though. I'm just a kid to them."

"I'd be happy to be here no matter how they treated me."

He led me to a patio love seat. We sat side by side.

"Don't we have to get to the awards?" I asked.

"We've got time."

The bartender brought out two sodas. He placed them on the side table and then left.

"So, Callie, how do you feel?"

I looked up at the fluffy clouds in the blue sky. I felt like telling him everything.

"I'm all right."

He reached over and leaned his hand on the back of the love seat. He stroked the top of my head. He started to run his hand over the back of my head, but I stopped him.

"What's wrong?" he asked.

"Nothing," I said, letting go of his hand.

"Callie, come on." He leaned closer. "What is it?" He looked at my head.

"Just not there," I said.

"Why?" He seemed almost amused. He held his hand over my head like some game, and I grabbed it.

What to say? I went for the truth. "I had some surgery."

His smile faded. "What kind?"

I tried to think of a believable lie. It wasn't coming. "I don't want to talk about it."

I looked at him. He was so concerned for me.

"It's . . . personal," I said.

He took my hand. "I know we haven't known each other very long, but I thought you trusted me."

"It's not that, it's just that everything is so good between us."

"And you're afraid if you tell me what kind of surgery you had that I won't like you anymore? You think I'm that shallow?"

My lip quivered. "No, of course not."

He squeezed my hand. "There's nothing you could tell me that would change how I feel about you. I want to know you. Everything about you."

He had no clue how big this lie was. "Please don't make me talk about it. Okay?" I pleaded with my eyes. "It's just that sometimes, you do things you wish you hadn't."

"I don't think there's anyone who can't say that. You're not alone." He ran his thumb over my hand.

He was trying to be nice, backing off from pushing me to explain. If only things were simple. If only I had never gone into that body bank. But if I hadn't, I never would have met him.

Past the cityscape, the sun was making its exit. "Shouldn't we be going soon?" I asked.

Blake took my hands and pulled me to my feet. "Follow me."

He led me inside, down a hallway, and opened a door. The room was a girl zone, decorated in soft shades of pink.

"Consider this your personal boutique." He threw open the closet doors, revealing a shimmering rainbow of evening dresses, from gowns to little cocktail numbers.

"Whose are these?" I asked.

"My sister. She likes to shop." He rolled his eyes.

Many of the dresses were the latest in fabric technology, featherlight miracles of physics that changed colors. Others were retro gowns inspired by old films from the last century. On the shelf above, glittery heels and purses sat in clear cases.

Blake waved his hand over a sensor, and the cases rotated so that more came into view.

"I didn't know you had a sister."

"She's up north, with my great-aunt."

I ran my hand over the fabrics. "What's she doing there?"

"Shopping."

He leaned against the wall, near my shoulder. Looked straight into my eyes. I could tell he was about to pick up where he'd left off a moment ago.

His face was inches from mine. "Don't worry." He held up one hand and wiggled the fingers before putting it behind his back. "No hands this time."

I couldn't help but smile. He moved his face lower, slowly, and kissed me. And kissed me. I didn't want it to stop, ever.

Just when I thought it couldn't get any better, it did. I wrapped my hands around his neck and didn't let go.

Then he did hold me, slipping his hands around my waist. I pressed my back against the wall, pulling him closer, feeling breathless and dizzy. I leaned my forehead against his.

"We'd better go," I whispered. "Or we'll be late."

He nodded. We released each other and he slowly backed out of the room. "Call when you're ready."

I touched my lips after he left. They were warm and puffy.

I ran my other hand across the fabulous clothes. How could I choose? It was like picking only one flavor of ice cream. But there wasn't time to waste. I put on a sleeveless blue gown with a matching shawl. The dress shimmered all the way to the floor but weighed less than a handkerchief. It was pretty and appropriately unrevealing. I wanted the senator to believe me. I remembered hearing once that blue was a color that made people trust you.

After a few minutes, Blake knocked at the door.

"Come in."

Blake was wearing a tux. He looked fantastic. His eyes got big when he saw me, but he switched to cool mode. He picked up a metal wand that was hanging in the closet and waved it over my dress.

"We don't have time to play," I said.

"Just watch."

An airscreen in the closet came on. An image of the dress appeared in 3-D, twirling. Images of shoes, a purse, earrings, and a bracelet also popped up.

The clear cases of shoes rotated until the pumps shown on the airscreen were in front. I took them out—heels decorated with a small silver whale clipped to each shoe.

"Whales. Your favorite," he said.

"Wow." I slipped into them. "We're the same size. They're perfect."

He handed me the purse and then held up a beautiful antique bracelet, filigree with blue stones, and matching earrings.

"You sure she won't mind me wearing her things?"

"Look at all this stuff. We could clear out half of it and she wouldn't notice."

"No, but the computer would definitely remember."

He reached for my wrist and saw the charm bracelet. "Pretty."

I offered my other wrist and he put his bracelet on it.

I turned to the mirror to put on the earrings. When I caught Blake's eye, the look on his face was worth memorizing. First the left side of his lip curled up slowly. Then his eyes crinkled and sparkled as his mouth went into a full-on grin.

"You look so amazing, you're going to steal my grandfather's thunder."

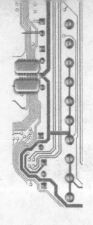

CHAPTER FOURTEEN

As we approached the Music Center plaza that night, I felt like a princess making her entrance at a royal ball. It was like a dreamscape, with tiny lights sparkling in the trees, larger ones highlighting the buildings, and spotlights illuminating the sculptural waterfall that danced in the center of the plaza.

We entered the Dorothy Chandler Pavilion, where chandeliers as big as minicars glistened over our heads. We climbed the grand staircase to the second level. The pre-awards party was in full swing. Ender waiters weaved through the glittery crowd with trays of champagne and punch. The guests were mostly rich Enders, but there was a sprinkling of wealthy teens like Blake.

And then there was me.

"Where's your grandfather?"

Blake handed me a glass of punch. "I'll go find him. You'll be okay here?"

"I'll be fine," I said, looking at the buffet table.

He craned his neck to look over the sea of silver heads and then disappeared into the crowd. I walked up to the buffet laden with shrimp and crab and lobster. Tyler's eyes would've bugged out of his head.

I was tempted to taste something when a voice surprised me.

Callie. You went after all.

It was inside my head. Helena. So she hadn't left the body bank.

"You're back," I said quietly. "I need an exorcism."

Everyone around me was too busy socializing or eating to notice me talking to myself. I didn't know whether to be angry or relieved.

I'm glad you saw the light.

"Don't thank me. I'm not here to kill anyone."

The senator is a monster. You let him get away, he'll be on that plane to Washington tomorrow, and the fate of thousands of teens will be sealed.

Her drama was not working on me. "You don't know that."

They say you can judge a man by the company he keeps. Well, the senator is in cahoots with the man who heads up Prime Destinations. The Old Man. He's the worst excuse for a human being in the universe.

"Then maybe I should kill *him*." I hoped the sarcasm was drippy enough for her.

You should. But he has too much protection. The senator is our immediate concern.

Sounded like her kill list was getting longer.

By stopping the senator from getting on that plane tonight, we can prevent this thing from exploding. I'll pay you five times what Prime offered you. And I will give you a home.

I made a point of not reacting. I stepped out onto the

balcony. I walked past the red glow of cigars held by Enders no longer afraid of early death. When I reached the far end, I stopped and looked at the evening skyline. Beyond the borders of our luxurious surroundings, the graffiti-ravaged buildings were a harsh contrast.

That was some offer Helena had just given. I hated even considering it.

"Even if I wanted to do what you're asking, I don't have a gun."

You do. I planted it earlier. This was my original plan, remember?

I felt sick to my stomach. This was Blake's grandfather she was talking about.

I'll tell you where it is.

"Don't tell me, I don't want to know." I wanted to put my fingers in my ears and sing nonsense syllables, but that wouldn't block her out.

I heard footsteps coming up behind me. I turned around to see Blake.

"Here she is," Blake said. "Grandfather, this is Callie."

Senator Harrison.

This was my chance. I could warn him. But I couldn't just jump in. I'd sound like a lunatic.

"We've been looking for you everywhere, young lady," the senator said, extending his hand.

Not the best introduction, having to be hunted down. As I shook his hand, I noticed he had the oddest expression. It was almost pained, as if he felt sorry for me.

"So where did you meet my grandson?"

"At a nightclub," I said.

He turned to Blake. "Nightclub? Which nightclub?"

"Grandfather—" Blake said.

"Club Rune," I said, probably too hastily.

"Club Rune." The senator stiffened.

I guessed he didn't approve. I should have let Blake answer. I glanced at him but he was poker-faced.

Blake turned to me. "Aren't you freezing out here?"

I shook my head. Then I looked into his face. Had I missed a cue to go inside?

The senator cleared his throat. "Lovely dress you're wearing."

"Thank you." I looked down and smoothed the fabric.

"And those earrings. The bracelet? Heirlooms? Very familiar."

"Your grandson picked them out for me."

The senator shot Blake an angry look. "Yes indeed. Take good care of that jewelry tonight. It's been in our family for several generations."

An aide approached and whispered in the senator's ear.

"We have to go backstage now. The ceremony starts in thirty minutes," Senator Harrison told Blake.

"I'll be right there," Blake said.

The senator huffed out a breath of air. "Appearances, Blake. Appearances."

"I'll be there."

The senator turned on his heel without a goodbye.

"I don't think he likes me," I said to Blake.

"Nah. That's his 'I'm really excited about her' face. Couldn't you tell?"

He squeezed my hand.

I had to smile.

"You've got your ticket. I'll meet you after the awards. There'll be a dessert reception in the ballroom." Blake stuck his tongue out the side of his mouth and rubbed his stomach before running off.

So now you know what the senator looks like. Don't let his charm fool you. He's a politician; they charm you in their sleep.

"You were there the whole time?" I asked Helena. The thought gave me the creeps. I had zero privacy.

Now listen carefully. The gun is in the last stall on the right in the women's bathroom on the second level.

And that's where it will stay, I thought but didn't tell Helena. Of course she could see that I wasn't heading that way.

You've got to get the gun, Callie.

"I'm not going to use it."

You can't leave it there.

"Why not?"

Because it has your fingerprints on it.

I stood in line at the women's bathroom on the second level. Elegantly dressed Enders primped in the wall-to-wall mirrors as they pretended they weren't holding their stomachs in. Ahead, to the left, were two rows of stalls, each with its own line.

Go to the right.

I moved to the right and waited. I counted four stalls, the last one a handicapped.

The middle stall opened up first.

No. It's the last stall.

I let the Ender behind me go ahead. Finally, the last stall opened and I went in. I locked the door and looked around.

"I don't see it." I whispered to Helena.

Look under the little trash bin.

There it was, low on the wall. I crouched down, trying my best not to get my beautiful gown in the toilet. I reached underneath it and felt a bulge.

She'd taped a small handgun to the bottom.

There.

I had to work at it to break through the tape. Chimes began to sound, alerting us that the ceremony was about to begin. Finally, I got the gun loose and put it in my purse.

As I rushed out of the restroom, I realized that I hadn't taken the bullets out of the gun. The ushers were closing the doors. I slipped my hand into my purse and clicked on the safety lock just as I entered the theater.

That's not necessary.

"Safety first," I whispered.

I sat by myself through the awards ceremony speeches. The senator was presented as a respected statesman. He went on about how his mission in life was to keep young people out of trouble by keeping them active. Helena added her running commentary, turning around every phrase to reveal Senator Harrison's true, malicious meaning.

She wasn't going to give up.

You have the gun. Shoot him.

If I could have spoken back to her, I would have told her to shut up. All through the world's longest presentation ever, the gun felt like it weighed a hundred pounds in the purse on my lap.

Once the ceremony was over, I poured out with the crowd.

"One question, Helena," I asked under my breath. "Why here?"

The bigger the scene, the better to expose the body bank.

I wandered around the ballroom waiting for Blake. Helena went silent, which gave me a break. I admired the mountain of desserts at the buffet table. I had no appetite, though, and I seemed to be in everyone's way, so I moved off to the side by the large windows.

I'd been there a few minutes when someone tapped me on the back. I turned to see the senator. Alone.

"Callie, isn't it? Enjoying yourself?"

This was my chance; I could warn him. "Mmm, not exactly. I—I wanted to talk to you."

His eyes narrowed. "You're so beautiful."

Somehow, he made it seem like an insult. It wasn't just that he was so direct, it was his tone that put me on edge. He stepped closer, way beyond the comfort zone, and examined my face like a doctor. I felt like a bug under a microscope.

"Something wrong?" I asked.

"No, you're just about perfect, in fact." He took my face in his hand and turned it to one side.

My heart was pounding. I wanted to move to the center of the room, where there were more people.

"You are perfect." He picked up both my hands and examined the backs. "Not a single scar, mole, or cut." He looked back at my face. "Not even the memory of a pimple." His lip curled.

He moved even closer, his face so near I could smell the residue of bitter cigar smoke on his breath.

"I know what you are." He gripped my arm.

I tried to pull away, but he held on too hard.

"Why are you here? Did Tinnenbaum send you?"

"No." I struggled.

"Who else is here?"

"No one, just me."

"I want you to get out of here, now. And stay away from my grandson." He shook me. "What kind of woman are you?"

"You don't understand. I have to tell you something important."

"Nothing you could tell me would change anything." The veins in his temples bulged like worms under his skin.

Where we stood in the corner, only a few people were close enough to notice us. An Ender woman maneuvered through the crowd with purpose. I recognized her face from somewhere.

"Senator Harrison, that's the girl who came into your office," she said.

That was where I had seen her before. Great.

An elegant Ender accompanied her. Blake's grandmother, I guessed. The one he didn't like.

"Clifford," the grandmother said with warning eyes. "Don't." She grabbed his arm.

As she tugged, he released me. He took the elbow of the office woman and led her away.

"Excuse us," Blake's grandmother said.

As they left, it felt like the room was closing in on me. I stared back at all the eyes and rubbed my throbbing arm. My heart was pounding.

You see? You see his temper? You're foolish to trust him.

I saw it. And felt it. But I was pulled away from my thoughts as new hands grabbed me, tugging on my arms. I was sure it was guards.

"Let go of me." I struggled to pull away.

"Calm down, Callie, it's me. Briona."

It was the trio of renters I had met at Club Rune, the ones I had gone to the bridge with. Briona, with Lee and Raj, both in black tie. The three of them were trying to escort me toward the exit.

But I couldn't leave. Not yet.

"Stop," I said.

Enders stared at us. Briona and the guys let me go, but they circled me, corralling me like a lone calf.

"You can't stay here, darling," Raj said in a low voice.

"Senator Harrison called you out," Lee said.

Briona put her lips close to my ear. "He knows you're a renter."

"We all have to get out of here," Raj said. "He's talking to security now."

"But Blake will be looking for me." I unclasped the antique bracelet.

"What are you doing?" Briona hissed. "We've got to get out of here."

"I have to give these back to Blake." I removed the earrings.

"I'll do it," Lee said, taking the jewelry.

"There's no time," Briona told him.

"We can't let the senator catch her with his grandson—he'll go neutron ballistic. I'll be quick." Lee pocketed the jewelry.

"Please be careful," I said. "They're heirlooms."

"With us seniors," Raj said, "what's not an heirloom?"

"No worries," Lee said to me. "I used to be a banker forty years ago. I'm good with valuables."

He turned and snaked through the crowd. Briona hooked her arm through mine. "Come on, sweetie, let's hustle."

Raj took my other arm. Guards eyed us, mumbling to each other.

"Hurry," Briona said.

We went out one of the many exits and turned left, rushing to the grand stairway, which faced a mirrored wall. Others were leaving too, and we blended into the crowd going down the stairs. My high heel twisted on the stairs in the rush and my left shoe came off.

"My shoe." I turned back to see it lying there.

Raj held me up to keep me from falling. "Don't stop."

I followed Briona's gaze and looked up. Security guards leaned over the railing above, looking down on us.

"Go!" she said.

We ran across the marble entranceway, me rising and falling with only one heel. At the last exit door we had to let go of each other to fit through. Briona went in front of me and Raj behind me, pushing me all the way. Once outside in the plaza, I removed my remaining shoe. Briona grabbed my hand and we ran past the fountain to the street.

"Where are we going?" I shouted.

"There!" Briona pointed to a silver SUV waiting by the curb. "Keep running."

I looked back and saw people, guards, running after us. Briona and I jumped into the backseat; Raj got in the front. Lee was already inside, sitting in the driver's seat.

"How'd you beat us?" Briona asked.

"Side exit," Lee said.

As my seat belt whirred into place, I looked out the tinted windows and saw several uniformed guards and some plainclothes people slowing, realizing they were seconds too late. And then I saw him—Blake—running up behind them, alone.

I started to lower the window so I could shout to him, but Briona reached over and stopped me.

"No."

The windows and doors locked with a loud click as Lee pressed the master lock.

I wanted to say something, at least wave goodbye. Blake couldn't see me through the dark-tinted windows. All I could do was watch him stare at the windows, searching, finding nothing. Deep disappointment fell across his face as our car pulled away.

It wasn't until we had a little distance that I noticed he was holding something in his hand.

My shoe.

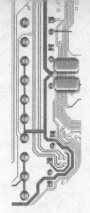

CHAPTER FIFTEEN

I pressed my hands against the window and watched Blake until he became a small blur. Raj and Briona both barked at Lee to drive faster—but the senator's guards weren't chasing us, so who were we running from? The marshals? Were renters afraid of the marshals the way unclaimed minors were? I figured renting was technically outside the law, but I'd always assumed that vast quantities of money in the right palms could solve anything.

Apparently not, or Briona, Lee, and Raj wouldn't have run out of the Music Center so fast.

Briona sat beside me, holding my hand tightly. I figured it was an Ender thing.

"How are you feeling, Callie?" Her mocha eyes searched my face.

"Okay." I gently wriggled my hand away.

Raj leaned his arm on the back of Lee's seat and turned around.

"You sure? You look a little pale," he said.

"Yeah, she looks pale," Lee said, "compared to us." He smiled at me in the rearview mirror.

I couldn't manage a return smile. I turned to the window, my mind still on Blake.

Once we were on the freeway, with no sirens to be heard, everyone took a collective breath and sat back.

"So now where?" Raj asked.

Ask them about Emma.

It was Helena. I knew she was angry that I hadn't killed Harrison. Maybe I could help find out something about her granddaughter.

"Raj, did you ever meet a renter who went by the name of Emma?"

"That was her donor's name?"

"Yes."

"I don't think so."

"Remember?" Briona turned to me but said in a voice loud enough for the guys to hear. "Last time you asked me that, I told you the guys wouldn't know."

"You sure?" I asked Raj. "Blond, tall. Here, I've got her photo." I pulled out my cell phone and held it up.

"Wish I had met her," he said. "But nope."

"What about you, Lee?" I held up the phone.

He looked in the rearview mirror and shook his head.

"Well, I tried," I said, mostly for Helena's benefit.

Thank you.

She sounded sincere but disappointed.

We drove around the city for a while. I thought it was funny that they didn't ask me why I wanted to know about Emma.

Briona put her fingers on her temples and groaned.

"What's wrong?" I asked.

"Just started getting these awful headaches. Never had them before. I think they're from the donor body's chip implant." She stopped rubbing and leaned her head back. "Do you ever get them?" she asked.

"No," I lied. "I don't have any problems."

When it was time to call it a night, I asked them to drop me off on Madison's street.

"Night." I got out and they drove off.

I looked up at Madison's house. I was too drained to go back inside and face her. When I'd left earlier, after calling Blake, I'd just snuck out the side door. It wasn't the nicest thing to do, but I'd been in a hurry.

I turned and walked to my car.

Back home, I lay in Helena's bed, staring up at the silken canopy, thinking about the mess I was in. Blake was on the plane to Washington, with his grandfather telling him I was really an old woman renting a young body.

He would never want to see me again. Who could blame him? And even if he knew the true story, that it was really me inside, could he forgive me for lying and pretending to be wealthy when the whole time I was really a street kid?

I clenched the sheets in my fists. The whole reason I was in this mess was because I was just trying to make a life for Tyler.

Tyler.

What was I going to do for him if Helena was right about the body bank? I probably wasn't going to see any payment from them. Helena had offered to pay more, and give me a home.

If I killed Harrison.

I loved my brother, and I wanted him safe and warm and healthy. But murder wasn't even in my vocabulary, never mind that the person in question was Blake's grandfather and a senator. I was a Starter, not an assassin. I didn't know what to make of Helena. How much of what she said was true? I understood she was angry over losing Emma, but lots of kids went missing these days. Some ended up dead. Was it really the body bank's fault?

Although Senator Harrison had mentioned Tinnen-baum. . . .

I sat up in bed. The senator had been upset by the thought that Tinnenbaum had sent me there. If Helena was right and the senator was going to talk to the president about some agreement between the body bank and the government, why would he be so upset thinking that Tinnenbaum might have sent me? To do what? To cancel the deal?

Callie?

I stiffened. Helena's voice in my head startled me. She hadn't spoken to me since we got home. "What?"

Why did you sign up at Prime?

"My brother's not well."

I'm sorry. She paused. *And you have no grandparents.*

"No."

So he's the one you wanted to give the money to before. Through your friend.

"Yes, exactly."

I wish we could bring him here, but it wouldn't be wise. But I will do something for you.

I waited, eager to hear.

Go to my dresser and open the bottom drawer.

I crawled out of bed and padded over to the antique dresser. I pulled out the last drawer.

Reach underneath the bottom of the drawer.

I felt a packet taped there. I pulled it off and saw that it was an envelope.

Open it.

It was filled with money. My arms felt tingly.

Get your brother a place to stay for now. A hotel.

"Minors can't do that."

I will tell you where to go, whom to talk to.

"I can't go to him. The body bank knows the address. If they track me and see I went there, they'll say I broke the contract."

There's a fix for that. Open the top drawer and look for the blue box.

I pulled out a small blue box and opened it. Inside was a pendant, a circle with a blue and green stone.

"Pretty."

It's a reception blocker. It jams the signal. It's not always consistent.

I started to put it on.

Don't. We have to limit the time you wear it; otherwise Prime could notice they're being blocked.

"Who made it?"

My tech. Once I'm out of Prime, I'll take you to meet him.

There had to be a price. "Why are you doing this?"

I still need your help. I want to find out what happened to Emma. If I can learn that, I might have the proof I'll need to shut down that horrid place. And our deal still stands.

"How could we do something like that? Even if we found out what happened to Emma?"

We have an advantage now. No one knows I can talk to you. We are two brains in one body.

She sounded so different, calm and thoughtful. Her frantic tone was gone now that she'd given up on the assassination plot.

Get some rest. We'll start in the morning.

I put the necklace on top of the dresser and climbed back into her big, soft bed. But I didn't feel like sleeping. My mind was filled with images of Tyler in a hotel room, with a real bed and heat and room service.

I turned off the lamp, and moonlight cast the room in a silvery blue.

"Helena, what do you see when I dream?"

Nothing.

At least my dreams and my thoughts were still my own. I lay there in silence for a few moments.

Callie? What was your mother like?

My mother. I pictured her smiling face. I didn't know what to tell Helena about her—there was so much.

Was she like you?

"No. She was one of those people everyone instantly liked."

I'll bet people like you.

"Not the way they liked her. People treated her like their long-lost sister. She fit in everywhere. She was on the archery team in the Olympics one year." A little childhood memory flashed into my brain. "She used to make me macaroni and cheese when I was sick."

It was funny, the things you remembered.

"What was Emma like?"

Emma was headstrong and determined. Maybe all sixteen-year-

olds are, but she was especially defiant. Knew what she wanted. It was hard for me, trying to take over raising her after the war. I couldn't be her mother or her father. And she was angry about all that. Who could blame her? You remind me of her, a little.

Helena didn't seem half as crazy as before.

I felt my eyelids close. I was exhausted.

Good night, Callie.

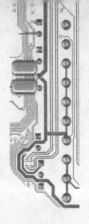

CHAPTER SIXTEEN

I parked on the side street near Michael's building and checked the area for renegades. It looked empty, but anyone could be hiding in a doorway. I grabbed the pack of food, water bottles, and meds I'd brought and rushed out of the car. I hoped Helena's necklace really would work and prevent Prime from tracking me.

I entered the lobby. Would Michael and Tyler still be there? With life on the street, sometimes we had to bolt. I tiptoed to the reception desk to be sure no one was hiding, ready to attack.

No one was there. All clear. I turned to the stairs in the middle of the lobby.

As I climbed the windowless stairway, I realized I didn't have my handlite anymore. It was too dark to see. How could I have forgotten so quickly what it was like to live this way? I felt my way down the hall. Then I remembered—I had Helena's cell phone. I pulled it out of my purse and used it to light my path. When I got to the end, I looked at my choices. Was their room to the left? I turned and walked down the long corridor.

A scruffy guy popped out of a doorway, holding a metal bar. My heart skipped a beat until I realized he was just as surprised by my clean appearance as I was by his hairy one. You don't see clean, well-dressed people in dark squatter buildings.

"I'm a friendlie," I said. "Here to see Tyler and Michael."

He pointed to the end of the hall.

"Thanks."

The last time I had been there had been almost two weeks ago, when Tinnenbaum had allowed Rodney to escort me. But that felt like another lifetime. As I entered, I saw that they had made changes. They'd moved the furniture and collected a lot more stuff. It felt homier. There was a scrap of yellow fabric draped over the table and a jar with acrylic flowers. More fabric scraps were stapled over the windows, giving a muted golden glow to the room.

"Tyler?" I called out.

I walked around the fort. He was sitting there with a girl bent over him. I dropped the backpack.

"What are you doing?" I said. My tone was accusatory. On purpose.

The girl turned her head to me. "Just handing him some water. Have a problem with that?"

I recognized her. Florina. The girl Michael had introduced me to just as I'd been leaving for the body bank. She looked like she was about to throw that cup at me, but Tyler called my name. I ran in and fell to my knees in front of him, throwing my arms around him and holding him close.

"I missed you so much." I stroked his soft hair.

"You're back," he said. "Finally."

I pulled away to look at his face. "I wish."

"Not again. You said that last time."

"I know, Ty, but this time we're almost done."

Florina looked at him. "You can be patient, can't you, sport?"

What was she doing, butting in like this?

"That's Florina." Tyler tilted his head toward her.

I looked at her. "We met before I left. Where's Michael?"

"Not sure." Her eyes focused on the floor.

An uneasiness turned in my stomach. But I ignored it because Tyler was there, playing with my hand. "And you. I have a surprise for you."

"What?" he asked.

"If I tell you, it won't be a surprise."

He groaned.

"How are you feeling?" I pushed his hair away so I could see his brown eyes. He looked pale, but it was hard to tell in this dim yellow light.

"We've had some rough days," Florina said.

So Florina had been taking care of him for a while. "You okay now?" I asked him.

He nodded and pinched my arm. "You got fat." He pulled on Helena's necklace I was wearing.

"No, don't touch that. Look, I brought your favorite yummies." I raised my brows to Florina. "So how long has Michael been gone?"

"He didn't come home last night," Tyler said.

That wasn't like Michael. I didn't want to ask the obvious in front of Tyler, but Florina and I traded looks. Had the marshals picked him up?

"We had a little spat," she said. "He stormed out."

"Then maybe he's cooling off somewhere." There were endless possibilities. Maybe he ran into someone he knew, maybe he was beaten up and lying in an alley. Maybe . . .

"What did you guys argue about?"

"Nothing important."

"Then why didn't you go after him?" I asked. "Did you look for him at all?"

She shook her head. Then she motioned with her eyes to Tyler. I realized she couldn't have chased after Michael because Tyler would have been alone. I felt like a jerk for being so cool to her before.

"I'm grateful you were here for my brother," I said. "It means a lot to me."

She stroked his hair. "Of course. We're old friends now, aren't we, Tyler?"

"We play games," he said.

"I'll bet she beats you," I said.

"No way. I beat her."

After Tyler and Florina had eaten the little feast of cheese and fruit and sandwiches I'd brought, Florina and I sat on the stairs to talk privately. From this position, we could see if anyone entered the building, so we felt safe leaving Tyler. And with that hairy friendlie on our floor, Tyler had some protection.

"Last week Tyler ran a fever," Florina said. "We were able to get children's pain reliever—Michael had some money hidden away."

That must have been the money I had given to Blake to deliver.

"Still, it was bad. I kept changing the cold cloths on his forehead because they heated up instantly."

I put my head in my hands. "I'm getting him out of here, tonight."

Florina straightened. "Really? Where are you going?"

"To a hotel. You come too."

"But you said you weren't done. Where'd you get the money?"

"I got an advance." It was sort of true. "When Michael comes back, he can join you guys."

That put a smile on her face. "I'll leave a message for him."

It sounded like they were more than just friends. I'd been gone in total for almost three weeks. A lot could happen in that time—look at Blake and me. I felt a pang. I was a little jealous but knew I had no right to be.

We went back inside and packed up what was most important. Tyler was feeling energized by the food and my presence, so he was helping. He picked the things he most wanted to bring and packed them in a duffel bag.

"Where are we going?" Tyler asked.

"To a nice place where you'll have a big fluffy bed and an airscreen and lots of hot chocolate."

"No kidding?" His eyes opened wide. "Really? How long can we stay?"

"I'm not sure. Depends."

"On what?"

"On how good you are." I went over and tickled him until he bent over laughing, begging me to stop.

"Should we bring the water bottles?" Florina asked.

I shook my head. She raised her brows. "Sure?"

"Okay, just in case."

We all packed quietly, looking at our few possessions.

Florina stood with her hands on her hips, no doubt wondering if her memories were worth the weight. Then she picked up something that caught my eye. It was a drawing of her, taped to cardboard.

I knew who had drawn it.

I turned away before she could notice. There was a moment, a frozen moment, but then I pulled myself back from falling into the abyss called pity. It was a place I refused to go.

The three of us went downstairs with our bags. Two younger Starters were leaning on the car. I waved them away, looked around to make sure no one else was hovering, and then opened the trunk.

"A car?" Tyler shouted.

I put my finger to my lips. I wanted to get out of there without having to dodge unfriendlies. I'd brought Emma's car, the least flashy one.

"Where did you get this?" Florina asked.

"Can you really drive it?" Tyler asked.

I closed the trunk and rushed everyone inside.

"Work loaned it to me," I said, after I locked the doors.

"Wow, that place is pretty cool," Tyler said.

As the seat belts whirred over their shoulders, both of them oohed and aahed at the interior. Even though this was Helena's least ostentatious car, it was still state-of-the-art. From the backseat, Tyler pressed every button he could reach.

"What's this do?" he asked, pressing a button on the door.

"It would open the door, but I have the childproof lock on," I said, looking at him through the rearview mirror. "Because we clearly have a child in the vehicle." I stuck out my tongue at him, and he responded in kind.

"Copycat," I said.

"Monkey-Face," he said.

I started the engine and pulled out.

"Look. Monkey's driving!" Tyler said.

At the hotel, Tyler and Florina stared at the luxurious lobby and its gigantic floral display. Helena hadn't let us down: she had led us to a top-notch hotel. The desk clerk looked at us strangely: all minors, one apparently rich, accompanied by two urchins with ratty baggage. But I asked for the manager, a woman Helena knew, and everything was easy. I showed her my ID with the name "Callie Winterhill," explaining I was Helena's grandniece. She was happy to take my cash and gave us a room on the fifteenth floor.

When I opened the door, Tyler's jaw dropped. It had been a long time since he'd been in a room this plush. It was huge, with two queen beds and a couch that opened to a third bed.

"Michael can have the couch," Tyler said. "'Cause he's not here to claim a bed."

Florina and I traded a look. "If he shows up," she said under her breath.

Tyler went for a jar of nuts on a table. "Nuts."

"There's more than that. Look." I opened the minibar.

"Wow!" he said, grabbing a Supertruffle.

Florina came over and I handed her a bag of chips and a soda. She guzzled the soda and tore into the chips.

"I call the bed by the window," Tyler said, chewing the candy.

I held him back. "Just a minute, buddy. Bath first."

"With bubbles!" he said.

After he had his bath, Florina took a long shower. Tyler looked so thin in his underwear, it frightened me. I pulled back the clean white duvet and tucked him in.

"It's so soft, I'm going to float away," he said.

"You stay right here," I said, pinching his nose.

Seeing his little head against those fluffy pillows brought back memories of us being kids again, in our own rooms, in our own beds, with cowboy lamps and stuffed animals and parents who came in and kissed us goodnight.

It was a world that I'd long since left, but maybe Tyler still had a chance to return there. I felt a hole in my heart. I couldn't hold back the tears that followed.

"Hey, Callie. This is a good thing."

He took my hand. His was so bony.

"Really good," I said.

Leaving was harder than I had expected. I hoped to see Tyler again soon. And then no more leaving. If Helena kept her promise to pay me and give me a house, then my brother and I would be a family together again. I'd find him a good doctor and he'd get better every day. I always pictured Michael joining us, but maybe he wouldn't, now that he and Florina were close. It didn't seem fair. I'd taken off to earn money. Michael and I hadn't had a chance to see where our relationship could go yet.

Since Blake was probably lost to me forever, the thought of losing Michael as well was impossible to accept.

I gave Florina enough money for three nights at the hotel, and extra to cover room service. I snuck some money into Tyler's bag as well. He wanted me to stay longer, but I was aware of the clock ticking away and Helena needing my help. I was able to leave without a scene when Tyler conked out from an overload of food from the minibar raid.

As I waited out front for the hotel valet, Helena came back into my head and planned our next move.

I need you to go talk to a girl who may have some information about Emma.

"Where is she?"

Someplace you're not going to want to go.

My mind went through an inventory of bad places. A rough neighborhood? They were all rough now. She certainly wouldn't send me to the body bank; she'd begged me not to go there before.

"I give up. Where?"

Institution 37.

I felt a hitch in my breathing. I leaned back against the wall.

"Could I pick hell instead?"

I know. The institutions are horrible—prisons, really. I visited many, looking for Emma. I found out about this girl, Sara, who knows something. But the day I went, she was out on work detail.

"I can't. I can't go there. I could meet her outside, anywhere. Just not there."

No. If we did that, she'd have to have an escort. She wouldn't be free to talk.

My palms were wet. I wiped them on my pants.

You'll be all right. We'll go home first and get some clothes to donate. You're going to drive up in a nice car, well dressed and groomed. They'll treat you like any wealthy claimed minor.

This wasn't just someplace I didn't want to go. It was my worst nightmare. I sighed.

It will be all right, Callie. Just remember who you are—Callie Winterhill.

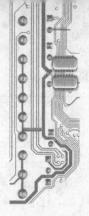

CHAPTER SEVENTEEN

I stood across the street, staring at the gates to Institution 37. I wanted to be anywhere else on the planet. Anywhere. It killed me to think I could be back in that fancy hotel with my brother and Florina.

Callie, why are you just standing there?

"You sure this is going to be safe?"

Face it, you're not safe anywhere at this point. But you're probably safest in there, because no one can get to you.

"That's so reassuring."

I had left the necklace at Helena's. She didn't want to use it too much for fear the body bank might notice my chip wasn't tracking. I crossed the street, balancing two shopping bags of designer clothes, many with the tags still on them. They came from Helena's closet, new pieces bought for Emma, never worn. Helena couldn't bear to give away the clothes her granddaughter had worn, even though she was never coming back.

A high gray wall surrounded the compound. I stood at the gate and spoke to the guard through a dirty metal screen.

"I'm Callie Winterhill," I said. "I called about donating."

The Ender guard scanned a list until he found my name. He pushed a button and the gate made a loud click before it opened. I froze. My feet wouldn't move.

Go!

I needed that nudge. I took a breath and entered. The gate closed behind me with a slam, metal hitting metal so hard it hurt my teeth. The road led directly to the administration building in front of me, with its dark gray walls. Back before the war, when there were public schools with admin buildings, they were never this frightening.

"Lovely," I said under my breath.

I walked down the path alongside the road. I slowed my steps, taking my time.

Don't go all the way. Turn right there.

Relieved, I followed Helena's instructions, heading toward the dormitory buildings, which had bars on every window.

"But won't they be expecting me? Back in the main office?" I asked Helena quietly.

Yes. But we have to find Sara first. I was told she's in this first dormitory building. Hurry, before someone stops you.

I climbed a few steps and pushed open the heavy doors. Inside, there were two hallways joined by a short corridor. A sour smell overwhelmed me. The paint was peeling, flecks of it littering the bare concrete floor.

"Now what?" I whispered.

Go down the first hallway.

I turned to the right and looked in the first door. Sixteen metal bunk beds were crammed into a gray room. An open wooden box was by each bed, holding a few meager belongings: a frayed hairbrush, a worn book. It reminded me of pictures of army barracks, with sad olive blankets drooping over the foot of each bed. Only this was worse, because these kids had no family to return to someday.

Everything they had was in those little boxes.

"No one's here."

Keep going.

I passed several rooms, all empty. I had come to the end of the hall and was ready to give up when I saw feet sticking out from under a bed.

I leaned down. A girl was lying on the floor, trying to hide. "Hello," I said.

She scooted backward, away from me.

"It's all right." I went closer. "I've brought some nice clothes."

I straightened up and waited.

"Clothes?" Her voice came from under the bed.

"Beautiful clothes. Pants and skirts and sweaters." I put down the bag and pulled out a sweater. "Here's a pink cashmere one."

"Cashmere?"

She crawled out and stood up. She looked about twelve, with a pretty face and a little gap between her teeth. Her uniform, a frayed white shirt and black pants, hung loosely on her bony figure. Her gauntness was typical for an unclaimed minor, but she wasn't living on the street anymore. It was clear they weren't overfeeding the kids.

Ask her what her name is.

I handed her the sweater. She stroked it like a kitten.

"Soft." She held it to her cheek.

"It's yours."

"Really? You mean it, really?"

I nodded.

"Oh, thank you so much." She slipped it on.

"What do you think?" I asked.

She answered by putting her right fist over her heart and cupping it with her other hand. She slapped her hands together, mimicking a beating heart.

"That means I love it," she said. "See, it sounds like a heart. You do it."

She picked up my hands and made me imitate her. I felt silly.

"More like a heartbeat, like this," she said. "It's better if you push your fist into your other hand." She forced my hands to mark the *thump-thump* rhythm.

"It's okay, I got it." I stopped and waved her hands away. "What's your name?"

"Sara."

My pulse quickened. Helena let out a gasp only I could hear.

"How long have you lived here?" I asked.

"Almost a year."

"Where are the others?"

"They're out doing brush clearance today." She sat on the edge of the bed.

"But not you?"

She pointed to her heart. "Bad valve."

I didn't know what to say, other than to dig up some standard apology.

"'S'okay. Doesn't hurt, and it gets me out of the worst work." She hugged herself in the sweater. "Was this yours?"

I shook my head. "A friend's. It looks good on you. I'm sure she'd be happy you got it."

She beamed and caressed the sleeves. "It feels so good." She patted the bed. The bed sagged as I sat next to her. The blanket felt rough and smelled moldy.

"When I came in, you were hiding. Why?" I asked.

She shrugged. "You never know around here." She looked down.

I reached into my purse and pulled out a Supertruffle. I offered it to her. She raised her brows.

"Go ahead." I moved it closer to her.

She took it with both hands and bit into it. I wondered when her last meal had been.

"Sara, I heard you might have met a girl named Emma? She looked like this." I showed her the picture on my phone. "Do you remember her?"

Her small fingers took the phone from me and examined it. "She came in here once as a volunteer, like six months ago. She did my hair. It was a beauty clinic."

She gave me back the phone.

"I saw her again, a couple of weeks later. My wrist got broken—don't ask—and I had to go get a scan. I saw Emma on the street, but it was weird."

"Why?"

"She didn't recognize me. I called her name, 'Emma!' She looked right at me but didn't remember me. She did look a little different, prettier, but I knew it was her. She had on the same jewelry. I guess she was embarrassed. Didn't want to be seen with me." She picked at the sweater. "And after we'd spent that nice day together."

I wanted so much to tell Sara she was wrong. That it wasn't the real Emma, but some Ender renter.

"Where were you, when you saw her?" I asked.

She shook her head. "I don't know. Somewhere not far, here in Beverly Hills."

I put my phone away. "I'm sorry." I said that for Helena's benefit. I wished I could have come up with more information.

"It's okay," Sara said. She moved closer to me on the bed. "Can I ask you something?"

"Sure."

"Do you think I'm pretty?"

"Of course. You've got a beautiful face. Why?"

"We found out last week there's going to be a special program. They're going to take some of us and make us over and give us important jobs. We'll be able to earn money. They've gotta pick me. I really, really want to get out. I've been here forever."

"When? When is this happening?"

"Don't know. They said we were getting showers tomorrow. We usually only get them on Sunday."

A look of fear shaded her face. Her eyes focused on something behind me as she stood. I turned around and saw a mean-looking Ender at the door. She might have been elegant once, but now she wore a stern gray suit and a ZipTaser on her hip.

"What are you doing here?" She came into the room.

I stood and pointed to the bags. "I brought donations."

Her badge read "Mrs. Beatty, Head of Security."

"All donations go through the headmistress. You can't just waltz around, tossing out gifts like beads at Mardi Gras." She picked up both bags. "It would only cause jealousy and fights, and we certainly don't need any more of that."

I was foolishly hoping she wouldn't notice. But the

sweater that Sara had on wasn't regulation gray or black; it was noticeably pink. Naturally, it caught Beatty's eye.

Sara crossed her arms over it in a futile attempt to hide it.

"Take it off," Beatty said. "Now."

"It's mine, she gave it to me."

"That's true." I stepped in front of her. "I did."

Don't get involved, Callie, Helena urged me.

"You'll hand it over right now." Beatty dropped the shopping bags and moved around me.

She pulled it over Sara's head and yanked it off.

"You can't take it, it's mine." Tears flowed from her red eyes. "It's the first thing anyone's given me since forever."

Don't stay, Callie, just get out of there.

"The headmistress does any and all distribution." Beatty nodded at me. "Let's you and I go see her."

No! Whatever you do, don't go there.

Helena's voice made my body tense. Beatty gestured with her head for me to go first. She cast a stern look at Sara, as if she would deal with her later, when I was no longer a witness. I walked to the door and stopped. I turned in the doorway and got one last glimpse of Sara's fragile little body. Bits of pink fuzz stuck to her white blouse, a sad reminder of what might have been.

There was nothing I could do for her.

Beatty and I walked down the hall. Beatty wore heels, not spiky ones, but chunky ones that made a certain clopping sound. I had a strange notion to run back and punch Sara in the face. If she had a black eye or a broken nose, then maybe the body bank people wouldn't pick her.

It was sick that it had come to that. As we left the building and climbed down the steps, I couldn't get Sara's face out of my mind. She was just a younger version of me, the me I had been for the last year. A desperate, starving orphan, eager for scraps, at the mercy of a system that cared less for unclaimed minors than for stray dogs.

When we came to the entrance to the main building, Helena spoke to me.

Go to the left. Just walk out like you own the place.

I did what she said. Beatty's clopping stopped.

"Miss. The office of the headmistress is this way." She pointed to the right. Her voice was so sharp, it hurt my ears.

"I know. But I'm not feeling well. I'm leaving."

"We have a doctor here. A good one. I'll call him."

"No thank you."

Beatty chuffed, her lips turning down into a sneer. But I kept walking to the main gate, holding my head high, never looking back. I was learning the posture of the entitled.

When I reached the gate, the guard looked at me from inside his little cage. I stared at the gate, expecting it to open. It didn't.

The phone rang and he answered it. It was all old technology there.

He stared at me and then hung up. He motioned for me to approach. I stepped closer to the mesh grating.

"Have a nice day," he said. "See you again."

The gate opened and it took all my will not to run through it. When it closed behind me, my breathing resumed and I walked across the street. I turned back and looked at the compound. The dormitory rose higher than the wall, and something there caught my eye.

Sara was in one of the windows, looking very small, waving at me. I swallowed whatever had gathered in my throat.

Now you see how bad it is in there. Now you know.

"It's even worse, didn't you hear her?" I said to Helena. "The body bank's going to cherry-pick the prettiest kids and start using them. We have to stop this."

Finally. You get it.

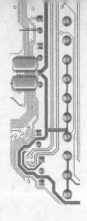

CHAPTER EIGHTEEN

I was so glad to be out of that horrible place. I wondered if Helena had ever expected Sara to have any clues about Emma's death, or whether that was just a lie to get me into an institution.

Before I could think any more about it, my cell phone rang. I got into my car and locked the doors. It was Madison. She'd left a message for me to come over and pick up the stuff I'd left there yesterday. Helena gave me the okay to stop by, as long as I was quick. It wasn't far, and I arrived in ten minutes.

I had barely stepped onto Madison's porch when she pulled the door open.

She stared blankly. "Do I know you?"

Uh-oh. Was this a different Ender inside? "Of course you know me. Pinky friends, remember?" I waved my little finger.

She folded her arms. "Well, you could have fooled me. I thought you were the one who disappeared in a puff of smoke last night."

"I'm so sorry. Really."

"I was imagining all kinds of horrible things that involved accidents and blood and humongous fines for damaging the rental body. "

"It was an emergency."

"I figured. A Blake emergency. Come on in."

I followed her into the house.

"I had to join him at an awards ceremony for his grandfather. It all happened pretty fast." I looked around the room and didn't see my overnight bag.

"I'll bet. They're in Washington, you know?" Her eyes sparkled. "He's on TV right now, with the senator."

"Now?"

"The six o'clock news," Madison said.

The senator? Helena's voice was sharp in my head. *I want to see.*

I moved past Madison to the game room.

She followed me. "Silly, you thought I called you just to pick up your stuff? I knew you'd want to see this."

In the middle of Madison's game room, Senator Harrison filled the airscreen, larger than life. A group of reporters were in the foreground, below his podium, and the White House was in the background.

"Today, the president came to a historic decision," Harrison said into a row of microphones. "As you know, employment for minors was forbidden by the Senior Employment Protection Act. As our senior population was living longer, they needed to be guaranteed they would not be forced out of the workplace. The decision then was to ban anyone under nineteen from working. Then the war came. It's been over for a year now, and many of us feel it is time to ease into a change. I am proud to announce the Special Circumstances Youth

Employment Act, which will allow certain teens to work for a select group of sanctioned companies. Phase one will address the institutionalized, unclaimed minors. The first company will be Prime Destinations, on the West Coast. By doing this, we will give meaning to the aimless lives of countless minors."

So Helena was right. We were all in big trouble.

As the senator concluded his statement and began to take questions from reporters, the camera moved and I noticed Blake standing beside him. Immediately my heart started pounding. What did he know about me? Had his grandfather told him I wasn't who I pretended to be? And if Senator Harrison was doing business with Prime, did he now know that I wasn't your regular customer, but a donor trapped in a mind lock with the renter?

Did Blake hate me? I scanned his face as if I could get the answer.

Then I noticed it. His tie clip.

It was the whale clip ornament from my shoe. He'd removed it from the shoe I dropped at the Music Center and was using it as a tie clip. That meant that whatever he knew— or didn't know—he wasn't mad at me.

He must have liked me, to do something like that. I moved into his holographic space, but he was no longer there, having been replaced by a reporter doing a wrap-up directly into the camera. It didn't matter, I was still basking in the memory of his face and his symbolic gesture.

"Isn't that something?" Madison said. "Prime's the first company to hire. Well, la-dee-dah. At least it'll be official now. Maybe we won't have to be so secretive."

"You think?" I noticed a blue flashing light in the corner of the airscreen. Below it was the number 67. "What's that blue light?" I asked.

"SPC. Special privatecast. From one of the many services I subscribe to. I can watch it later." She got up and looked at the airscreen. "Sixty-seven—that's Prime Destinations. Right after Harrison mentioned them?" She wrinkled her nose. "Odd."

"It's no coincidence. Turn it on."

Madison air-touched the icon. A bulletin flashed across the screen: *Stand By for Special Announcement from Prime Destinations.*

The screen showed an empty set, with marble columns in the background.

"Who else is watching this?" I asked.

"Only Titanium Premium subscribers of Prime."

"How many of you are there?"

She shrugged and sat down on the couch. "Don't know. Most of them are like you, Silver subscribers, right?"

"Yeah." I nodded. "Silver."

"Shhh." She tucked one leg under her and fluttered her hand. "It's starting."

Tinnenbaum stepped into frame from the left, with his TV-host posture. From the right edge of the frame, Doris entered, beaming.

"Hello, friends," Tinnenbaum said, addressing the camera. "Thank you for letting us into your home."

"We're thrilled to be here," Doris said.

"This is a special announcement exclusively for our Titanium Premium subscribers, private and confidential to you," Tinnenbaum said.

"So if you have others in the room, you may wish to watch this later," Doris said.

Madison and I traded a look. This sounded important.

Tinnenbaum and Doris smiled at each other, pausing to

let people turn off the program if necessary. Then Tinnen-baum nodded to someone off camera, as if he'd been signaled to proceed.

"We have a special surprise for you," he said. "The head of Prime Destinations is here to make an important announce-ment."

Madison sat up straight. "We've never seen him before."

That's him, Callie. Helena's thoughts rang in my head. *The Old Man himself.*

I locked my eyes on the airscreen. The picture cut to a dif-ferent camera. In some other place, possibly another location entirely, the camera moved closer to a darkened booth with windows. It was raised on a platform. Inside was the three-quarter silhouette of a man.

"Looks like we're still not going to see him," I said.

The camera moved in closer, framing him from the shoul-ders up. The lights in the booth came on, but the face we saw was not that of a 150-year-old Ender. Instead, it had a strange electronic shimmer to it, as if thousands of pixels slithered over his features. Parts of his face looked like the features of a woman, parts like those of a man; some pieces were young, some old. All were constantly moving, racing and chasing each other.

The effect was eerie, but I couldn't take my eyes off it. I'd never seen this technique before.

"Thank you, Chad and Doris." The Old Man's voice was electronically disguised as well, and had a quality that I could only describe as liquid metal.

Fluid tones with a metallic edge.

"To my loyal Titanium Premium subscribers, you are the special ones who have supported us from the beginning. We want to let you be the first to know of our newest service. First of all, we will be extending our product line so our inventory of body types will include more nationalities to fulfill your specific youth fantasies."

"Oh, that'll be fun," Madison said. "I'd love to try Chinese."

I wanted to gag. Madison made an entire nationality sound as trivial as a menu selection.

The Old Man's face continued to morph and shimmer, as if he wore a 3-D mask. I could make out the shape of his features underneath but could only guess at what he really looked like. The camera moved in closer, signaling something big. "But the more important, the more revolutionary advancement is going to be available much sooner than we had ever imagined." He paused to get our full attention. "Permanency."

Madison gasped and put her hand to her mouth.

"Instead of renters, you will be able to become owners," the Old Man said.

No!

That was Helena. Screaming in my head.

The Old Man continued. "You can choose a body, complete with a specialized skill set, and maintain that body for the rest of your life. You will in effect become that new and vibrant person. You can build relationships that last. Live the fantasy forever."

My heart pumped so hard, I could hear it pounding in my eardrums.

"As we all progress with advancements in prolonging life, your experience will expand. We can already keep your birth body in that chair until it reaches two hundred years. Soon it will be two hundred and fifty. One of my employees likes to say, 'Two hundred fifty is the new hundred.'"

A quick cut to Tinnenbaum and Doris, looking down as if watching the Old Man on a monitor. They laughed politely before the camera cut back to the Old Man.

"You can enjoy the best years of life as this new body ages beautifully through its twenties and thirties and beyond," the Old Man said. "At Prime Destinations, our visions for you are endless."

The lights faded to black inside the booth, and the camera cut back to Tinnenbaum and Doris.

"As always, we will maintain the strictest rules of privacy," Tinnenbaum said. "And we ask the same of you. While we are planning on expanding our inventory, we also have our internal waiting list of Titanium subscribers eager to jump in and test the waters."

Doris smiled. "You could be one of them, so don't hesitate. Come in soon to discuss the possibilities for your permanently youthful future."

Their images faded to a black screen with an endless scroll of warnings and disclaimers, complete with a female voice-over reading the list so fast it was almost comical.

Madison muted the sound. "Can you believe it?"

"No." My chest tightened, as if a fist were inside squeezing.

"I can't wait." Her eyes lit up. "That man is a visionary."

I rocketed off the couch. "What are you saying? That you'd do it?"

"Why not? Of course it's fun to try different bodies, but instead of all the back-and-forth and in-and-out, it would be nice to settle with one and be done with it."

"Madison, listen to yourself. It's not like picking out a

new dress or a car or a house. These are people. Living, breathing teens who have their whole lives ahead of them. But not if you steal it from them."

She pouted.

"Do you really want to be in someone else's body for the rest of your life?"

She was quiet for a moment. "When I did my first rental, and I was in that young body, I felt like I was home again. More like myself, the way I used to be, healthy and fit and spry. Don't you feel the same way?"

I folded my arms. "No. I don't. This was just a lark. Temporary. But if you or I are permanently in someone's body, it means that girl will never get a break. It's not like she's out for a month and then gets her life back. She'll never know what it's like to go to college, fall in love, get married, have children. You might have those experiences—again—but she won't. Her brain will be asleep—forever."

"Oh dear." Madison slumped back on the couch. "That sounds so horribly inhumane."

"You're robbing them of the most precious thing—their lives." I looked around and spotted my overnight bag against the wall.

"When you put it that way . . . it sounds like kidnapping."

"It's worse than that." I picked up my bag. "It's murder."

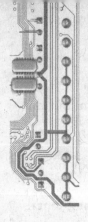

CHAPTER NINETEEN

I was so mad I could barely think. I shoved my overnight bag into my car, drove out of Madison's driveway, and then parked on the street where she couldn't see me. It was dark now, eight-thirty p.m. I sat there with locked doors, my car parked near the hedges that separated her estate from the next one.

I leaned my head back against the leather headrest. "You were right, Helena. About Harrison. I didn't believe you before, but it's all true."

It's even worse than I thought.

"Treating us like we're property. Slaves. It's not our fault, it's all because of that stupid war that we never wanted."

You're right.

"I've seen what they do with the rented bodies. They call it joyriding. They jump off bridges, do stupid stunts. They treat their cars better than they treat us. And your poor Emma . . ."

I gasped and put my hand to my mouth as a new possibility occurred to me.

"Helena. Maybe Emma's not dead."

What . . . are you saying?

I looked out the windshield of my parked car. The streetlight cast harsh shadows, making the bushes and trees seem hyper-real.

"Maybe," I said slowly, "she's been taken over as a permanent."

My God.

"They must have tested it before they would announce it to their subscribers. She could be alive. Maybe that's where the missing kids are."

Oh, Callie, if only . . .

"You were right, Helena. Harrison has to be evil to do this to all the unclaimed minors. And the Old Man behind it all is ten times worse. Watching the airscreen, his face hidden, hearing his mechanical voice . . . it was like tarantulas crawling up my spine." I rubbed my arms and shuddered.

We'll make a plan—

She stopped talking in the middle of her thought. I waited a moment.

"What?" I asked.

Silence. Then, for the first time, her voice sounded terrified.

No. No. Stop.

I sat up straight. "Helena? Helena, what is it?"

Please . . . don't . . . Her voice became strained and faint.

"What's happening?" I screamed.

I felt her power draining. I wanted to reach out to her with my mind, to give her some of my strength.

I waited forever for some response. When it came, it was as faint as a whisper.

Callie, run!

That was her last word. And then nothing. The sound in my head went completely silent.

Our connection was severed, I knew it. I felt it.

A cold fear took over my body, making me shiver. I couldn't stop the shaking.

She was gone. Helena was dead, I felt it in my bones.

I was alone.

Suddenly I heard a noise like a high-pitched ping and a crack. I looked to my right but didn't see any unfriendlies. I turned to the left and saw a boxy SUV slinking away in the night.

Then my focus changed as I saw a small hole in my driver's side window. Surrounding it, a web of cracks radiated out, growing as I watched.

The hair on the back of my neck rose. I looked up and saw the red brake lights of the SUV. They'd stopped.

They turned around. They were coming back.

I started my car and pulled out. The SUV was barreling down the middle of the street, heading right for me. I stopped my car and pressed the reverse button. I floored it, retreating from the approaching SUV. As it got closer, its high beams came on, blinding me with the blast of white so I couldn't see who was behind the wheel.

Only a few feet separated the hoods of our cars. I checked the rearview mirror, hoping I wouldn't hit anything. My palms got so sweaty my grip on the wheel became slippery. I held on tighter as I raced backward. Houses, lawns, hedges, flashed by me on either side. At least there were no other cars driving in this residential neighborhood.

The SUV got close enough to bump my hood. I flicked the wheel back and forth and pressed the gas pedal to the floor. I pulled away, but the SUV caught up and hit me again.

A small intersection was coming up in my rearview mirror. I made a quick decision and pulled hard on the wheel, whipping back into the side street. The SUV's momentum kept it going through the intersection and beyond. I switched into drive and raced straight across the intersection, staying on the side street, knowing it would take the SUV time to back up and turn around.

I floored it and hung a right, then a left, making my getaway. I turned off my lights and searched for a place to hide. One house had its gates open, and I pulled into the circular driveway, hiding my car behind the tall hedges. I shut off my engine and listened. A moment later, I heard the screech of the SUV as it raced through the streets. The sound faded away to the quiet residential night that mansion neighborhoods enjoyed.

Lights came on in the home of the driveway I was borrowing, so I started my engine and left. As I drove off, I wondered where I could go. My brother was at the hotel, Blake was in Washington, and who knew where Michael was? I couldn't tell Madison.

I wanted to run to my brother and Florina for refuge. But someone was shooting at me. The last thing I wanted was to lead danger to my brother's door.

Run, Helena had said. But where? Before I went anywhere, I had to go to Helena's place.

For the gun.

I got to Helena's home and went straight to her bedroom. I threw open the dresser drawers, digging through the scarves, searching for the gun Helena had had waiting for me at the Music Center. It was gone.

Had Eugenia moved it?

I went out to the hall and shouted for her. "Eugenia!"

Her heavy shoes clunked as she climbed the stairs. "Coming."

Her voice sounded bored. I didn't wait but shouted down the length of the hall as she approached, taking her own sweet time.

"Did you take anything out of my drawers?" I asked.

She waited until she stood in front of me before she answered. Her expression could only be described as stunned. "You know I never, ever touch your drawers."

"You took it. You took the gun, didn't you?"

She put her hand to her mouth. "A gun? No. I'd never touch a gun."

"People will do anything if they have to."

"It was here, in your bedroom?"

I turned around and looked at the room. Then I winced.

I'd remembered where I left the gun. I went to the closet, opened it, and saw the evening bag there. Eugenia stood in the doorway. With my back to her, I squeezed the bag.

The gun was inside.

I turned around. "I'm so sorry. I haven't been myself. I've had headaches. I was going to go see my tech, to look at the chip." I was reaching, praying that she knew who Helena's tech was.

"Why don't you just go back to the place where they put it in? You sure paid them enough."

She was still angry. But that was nothing compared to how she'd feel if she knew she might be in danger. Helena had only told her about the rental, nothing else.

"Eugenia, listen carefully. Don't answer the door for anyone. If someone calls, you don't know where I went."

Eugenia stared at me, her face long and serious. "You mean business as usual?"

So Helena had been cautious. But it was never as dangerous as this. My life was at risk every minute I stayed. Eugenia knew nothing, which would serve to protect her.

"I have to go," I said. "Please be careful."

I got into Helena's sports car and turned on the engine. I pulled up the navigator's listing of Helena's history. The long list made me want to give up, but then I recognized one of the names. Redmond. That was the person Eugenia had mentioned my first night at the house. She said he'd called Helena.

"Redmond," I said to the navigator.

"Redmond. Right away," the navigator chirped.

The navigator led me to a warehouse in an industrial area of the San Fernando Valley. It wasn't exactly a neighborhood I would have chosen for a nighttime drive. I passed chain-link fences holding back dogs that warned me to keep driving. The address popped up on the navigator. It was a complex of warehouses with pools of light coming from roof-mounted lamps. I parked inside the compound so my car wouldn't be visible to any renegades on the street.

Redmond's address was the last warehouse. The door was locked. I pressed an old-fashioned metal buzzer. Above it was a tiny hole with a shiny center, a camera, most likely. Redmond was crafty, making the exterior look old and cheap. A moment later, the door opened with a loud clunk.

Inside, it was very industrial, the kind of place you'd expect a sculptor to live and work. Concrete floor, a basic hallway created out of a plain white wall. I saw the cool glow of fluorescent light at the end of the hallway. I took out my gun.

My heart was pounding. Was this a trap? I wished I had Helena in my head. She'd know; she'd tell me. I should have pressed for more information about Redmond when I had her.

I came to the end of the hall. I turned left and stepped into a large space broken up by rows of tables and counters of electronic parts, computers, and monitors, some working, some with guts exposed. There was so much that some of it was fastened to bars suspended from the high ceiling. A chemical odor hung in the air.

An airscreen above a cluttered counter showed the outside door, where I had rung the buzzer. Below it, a silver-haired man sat slumped in front of a bank of computer monitors. Ender.

What I couldn't tell was whether he was dead or alive. He was motionless as I crept up behind him, both arms holding the gun in front of me.

"Redmond?" I said.

"Helena," he mumbled with a British accent. "You took so long, I almost dozed off."

He lifted his head. I could see his face reflected in two black-screened monitors. He looked back at my reflection in them, speaking to me without turning.

"Helena, what's that for?"

"I've got a request."

"Usually you ask without pointing a gun at my head."

He started to swivel his chair around. I slammed my foot on the metal ring, freezing it in place.

"Put your hands on the back of your head," I said.

Everything I was doing I'd either learned from my dad or from the holos. It worked, and he obeyed.

One of the monitors beeped in time to a pulsating red dot, part of a map of the city. The dot looked like it was right at the spot where we were.

"What's that?" I pointed to it.

"It's you. Your tracking device. But you know that." His eyes narrowed.

He was thin and gangly, with mad-scientist hair. His bone structure was nice—you could tell he had been handsome when he was young.

"Everyone knows more about my body than I do," I said. "Well, now I want you to remove the chip. I'm finished."

"How did it go?"

"What?"

"Your big plan."

"All these monitors and you don't get the news here?"

He stared at me and rolled his chair forward, hands still on his head. He was reading me, examining, searching to see who was really inside me.

"My God." He lowered his hands and moved in so close that I could smell mint on his breath. "That's not Helena in there, is it?"

My gun hand shook. "No. She's dead."

He wrinkled his brow. "How?"

I shook my head. "I don't know. But I heard it happen. She was inside my head at the time. I think someone killed her."

His eyes grew wider as he hung on my words.

"We were getting close," I said. "I thought I'd get to meet her, in person."

"Helena was a fireball." Sadness washed over Redmond's face. "We met in college, must be over a hundred years ago now."

"How much do you know about the body bank?"

"I know what I need to know."

"Then I'll give you the dummy's version. The body bank killed her. She warned me they would kill me too." I aimed the gun again. "I need you to take out this chip."

"I can see why you don't want them tracking you. You're an eyewitness to Helena's death."

"An earwitness, anyway. So please, take it out."

"I can't."

"I could kill you." I straightened the arm holding the gun. "You should know that better than anyone. You're the one who flipped off my stop-kill switch."

"The question remains whether Helena's plan would have worked," he said. "Would you have been able to do it? It's not clear whether I was successful or whether I failed at that too."

"Do you really want to be the one to test it? For the last time, I'm begging you to remove the chip."

"I want to. I do. Because I'm concerned they may have built in a drop-dead command."

"And that is?"

"They send a signal to the chip to make it explode."

I squeezed my eyes shut for a second. That was one I hadn't thought of.

"Don't worry. It's more likely they'd continue to use the chip—with another senior, someone else there at the body bank, wired up the way Helena was."

I didn't know which was more frightening: someone else taking over my body or my head exploding. "But since you've altered the chip, I haven't had any more blackouts. Helena was unable to take over."

"Right. But someone else could reach the level that Helena had with you at the end—that kind of mind-to-mind connection."

"So take it out!"

"I would if I could. But it's impossible. It's located in your brain."

"But you went in and altered it. Twice."

"And it wasn't easy. But I can't remove it. They embedded it in you in a complex webbing pattern so that if anyone tried to take it out, it would self-destruct. You would almost certainly hemorrhage at the least and be blown to bits at the worst. Think of it as a tiny bomb in your head."

"A bomb? In my head? You've got to be kidding."

"Sorry."

Hemorrhage. Exploding head. I was feeling dizzy.

"It's horrible." I lowered the gun. "Why did they do this to me?"

"They probably did it to all the donors. As a fail-safe. This way, no one can kill a donor and steal the valuable technology."

"So I'm stuck with a piece of metal in my head that links me to them for the rest of my life?"

"I'm afraid so."

I would never be the same. Never be safe. The girl who had walked into the body bank was gone forever.

Redmond cleared his throat. "There is some good news."

"What?"

"You're the only one with an altered chip. That makes you a unique subject."

I let out a bitter laugh. "What's so great about that?"

He stared at me. "The body bank might want to keep you alive."

Redmond fashioned a magnetic plate that covered the area of my head closest to the chip. I didn't feel any pain, thanks to a local anesthetic. As I lay on a table in his sterile room in the back, I couldn't help but admire his precision. Redmond felt to me like a young soul in an old body. I trusted him. Truth was, I didn't want to leave his lab. There was a deep feeling of safety, being with someone who knew my inner workings the way he did.

He explained that his prior career had been as a brain surgeon. But when he retired, he went back to his first love, computers. He said working with hardware was like operating on a patient who never complained. And if anything went wrong, he could always start over.

I felt comforted in his hands. But I was dangerous to him. He was not a supporter working for the cause. He was there for the pay, for the allure of the unknown science, and maybe because Helena was an old friend.

But I was a stranger, and I knew he wanted me out of there as soon as possible.

"Now, I'll warn you, this isn't a permanent fix. It's just what I could do on short notice. This sealant I'm using will break down from the contact with the plate. Anything stronger would burn your scalp."

"How long will it last?" I asked.

"I don't know. Maybe a week."

He continued to work, applying a gel to the plate's metal edges.

"What do you know about the Old Man?" I asked.

"The one thing everyone knows is that he's kept his identity a secret. No one's ever seen his face. Rumors abound. . . . He used to be a software genius, he was in charge of Dark Ops during the war and sustained some injury. . . . Who knows if any of it is true?"

I swallowed, thinking of Helena and Emma. "I want to find him."

"So do a lot of people. Which is why he's so reclusive."

"I know he goes to the body bank sometimes. I saw him there once."

Redmond stopped and leaned over so he'd be in my line of sight. "Don't go after him. You're young and beautiful. If you stay out of their way, you'll have your whole life ahead as your reward. He is a bad, bad man."

He helped me to a sitting position. He handed me a mirror and, like a hairdresser, let me admire his handiwork in a second mirror on the wall.

"You can't even see it," I said.

He took my hand and placed it on the back of my head. "Easy," he said.

Underneath my hair, I felt a hard metal plate that was molded to the shape of my skull.

"I had to shave some of your hair by the scalp, but your outer layer covers it. You can't see anything strange unless the wind blows too hard," he said.

"And this will prevent them from tracking me? For a week?"

"Yes. And I won't be able to follow you either. You're on your own now."

"It's okay." I put the mirror down and stood. "I've been that way for a long time."

His expression became even more serious. "Come with me."

I followed him back to his lab. He pressed his fingers to a pad on a file drawer built into his desk. It opened with a click. He pulled out a small metal box about the size of his palm. On the top, it was labeled *Helena*.

"Now, if anything should happen to me, come and get this box."

"How will I unlock it?"

"It's already coded for your fingerprint. Helena did it."

I looked at my fingertips. Was anything mine anymore? The box was plain. A hard drive?

"What's inside?" I asked him.

"The key that has the information about how I altered your chip." His eyes softened and his lips almost formed a smile. "I guess you could say it's your birth certificate."

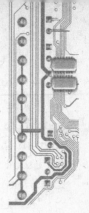

CHAPTER TWENTY

Now that the body bank could no longer track me, they would know that somehow I had defeated the chip. Because we couldn't remove it, there was no way for Redmond to put out a false tracker to mislead them. Up to this point, Prime might have thought that I was at the mercy of Helena's plot. But not anymore.

I sat in my car by Redmond's warehouse and pulled out a new cell phone he had given me—he was concerned that Helena's could be tracked. I turned on her cell phone just long enough to see Lauren's number, then shut it off. When I called Lauren, I got a recording. I left a message for her to call me—well, not me, she didn't know me, but Helena—and gave her the new number.

I started to call Madison, but a call came through Helena's phone. I saw that it was Blake.

Blake.

My heart was chasing my breath. The last time I'd seen

his face was on the airscreen, when he'd been wearing my whale clip. Had his grandfather tried to turn him against me, and Blake hadn't bought it? Or had the senator never said anything to Blake at all?

I took a deep breath. Then I used the other phone to call him back.

"Blake?"

"Callie."

Just hearing his voice made me feel like crying. "You're back."

"Finally." He took a second. I heard him take a deep breath.

"Listen, Blake, about that night . . ."

"I know. I missed you."

"I really missed you," I said.

"That's good. 'Cause it would be really bad if it was just me."

He made me laugh a little.

"Hungry?" he asked.

"Starving."

He Zinged me the address of an old-fashioned, all-night restaurant called the Drive-In. When I arrived, I was glad to see several armed Ender guards on the property. They were no longer the enemy. I saw them as possible protection.

Fancy cars filled every space by the food service center. No expense had been spared making this place, advertised on the walls in neon as BLAST FROM THE PAST. Fit Enders on blades held trays above their heads, carrying burgers and shakes and banana splits to your car, while quaint rock 'n' roll played from speakers. Outdoor airscreens played movies from the

1950s without sound, adding to the true sensa-round retro experience.

I pulled into a parking space on the edge of the property, far from the food service. I walked over to the restroom. When I came out, I didn't see Blake's car, so I walked back to wait in mine. A few minutes later he drove up close to my car and smiled. Nothing could have looked better to me. His passenger door opened with a click and a whirr, and I got in.

As soon as I was in my seat, he leaned over and kissed my cheek. "Hi."

It felt right to be with him, in his car.

"You look so good," he said.

He pulled into a space by the restaurant between two other cars. A trim Ender with a silver ponytail bladed over and took our orders.

After she left, Blake took my hands in his.

"I'm sorry," I said.

"Don't."

I breathed in his scent and for a moment took comfort in the familiar features of his face. But I knew if I let myself relax into him, tears would follow. I had to be strong to say what I needed to say.

He started to pull me toward him.

"There's stuff I have to tell you," I said.

"I know." He sat back in his seat. "Me too. I wanted to call you from Washington, but my grandfather took my cell phone away. I just got it back."

"Seems like you've been gone forever, so much has happened."

"I thought about you the whole time," he said. "The

hardest was at night, right before I went to sleep. During the day, there were all these distractions. But at night, it was just you."

Something glinted on his leather jacket. The whale clip from my shoe. I touched it.

"I should wear mine," I said. "We'll be a pair."

"We're already a pair."

He looked at me with such intensity I thought his eyes were going to smoke. Then he leaned closer and put his hand around my neck, pulling me to him. I felt his breath on my face—it instantly gave me chills—right before he kissed me.

I closed my eyes and let the kiss vibrate through my whole body. His scent—sort of woodsy and grassy—both calmed and excited me. His hair was so soft, almost too soft for a guy. His hands touched my face, my neck, my hair, as if he were discovering me, as if I were the first girl he'd ever touched. It made me feel so special. His hand stroked my hair and then stopped . . .

. . . right where that metal plate was placed on the back of my head.

He froze. "What is that?"

I pulled away, a gasp escaping my lips.

"I'm sorry," he said, "I'd forgotten. You told me. That's the . . . surgery?"

The waitress bladed over with our food, interrupting us. The conversation halted while she fixed the tray to the car's window edge. After she left, the food just sat there.

"What you felt," I said. "That's what I have to tell you."

He looked at me. Waiting.

I felt my stomach drop, as if I were in a fast elevator. Why was this so hard?

Because it was so complicated.

He took my hand. "It's okay. Really."

"I'm not who you think I am."

A nervous half smile came over his face. "So who are you?"

"Don't hate me."

"Never."

I wanted to stop time. He still liked me, still believed in me. And that might all end.

He touched my cheek. "It's okay, Callie. This has to do with that surgery you talked about before, right? There's nothing you could say that would make me hate you."

"Well, let's see how you feel when I tell you everything." I took a deep breath, exhaled, and then went for it. "I lied. My name isn't Callie Winterhill. It's Callie Woodland. I'm not rich, these clothes aren't mine, that car isn't mine, and the house isn't mine."

He stared for a second, and then shook his head. "I couldn't care less if you're rich or poor."

"I'm not just poor. I'm an unclaimed minor. I live on the streets, on the floors of abandoned buildings. I eat scraps."

I didn't look at his face; I didn't need to. I felt tension fill the car like a poisonous gas. I continued before fear could lock my mouth shut.

"I needed money for my sick brother. He's only seven. So I signed up at this place, Prime Destinations. We all call it the body bank. I was a donor, renting out my body to a senior named Helena Winterhill. It's her house, her car, her life. She wanted to stop your grandfather from going through with the deal with Prime Destinations. I thought she was crazy but it turned out she was right, that the plan's even worse than she imagined."

I rattled on, telling him everything, probably much too fast. He let me talk, never interrupting me. I left out one thing. I didn't mention Helena's plan to shoot his grandfather. Now that she was gone, I wasn't about to unload that on him. This was a major info dump as it was. Why worry him over something that was no longer an issue?

When I finished, I turned to him. He was still looking at me, and his expression wasn't full of disgust, the way I had imagined. He did look solemn, though, and was totally silent. The waiting was torture. My throat went dry waiting for him to say something. Finally, he spoke.

"This is so . . . I don't know what to say."

"Do you believe me?" I asked.

"I want to."

"But you don't."

"It's just kind of a shock, you know?"

I pushed aside the hair on the back of my head and showed him the plate that Redmond had placed there. It felt like the most personal part of my body to expose, even more so than any private parts. This is me, I was saying to him. This is who I've become.

"Under that plate, that's where my chip is."

He didn't say anything. I lifted my head and smoothed back my hair.

"If you could convince your grandfather to renege on this partnership between the government and Prime . . . if you can show him how awful this will be, how it's sending these unclaimed minors to their deaths, wouldn't he want to take it back?" I blurted out, daring to hope I could have it all, the truth and Blake.

There was a slim chance that the senator didn't understand what Prime had in mind. Maybe he didn't know about the permanency factor.

Blake didn't say a word. He seemed lost in thought, troubled.

"Blake?"

He wiped his hand over his face. "I'll talk to him. No, wait, you talk to him. You can explain this better than I can."

"Really?"

"Tomorrow. It's Saturday, he'll be at the ranch. Come over before lunch. He's a lot easier to talk to there. It's his favorite place."

"He's not going to listen to me. He hates me."

"We'll do this together. He'll listen to me. I'm his grandson." He rubbed my hand. "All we can do is try." He looked thoughtful. I could see he was still processing this new way of seeing me.

We ate our meal in silence, and then Blake drove me back to my car at the other side of the lot.

"See you tomorrow," he said.

"Tomorrow."

He kissed me goodbye. It wasn't like before. It carried the burden of my lies, which separated our lips like a layer of wax. I got out and he drove off. It felt as if a thousand-pound weight were pushing my feet into the ground.

I got into my car and locked the doors. When I had gone to the restroom earlier, I had spoken to one of the Ender guards. I told him I was going to catnap in my car for a few hours and would appreciate it if he'd keep an eye on me. As I slipped him several large bills, he said he was happy to.

I woke up around six a.m., with the sun in my eyes. I raised the seat back up to the normal driving position and ran my tongue across my teeth. I felt the back of my head where the plate was. It was throbbing in a nasty reminder of how it had betrayed me to Blake. I swallowed two of Redmond's painkillers.

The new phone was blinking. A zing had come in from Lauren.

Lauren was still in Reece's fabulous body, her long red hair glistening in the morning sun. "Tell me you have some good news, Helena. I've learned nothing about Kevin."

She inserted a card key into a gate, letting us into a small private park near her home in Beverly Hills. I was apprehensive about meeting so close to the body bank, but in addition to being gated, the park was also guarded.

"People have seen him, even spoken to him, but no one's spotted him in the last month," she said.

I knew I had to clear up who I was right away. I wasn't going through the torture of indecisiveness again.

"I'm not Helena," I said.

Lauren continued to talk, my words not registering at all. I had to interrupt her.

"Listen to me. I'm not Helena."

Her mouth opened. She folded her arms. "What are you saying?"

"I'm the donor. The body Helena rented. I'm really sixteen."

"Wait. When I spoke to Helena, she was in that body." She gestured at me.

"You were talking to me then. I was at Club Rune and at the Thai restaurant."

"That was you?" Her eyes flashed at me. "What happened to Helena?"

I felt my heart sink as I was forced to recall Helena's last moments. "She's gone."

"She's dead? Helena's dead?" She put her hands on my shoulders and shook me. "What did you do to her?"

"Easy, I didn't do anything." The armed guard looked our way. "It was someone at the body bank, at Prime."

"Who?"

"I don't know."

"Then how do you know she's dead?"

"I heard her screams in my head."

"You what?"

"Helena had the chip altered. By the end, I could hear her thoughts in my head. We were able to communicate."

Lauren let go of me with a shove. "I can't believe it. I knew her for eighty-five years." She took out a hanky and wiped away angry tears. "And now she's gone."

"I'm sorry. I was getting to know her myself."

"How dare you say that!"

"I learned a lot from her," I said.

"About what?"

"About the senator. The Old Man."

She turned away. "I can't do this. I can't look at you. You lied. You let me think you were her. And now I find out she was dead all along."

"No, it's not like that. It just happened."

"Why isn't anyone who they seem to be anymore?" she said through gritted teeth.

I looked at her, hiding in that teen body. I didn't dare remind her that I could say the same thing about her.

"At least . . . ," I said, "I believe Kevin is alive." I thought bringing up good news about her grandson might soften her.

"How would you know that?"

"Because the Old Man is going to let subscribers do more than just rent—they're going to be able to buy the bodies. My guess is that they've been testing this already. That would explain the missing teens, with no signs of struggles, no bodies."

A flicker of hope danced across her eyes. Then she scowled.

"You don't know anything. How can I trust anything you say? You're wearing Helena's jewelry, driving her car. Have you no shame?"

"I want to help her."

"You can't help a dead woman. *You* can't help anyone."

She turned and walked away.

"Lauren." She didn't turn around. "Or is it Reece?" I shouted.

She kept walking.

I stood there shaking. I'd thought she'd help me; she was Helena's friend. She was the only one I could talk to about the missing teens.

The guard stared at me. He put his hand over the gun on his hip and started walking toward me. I had been a guest of homeowner Lauren in this private park, and now that she was gone I had no reason—or permission—to be here.

I headed for the gate.

I pushed it open and ran out, letting it slam behind me. Just as I was about to get into my car, I looked across the street and saw someone I recognized.

Michael.

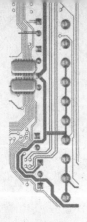

CHAPTER TWENTY-ONE

I ran across the street, dodging cars and bikes, waving both hands, but he didn't notice me.

"Michael!" I shouted, chasing after him as he walked away. "Michael, wait!" I ran up behind him and poked his back. "It's me."

He turned. The sight of his face warmed me. I hadn't realized how much I had missed that long blond hair, those soft eyes. He smiled, and my shoulders melted.

"Wow, you look great," I said, touching his expensive-looking jacket.

"So do you." He looked me over, undressing me with his eyes. "What's your name?"

The voice was Michael's, but the words weren't. I stared at his perfect face, his mouth, his eyes, his nose. No sun freckles or moles, no street-fight cuts. Just flawless skin and pricey clothes.

A chill ran through my veins.

This wasn't Michael. It was a rental.

Some Ender had rented his body. He hadn't waited like he'd promised. He'd gone through with it before I was finished.

"Who are you?" I asked, trembling.

"Hey, I'm a sixteen-year-old stud. Like what you see?" He held his arms out and spun around 360 degrees. "Pretty cute, huh?"

My breathing started getting faster. I couldn't control it. I grabbed his fancy jacket in my fists.

"Hey, easy," he said. "That's real Russian alpaca."

"I don't care if it's from Mars. How long have you had this body?"

"I don't know what you're talking about."

I pulled him closer, tugging hard, making it hard for him to breathe. "If you're going to lie, do it with your own wrinkly mouth. How long?"

"I just got it." His voice came out hoarse. "I just came out of Prime."

I released him. I couldn't risk attracting so much attention. Already Enders were turning their heads.

He straightened his jacket. "And I paid plenty for this body," he said, his voice low. "So that makes it mine."

The guard in the park across the street stared at us through the gate.

"You better take good care of it," I said.

"What, you know this guy or something?" He motioned to his body. "Honey, I'm going to have a great time with it. Why do you think I did this? I'm gonna go wild. Nothing's gonna hold me back." He roared with laughter.

I was breathing so hard I was afraid fire was going to come out my nostrils.

It just made this lowlife grin. Whoever he was.

"You're really sweet. You his girlfriend?" he asked. "Then maybe I got a bonus with this body, huh?"

He put his arm around my shoulder. I threw it off.

"Don't touch me," I said. "Because I don't want to bruise that body."

Passing Enders stared at us. Then the creep did something I never would have imagined. He leaned in close, stuck out his tongue, and gave my cheek a long lick from jawline to eye. I pushed him away hard and wiped the slime with the back of my hand.

"Stop it," I said, gritting my teeth. I wanted to punch him so hard. But that was Michael's body.

"Well, it was fun having this little reunion and all, but I gotta go," he said. "So much excitement, so much life out there, waiting . . . for me."

He winked, backed away, and then turned to hustle off. The guard was still staring at me from across the street.

I'd found Michael, but I hadn't found him at all. The guy who I could always count on, the thoughtful, sensitive guy, wasn't there. Some slimy, ignorant old Ender, maybe two hundred years old, whose real body smelled like moldy cheese, was occupying Michael's skin.

Renting Michael. But he hadn't said "rented." He'd said, "It's mine."

What if he had bought Michael? Was this one of the first official permanents?

No. Please, no.

I looked down the street but couldn't see him anymore. I ran, pumping my arms. When I got to the corner, I looked up and down the cross street. Was that his brown jacket to the left? I opened my purse and snaked through the crowd of strolling Enders. My right hand slipped into my purse and gripped the gun.

When I caught up to him, I pressed the gun into his back, covering it with my body so no one else could see.

"Stop," I whispered in his ear.

I grabbed his arm to make sure he obeyed. He spoke over his shoulder.

"Please don't hurt me. I'll give you my wallet." The voice was too high.

I turned him around and saw an acne-scarred face on the verge of tears. This was some normal Starter.

"Sorry," I said, and let go of him.

He froze there on the sidewalk, in shock.

"Run," I said, and he did.

I spun around, scanning the faces of the sidewalk crowd, but it was hopeless. I'd lost Michael. I'd had one precious chance to protect him as his body left the body bank. But I'd let him slip away.

I wanted to cry, but all that came out were panicked breaths.

This was worse than if I'd never found him at all.

I stood in a daze while the sea of silver-headed Enders flowed around me.

Which way back to my car? I had gotten disoriented. The last thing I wanted to do was to get any closer to the body bank. I took a second to get my bearings and then went north. Ahead, in the crowd of Enders, three familiar young faces headed my way.

Briona, Lee, and Raj, their arms loaded with glossy shopping bags.

"Callie!" Briona waved at me.

They were wearing the latest fashions, from their ultra-hip sunglasses to their pointy designer boots.

"Briona," I said, trying to sound normal. "What a coincidence."

"No coincidence," Raj said. "Everyone knows the best shopping is in Beverly Hills."

Briona gave a bright smile to Raj. "We popped in at Prime," she said. "To ask about the new services."

"We just noticed your number came up on ours." Lee held up his cell phone.

"My phone's not on," I said.

"Uh. Yes it is," Lee said.

I opened my purse, angling it away so they couldn't see the gun. My old phone was lit.

"How'd it get on? I turned it off."

"Purse call, happens all the time," Briona said.

I shut off the phone.

"Did I see two phones in your purse?" Raj asked.

"Yeah, one's mine." I closed my bag. "And one's the donor's."

"Here, let's sit," Briona said.

Before I could protest, she pulled me by the elbow to a nearby table outside a small café. We were the only customers there.

"Raj, go inside and get us some lattes," she said, and he obeyed.

"I can't stay," I said.

"Only for a minute." Lee sat too close on the other side of me.

Nervous glances shot across the table. What was going

on? Briona tapped her nails on the tabletop. Lee stared at her and she stopped.

"So, did you hear about the announcement?" Briona leaned forward. "From Prime?"

"Yeah. What'd you think?" I asked.

"Can't wait to go permanent," Lee said. "Stop playing around, settle down and focus on building a new life."

"You have your eye on something special?" Briona asked.

"No," I said. "Do you?"

"I have my eye on a cute little blond sixteen-year-old," Briona said. "I could do a much better job of using her body than she could. And I'm so much smarter." She rested her chin on her palm.

Lee's legs bounced up and down nervously. That reminded me of someone. I tried to remember.

"It's like that old expression, 'Youth is wasted on the young,'" Lee said. "How about you, Callie, are you going to go permanent? With this body or another?"

"Something wrong with this one?" I asked.

"Nothing that I can see," he said. His legs continued to bounce.

"Going permanent sounds scary," I said.

"I guess if you're unhappy they'll let you exchange," he said.

"But then what happens to the donor body?" Briona asked. "I mean, you can't exactly let that little blonde come back to life three months later. She'd be all like, 'What happened?'"

"Maybe she wouldn't notice," I said.

"As soon as she looks at her calendar and sees she lost months instead of days," Lee said, "she'll know."

"The advantage to renting is you can try new things," Briona said. "If I had a permanent, I wouldn't dare do anything dangerous, like boxing, for example. But with a rental, it's no big deal."

"Except for the whopping penalty fee," Lee said.

"That's what rental insurance is for," Briona said. She winked.

"But permanency is a bargain," he said. "Huge savings over renting."

These Enders were driving me crazy. How could they talk about us this way? We were just vehicles for their pleasure, for their stupid fantasies. If we died, so what, it was covered by insurance.

They fell silent. Lee's legs bounced up and down and Briona drummed the table with her long nails. Where had I seen those habits before?

Lee caught me staring at Briona's hands. Nervous glances flashed like lasers. I pulled my purse closer to my body.

A chill washed over me. I knew who they were. They weren't some random Enders.

An SUV pulled up to the curb with Raj at the wheel. That was why all the chat. They were waiting for the car.

"Guess we're taking our coffee to go." Briona stood.

Lee also stood. He slipped his arm in mine. "Ready, Callie?"

I yanked away and opened my purse. "No."

"Come with us." Briona moved closer.

I pulled out the gun and pushed it into her side. "I don't think so. *Doris*."

"Now, careful," Lee said quietly. "Don't do anything stupid."

"What are you worried about? It's not your body, Tinnenbaum," I said.

Raj, in the SUV, looked over at us. He couldn't see the gun and was still pretending everything was fine. He held up a paper cup of coffee in an inviting gesture.

"All this time, you were hiding in those bodies," I said. "Spying on me."

Lee moved to block my way. He was on one side, Briona on the other.

"Just get in the car, Callie," she said.

"I don't need any coffee," I said. "I'm wired enough."

I pushed Briona away and she stumbled into Lee's arms. I ran into the shop and out the back entrance.

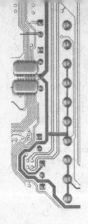

CHAPTER TWENTY-TWO

I didn't turn around to see if Lee or Briona was chasing me. No, make that Tinnenbaum or Doris, now that I had figured out who they really were. Who they had been all along. Raj, at the wheel, was probably Rodney, the guy who had escorted me to see Tyler and Michael. Why would the body bank have them spying on me like that, pretending to be normal renters? Had they known about Helena's plan all along? Or had it started after she altered the chip?

I came to the street where my car was parked and got in. As I pulled out, I saw a black SUV do a U-turn and follow me. Was that them? I couldn't see, because a truck got between us.

I pulled out the new phone and called Tyler's hotel. I wanted to tell Florina about Michael. "Room 1509, please."

"That party checked out this morning," the operator said.

"What? No, they couldn't have."

"I'm sorry, but they left this morning."

My stomach sank as if I were in an elevator with a cut cable.

I demanded to speak to the manager who had checked us in. She got on the phone and confirmed what the operator had said. My brother and Florina had left no word as to where to reach them. The manager also said she had seen them get in a car with a man, a senior. He had said he was Florina's grandfather.

I felt a numbness come over me like a wave. Florina didn't have a grandfather. She wouldn't have been living on the streets if she did. And she would have left me a note.

Someone had taken them. Who? A ball of fire blinded me. I'd heard of kids being taken for ransom. Had the car and fancy hotel given Florina ideas? Was her nicey-nicey routine all an act? A desperate Starter could do anything these days. Or maybe it was an undercover marshal? Some Ender in the hotel, a client or even an employee looking for side money, could have seen the poor unclaimed minors and ratted on them.

If that was it, they'd be locked up in one of the institutions. This couldn't be happening.

What if it was the body bank?

They wouldn't rent out Tyler, of course—he was too young and sickly—but they might use him as bait to lure me in. I clenched my fists.

I had an urge to go there, gun in hand, and demand to see my brother. But even in my surge of fire, I knew it was impossible to rescue anyone from Prime. They had guards. And big thick doors with locks. And it would be just what they wanted. Not to mention it would be a gamble, because truthfully, I didn't know where he was. I just knew in my gut it wasn't good.

Still, I had to do something.

I drove onto the gravel by the fence that surrounded Blake's family ranch and swung my car around so I would be facing the right direction when I left. Best to plan for a quick exit. When I grasped the car door handle to get out, my hand was shaking.

I rushed across the crunchy gravel path to the front door, keeping my purse over my shoulder, with the strap across my body. I needed easy access to my gun.

The housekeeper let me in and took me to the living room. It was in grand hacienda style, with a high ceiling and dark, exposed beams. The scent of coffee and tobacco, something that normally would be inviting, made me cringe under these circumstances. He was all money and power, Senator Harrison.

Blake and his grandfather were sitting in large sienna leather armchairs—until they saw me.

"What is she doing here?" The senator stood and pointed at me.

"It's all right, Grandfather. I invited her." Blake rose.

"Why on earth would you do that?"

"Because she's got something she wants to say to you." Blake came over to me and held my hand. I wondered if he'd said anything to his grandfather.

"Get her out of here now!" the senator yelled.

My blood was pumping so hard, I thought I heard it throbbing in my ears.

"Go ahead, Callie." Blake released my hand. "Tell him."

"Tell me what?"

"Are you aware that what you are doing is murder?" I said.

He flushed with anger. "Don't you talk to me that way, you old biddy."

I pulled out the gun and aimed it at him. "I'm not old, I'm sixteen. I'm the donor body."

Out of the corner of my eye I saw Blake's jaw drop, but I brought my focus back to the gun. I needed to keep my hand steady. I stood behind one of the couches so I could brace myself against something. I calculated the distance between me and the senator. Roughly twelve feet.

His face registered surprise. "Then why do you want to kill me?"

"Your deal with the government and Prime Destinations means that innocent unclaimed minors will be sold to the body bank. And the body bank will let seniors buy them to occupy their bodies for the rest of their lives."

The senator was hard to read. His face had a horrified expression, but it wasn't clear whether this information was news to him.

"I blame you for this." He pointed at Blake. "Do something."

"She's making sense, Grandfather. Is it true?" Blake asked him.

"Is it true?" The senator repeated Blake's words in a mocking tone.

"You are going to take me to the man behind Prime," I said to the senator. "The Old Man."

His jaw went slack. "No. I can't."

My palms were perspiring, I was so nervous. The sweat made my grip on the gun loose, slippery.

"You don't want to give me trouble, Senator Harrison, not now. My best friend's just been bought and my little brother is right behind him. He's probably in line for his surgery right now, like some dog at the vet. My only hope is to see the Old Man, and if you can't take me, then I have nothing to lose."

"I can't," he said. "I can't do that."

"You don't have a choice."

"Just take her, Grandfather," Blake said. "You know where he works."

"Let me put it this way," the senator said. "If I take you to him, he'll kill me."

"And if you don't, I'll kill you." I struggled to steady my grip. "I warn you, my arms are getting tired, so I'll give you to three. Isn't that what they do in the holos? You start walking to that door or on three, I shoot. One."

He licked his lips.

"Two."

He swallowed so hard, I could see his Adam's apple vibrate.

"Three." He wasn't going to move.

I had to shoot, but I didn't want to. I imagined the bullet piercing flesh, ripping it apart, the skin curling back in flower-petal shapes as blood spurted like a fountain, flooding the room. My finger quivered, and pulled. It was like I was trying to let go, let the trigger come back to position, but of course that didn't work, so I shot him. I guess I did want to.

The gun went off with a high, tinny pop.

At the same time, or maybe sooner, I'm not sure, Blake went flying over to his grandfather, pushing him hard.

"Blake!" I screamed.

They both ended up on the floor, blood starting to stain the cream-and-black Navajo rug. It was coming from the senator's arm.

I looked down at them. The senator groaned. Blake tore off his grandfather's jacket and applied pressure to the wound.

He looked up at me for a second, his expression one of pure shock and disbelief. "You shot him! You could have killed him."

I didn't know what to say. He was right. I would have killed him if Blake hadn't intervened.

"He should have done what I said."

"I didn't think . . . you'd do it," the senator said through his pain.

Neither did I. My heart was racing. I pointed the gun at the senator. "Get him up."

"What?" Blake asked.

"It's just an arm wound. Get him up on his feet."

Blake helped his grandfather to a chair. The senator leaned back, moaning in pain.

"I didn't want to do this. You forced me into it." I motioned with the gun. "So let's not make this all for nothing. I want you to take me to the Old Man."

The senator's face was pale as he drove his car with one hand. I sat shotgun. I wondered if that was where the expression came from. Or maybe they meant leaning out the window and shooting. In any event, I was sitting there holding the gun on the senator and Blake was in the backseat right behind him.

"What part of town are we going to?" I asked.

"Downtown," the senator said, wincing in pain.

We had covered his shirt with his jacket so the wound wouldn't be obvious.

"I'm not the bad guy here," I said. "My little brother is sick. I have to find out who took him."

"He could be anywhere." The senator spoke with great effort.

"You're right, I don't know where he is. So I have to search. The Old Man is my best guess."

"You seem like a smart young lady. Resourceful. Let me make a proposal. I'll pull over and let you go, and I won't report this."

"Do I look senile to you?" I asked.

He stared in the rearview mirror at Blake. I realized then that Blake had been awfully quiet. He hadn't said a word, actually. What was going on in his head? I guessed I had put him in a no-win situation. I turned around to look at him. Just then, the car swerved hard. The senator floored the gas pedal and turned sharply, crossing lanes until we were on the opposite curb. We rammed into an empty transport bench.

Airbags deployed, shoving the gun in my hand into my head. Hard.

When everything stopped moving, the bag deflated. I felt dizzy, and my vision was blurry. The senator opened the back door and pulled Blake out with his one good arm. I couldn't see if he was hurt.

I moved in slow motion. The side of my head was wet. I touched it—blood. I could make out the senator helping Blake as they ran away from the car. Blake tried to turn around, his arm reaching out, but his grandfather forced him to keep going.

I had to get out of the car. Where was the door release?

My hand found it, pushed it open. I fell out of the car, onto the road. Everything was out of focus. Shapes, people, ran toward the car. The last one I saw, before everything went black, was a man in uniform.

A marshal.

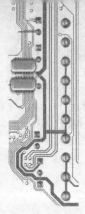

CHAPTER TWENTY-THREE

I came to on my back, beneath a bank of harsh lights. I had to squint, the light was so intense. An IV tube snaked down to my arm.

"She's awake," an elderly female voice said.

"Hello? Can you hear me?" A man's voice, also an Ender, hovered closer.

"I can hear you." I managed to croak out the words. "But I can't see you."

"That's all right," he said. "That's normal. Just take your time. Keep your eyes closed if it's more comfortable. We're just going to ask you a few questions, all right?"

I nodded. My brain felt heavy. Foggy. I wondered what drugs were pumping through that IV.

"What is your name?" the woman asked.

"Callie."

"Last name?"

"Woodland."

"What is your age?"

"Sixteen."

"Are your parents alive?"

Her voice sounded familiar.

"No."

"Do you have grandparents or any other guardians?"

"No."

"Are you an unclaimed minor?"

My head ached. "How long have I been out?"

"Not long. Just answer the question," she said. "Are you an unclaimed minor?"

I didn't have the strength to lie. "Yes."

The questions stopped. I heard her straighten.

I slowly opened my eyes. My vision was still unreliable. I could make out that the man was dressed in surgical greens, like a doctor. I expected the woman to be a nurse, but she wore gray, not white. She held a tiny metal button in one hand. A recording device.

"Would you like some water?" the doctor asked me.

I nodded. He held up a cup. I sipped from the straw.

"I had to give you stitches for that gash on the side of your head. There will be no scar, it was all under the hairline."

"The plate," the woman said.

"Yes, what's the purpose of that plate in your head?"

I looked around the room. Everything was coming into focus. This wasn't some state-of-the-art-medical facility; it was bare and dingy. The walls were gray.

"What hospital is this?" I asked.

"It's not a hospital," he said. "You're in the infirmary."

"In the institution," the woman said. "Now tell us about the plate."

I remembered her. Mrs. Beatty, the head of security. I

struggled, but something was holding me down. That was when I saw that my arms and legs were strapped to the table.

"Get me out of here." My head was clearing up fast. "It's a mistake. I have ID. In my purse. I'm really Callie Winterhill. You remember me."

They looked at each other.

"No purse was found in the car," Beatty said. "We did, however, find a gun." She pursed her wrinkled lips. "It tested positive for your DNA and prints."

A rhythmic pulsing pounded in my ears, getting louder by the second.

"And the ballistics report said it's the same gun that shot Senator Harrison," she said.

He had turned me in. Blake must not have been able to stop him. Or maybe Blake hated me, now that I had almost killed his grandfather.

Beatty put the recording device in her pocket. She nodded to the doctor and he added something to my IV. I saw a look of sadness on his face before he left the room. She watched him shut the door and then leaned close so she could hiss in my ear.

"I hate liars." She stared at me, a corona of moles around her eyes.

I could smell her ancient stink, a mix of mothballs and mold. I felt a heavy fog come over me. Panic bubbled from deep down in my gut, but it couldn't rise to the surface.

"What . . . did . . . you . . . give . . . me?" I pushed the words out one by one.

She straightened and looked down at me with a nasty smile.

"Welcome to the special private club in Institution 37," she said. "The incarceration ward."

CHAPTER TWENTY-FOUR

The next morning, I found myself on the cold concrete floor of a cell that reeked of mildew and urine. I pushed myself up to a sitting position. The right side of my head throbbed with pain. I touched it and felt a bandage. I remembered the doctor, the stitches, the car accident.

I was wearing a baggy gray jumpsuit. A prison uniform.

It was dark, the only light coming from a small window just below the ceiling. There was nothing to sit on. The tiny cell was empty. I stood and leaned against the wall. A hole in the floor in the corner made a constant vacuuming sound. A tight mesh panel in the metal door looked like it would open for food delivery.

Tell me this is not going to be my life.

I stared at the dirty walls and wondered if this was like the quarantine facility my dad was sent to, to die. For all I knew, they used the patients to experiment on. It was horrible, sending them far away from their families just to die out of sight and then be burned or buried in mass graves. We'd all heard the rumors.

As awful as it had been for my mother to die at home, it had to be worse to die in an institution.

Comparing places to die. Had it come to this?

I'd been with her that day. We were walking from our car to the grocery store when we saw the explosion in the sky. It looked like a giant dandelion breaking apart, daytime fireworks that spread and then rained. Toward us.

"Back to the car!" my mother yelled.

We turned and ran. The car seemed miles away, at the back of the parking lot. We should have gone for the store, but it was too late to change our minds.

Someone behind us screamed. I turned to see an Ender running toward us. She put her hands over her nose and mouth so as not to breathe in any spores. I couldn't tell if any had touched her or if she'd already inhaled any. Or if she was just panicked.

I was vaccinated, but still, there were rumors about some Starters not surviving a massive attack.

"Keep going!" my mother screamed. She was right behind me.

She aimed her alarm button like a rapier and I heard the sweet sound of our car doors unlocking.

Our car, our sanctuary, waiting. I opened the closest door and slid across the backseat. I held out my hand for my mother.

"Mom!"

A smile of relief beamed across her face as she grasped my hand. Her cheeks glowed, her eyes shone.

We'd made it.

"It's all right, baby, we're okay now."

She placed one foot in the car, but before she could get inside, a single white spore floated down between us.

It landed on her forearm. She stared at it. We both did.

She died a week later.

The hospitals had closed to spore patients, and every hospice was overflowing.

Days after she died, the marshals took my dad away even though he showed no symptoms, no breathing problems. They knew the odds. But he would Zing us daily from the facility to let us know he was all right.

Then one day I got a message: *When hawks cry, time to fly.*

It was a code he had set up before he left that meant Tyler and I had to run. The marshals would be coming for us. I wanted to know more. *Dad,* I Zinged back. *Are you sick? Do they know it?*

He just repeated the code.

I thought I was going to see him again. I thought he was going to come home. I stared at the stained wall of my cell. A muffled voice floated in from the hallway. A few minutes later, footsteps came to my door. It slid open with a mechanical buzz. Beatty entered my cell, leaving the door open. I could see the shoes of a guard standing just outside.

"Feeling better?" Hatred oozed like oil from Beatty's pores.

I looked at her mole-encrusted face. It was worse than I remembered. She looked a million years old.

"Are you moving me?"

That got a laugh out of her. "You would have gotten a dorm room, but you tried to kill a senator, if you recall."

"Am I getting a trial?" I'd seen them in the holos.

She smiled. "Surely you know unclaimed minors have no rights?"

"We have some rights. We are humans, you know."

"No, you're lawbreakers, squatting in property that doesn't belong to you. The state generously takes the unclaimed and boards you. But you're a criminal now, so you'll be here in lockup, the very center of the belly of the beast. And you'll stay until you come of age."

"Nineteen?" That was an eternity in here.

She nodded, and her eyes twinkled. "You'll be assigned a state lawyer then. Of course, they're overworked, and they don't have time to make much of a case for criminals like you. You'll almost certainly end up in an adult prison."

"Prison, forever?" She was lying. I struggled to breathe, but all I got was foul air.

"Assuming you survive the next three years here in lockup." She folded her arms and smiled. "Few do."

I covered my emotion as best I could. I didn't want to give her the pleasure of knowing what this information was doing to my insides. I wasn't going to ask about my brother, although I was desperate to know whether he'd been institutionalized.

Then, as if she could read my mind, Beatty said, "Where is your brother?"

"I don't know." How did she even know I had one?

"Perhaps I'll look into that. If he's not already institutionalized, then he should be rounded up."

I did my best to keep a poker face.

"I'll figure out what that plate is on your head too. We don't keep secrets here."

She left and the door slid shut. Was I all alone here? What

about those other cells—did they hold girls like me? Or were they empty? I couldn't hear anyone. Maybe they knew enough to keep quiet.

I clenched my fists. How could this be legal? I didn't have a bed; I didn't have a blanket. I spun around the cell, looking at the four walls. I spotted a single metal button on one wall. I pressed it, and a short pipe came out. Water. At least I had water. I took a deep breath. I turned my head, put my mouth under the pipe, and drank. The water was metallic and tasted of chemicals, but it was wet.

After three seconds, it shut off. I pressed it again, but nothing happened.

My home for three years. If I survived. I slapped the wall with my palms, over and over.

The next morning, I ached from sleeping on the concrete floor. My head hurt from the car injury, and no one was talking about giving me any painkillers. They did let me out into what they called the yard: an enclosed patch of dirt in the back of the compound. At three o'clock p.m., I was to get twenty minutes of exercise. The regular girls were allowed out for an hour, unless their work furlough duties were off-site.

The yard was filling up with maybe a hundred girls milling around. Some of them played with a ball or sticks. But most walked in groups of twos and threes, speaking in hushed voices. I was searching the crowd for a familiar face when someone tapped me on the back.

I thought it might be Mrs. Beatty, but it was Sara, the girl I had tried to give the sweater to.

"Callie. What are you doing here?" Her face was pained.

"I was arrested."

"Oh, no, what did you do?"

"Nothing." I was now a common criminal, denying my crime. It was easier than explaining everything to a twelve-year-old.

"So it's a mistake?"

"A big mistake."

She cast an eye at one of the armed guards stationed around the perimeter. She linked her arm in mine. "It's better if we keep moving. Is it horrible in lockup? Can the food possibly be any worse than what we get?"

"Is yours black and liquid?" I asked. My stomach growled. She shook her head.

"Listen, Sara, I'm looking for my brother. His name is Tyler. He's seven. Do you ever see the boys?"

"Sometimes they gather us for some presentation. Or to yell at us. Is he here, in 37?"

"I don't know. He could be."

"I'll ask around. But no promises."

A couple of girls bumped us, pretending it was an accident. I stopped and looked at them. The girl closest to me was the bully who had jumped me near my building and stolen my Supertruffle. Her right hand bore the scars from when she had smashed it into the pavement instead of my face. That was the night I came back from my visit to Prime. So much had changed since then, but not this bully's aggression.

She did a double take at my new and improved face, then recognized me.

"It's you," she said. "You better watch that pretty face."

"Never mind, Callie." Sara pulled me away.

"Bye, Callie." The bully said my name in a singsong voice, now that she knew it.

We glared at each other as friends pulled us in opposite directions. Sara took me over to the wall, where we rested our backs.

"Forget about her. Let's talk about something happy," Sara said.

There was a moment of silence.

"Do you have a boyfriend?" Sara asked.

My face warmed from my chin to my forehead. "I did. Sorta."

"So do you or don't ya?"

I sighed. "I wish I knew."

"What's his name?" Her eyes were twinkling now.

"Blake."

"Blake. He sounds cute." She grinned. "Bet he misses you." She pinched my arm. "Bet he sleeps with your picture under his pillow."

I glanced around. The last thing I needed was to give the bullies another excuse to tease me. "I don't think he has my picture," I said quietly.

"Not even on his phone?"

I looked up. She was right. He'd taken one on his cell phone, that first day at the ranch.

"Yeah, he does." I smiled.

"See." She reached up and pinched my nose. "Told ya so." Then a look came over her face like she remembered something. "How do I look?"

"Why?"

"Oh, no reason."

I shook my head. "Sara, does this have anything to do with what you told me before? About a man coming here?"

"Maybe."

"Did you hear the name Prime Destinations?"

"I'm not saying." But she smiled.

"Sara . . ." I buried my face in my hands.

"I really hope I get picked," she whispered.

My throat tightened. "When is he coming?"

"Soon. Is it true no one has seen his face, like, ever?"

I nodded.

"So what will he do, wear a bag over his head?"

"Maybe a mask."

"Like Halloween?"

I took her by the shoulders. "Where's the best place to hide here?"

"In the institution? Easy. The laundry room. It's buried in a funny corner of the basement, past the emergency exit. I hid there once to get out of garbage detail."

"What would you say if I told you I knew about Prime, that I'd been there before, and it's a bad place? You could lose your body forever."

She squinted, as if I was giving her a headache. "What are you talking about?"

"Just trust me. You have to hide when they come to pick out the girls."

"Hide? Why? It's my best hope of getting out of here."

I was about to tell her about how they had operated on my brain when a bell rang. Mrs. Beatty stood by the yard entrance staring a hole in me.

"Please. Think about what I said. I have to go."

"Already?"

"I only get twenty minutes. I'm the bad girl, remember?"

"Wait." She reached in her pocket and pulled out a tissue. Inside was something dark.

"What is it?"

"What's left of the Supertruffle you gave me." She smiled and offered it to me.

That had been days ago. The truffle had become dry and hard. I remembered it falling. She must have picked it up and saved it for herself to enjoy, little by little. And now she was giving it to me.

She placed it in my palm. I stared at it a moment.

"Go on, don't be shy," she said.

"Don't you want . . . ?" I gestured to it.

"No, no, you have it all."

I gingerly bit into the dried Supertruffle, hoping not to break a tooth. "Crunchy."

She beamed. Then she threw her arms around my neck and gave me a big hug.

"Is it selfish to say I'm glad you're here?" she said. "Because I am. I thought I'd never see you again and now here you are. My friend."

I smiled as best I could with my mouth full of brittle crumbs.

Sara was the one bright light in my day; the rest of it was agonizing. I lay on the cold floor thinking about Tyler, wondering where he could be and whether he was getting worse. I could handle this, no blanket and all, but he couldn't. Was he locked up in an institution like this one? Or was he with the Old Man?

I also thought about Blake and the time we had shared, and whether he'd ever find it in himself to forgive me. But the princess had lost her beautiful clothes, and her chariot, and had found herself imprisoned in the dungeon for life. The fairy tale was over. No prince was ever coming to rescue a princess who had tried to kill his grandfather.

The next day, I counted the hours until exercise period. When a guard came to escort me to the yard, I noted how his ZipTaser gun sat in the holster on his hip and imagined how I might steal it. But even if I did, I would have a swarm of guards on me, with many more ZipTasers. And a long way to the exit, where the gate was controlled by another guard. My odds of escaping were so small, there probably wasn't a fraction to express them.

And I wouldn't want to leave 37 anyway, not until I was positive that Tyler wasn't here.

Once I was in the yard, I scanned the faces, looking for Sara. Girls bumped me, and someone even slapped me hard on the back. I moved away. I stood in the corner where I'd seen Sara the previous day, and soon she appeared.

"Did you find out anything about my brother?" I asked.

She shook her head. "Sorry. But maybe he's here. Maybe they changed his name."

That thought just burned me up. Changing his name. Could they take anything else away from him? Where was he? Who was he with?

"Cheer up, Callie. I'll show you something."

She took my hand and led me to a barred opening in the wall. After she glanced around, making sure no one was watching, she squatted and pulled me down with her.

"Look," she whispered.

We peered out the opening and stared at a black bug of a heli-transport on the grass in the main quad. Beyond the heli, a tall metal ladder leaned against the external wall that separated the grounds from the outside. For a second, a delicious second, I imagined it as a means to escape. Except that there was an Ender standing on the thick wall, repairing the barbed wire that topped it.

Sara looked in the direction of a guard across the yard who was staring at us and pulled me up.

"That's the Old Man's heli," she said.

The Old Man. Here. My heart beat faster. Did he have my brother?

"Are you sure?"

"I heard the guards talking," she said. "They said no one could see his face. He wore a hat that covered it like this." She fanned her thin fingers and made a brim around her head.

She was smiling. The thought made me sick. "You're going to go with him, aren't you? I can't talk you out of it?"

"You're joking. I'd do anything to get out of here. And you come too. You're definitely pretty enough." She touched my cheek.

"Sara, would it be dangerous if anyone hit you, like on your chin? Or your nose? I mean, because of your heart condition."

She squinted. "No." Her eyes searched my face. "Why?"

I took a deep breath. "I really like you. Please remember that. Understand that whatever I do, it's because I'm trying to protect you."

She cocked her head at me, curious. Her innocence made it all the harder to do what I knew I had to. I pulled back my arm, curled my fingers into a tight fist, and punched her straight in the face.

"Ow!" she shouted. She fell backward on the ground. "Why?"

She got up and put her hand to her nose. Blood trickled from beneath it.

"I'm really sorry," I whispered.

And I hit her again to be sure.

This time, she didn't fall. Tears streamed down her cheeks. She looked so hurt, so betrayed, it cut me to the core. Girls around us stopped and stared. They asked what happened.

"I hit her," I said as loudly as I could without screaming.

Some called for a fight. The bully girl with the scarred hand came pushing through the crowd. I turned to face her and braced myself for what was to come.

Go ahead, do it fast, I thought.

I made no attempt to stop her. She reached into her pocket, then pulled out her fist. Something on her hand glinted in the sun. She punched me hard in my right cheek.

It stung. I reeled back but steadied myself. I took a quick look to make sure no one was coming at me from behind—I didn't want anyone hitting the back of my head—and went back for more. Suspicion darkened her face, but she hit me again, this time in the jaw, and one of my teeth was ripped out of my mouth.

The pain reached all the way back to my eye sockets.

I saw then that she had some metal rings wrapped around her fingers. Good, that had to have done serious damage. Some of the girls yelled warnings that the guards were coming. The bully slipped the metal device back into her pocket.

Sara stood a few feet away, crying, blood running down her face. I was happy to see that her eyes were already swelling up. My own face stung like I'd been hit by a cast-iron skillet. The bully came at me again, pulling my hair and dragging me to the ground. The guards ran over, swinging batons at anyone in their way. They hit the bully in the back and yanked her off me. Another guard hit me in the stomach.

I couldn't breathe. I fell to my knees from the blow.

A metallic taste filled my mouth.

Mrs. Beatty pushed through the crowd. I had thought her face couldn't get any uglier, but when she saw the blood, her expression was all wrinkles and frown lines.

"Girls. Not now," she said. "Just when we have a visitor."

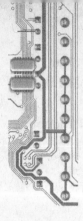

CHAPTER TWENTY-FIVE

A guard accompanied Sara and me to the infirmary. If I did want to escape, this would be a good time, with one guard and two girls, but Sara probably wasn't in the mood to help me with anything at this point.

She held a cold cloth to her face. She was crying. "I thought you liked me. What did I do to you?"

I couldn't say anything in front of the guard. When the doctor saw me again, he showed no emotion, just a flicker of recognition in his eyes.

The doctor pointed to a stainless steel exam table, and the guard put Sara on it. I sat on the adjacent one. The guard explained the situation and said he would stay to make sure there wasn't any more trouble.

"That won't be necessary," the doctor said.

The guard insisted that Mrs. Beatty wanted him to stay and the doctor shrugged it off, as if it didn't matter. But I had the impression that it did.

"So let me take a look at you," the doctor said to Sara.

"She hit me. Hard."

"I can see that. And she's bigger than you." He touched her nose gingerly with his thumb and forefinger.

"Can you fix me?" Sara asked.

"I'll do my best." He moved over to me, turning my face. "That cut on your mouth will need stitches. Your jaw took a pretty good beating. But the back of your head is fine."

I tried not to smile. That was exactly what I wanted to hear.

"Doctor," Sara said. "Can you fix me first? There's a man here, and I have to be beautiful." She shot me a look of 100 percent hate.

The doctor could do only so much with the limited resources in the infirmary. An hour later, I had stitches and Sara's nose was being taped. We were both sprayed with a pain blocker. Sara was beside herself, complaining that she had to get out there to meet the man from Prime. There was no mirror in sight, so she was unaware that besides having a bruised and bloody nose, the swollen skin underneath her eyes was decorated with a shiny purple and black rainbow.

I hoped the Old Man had come and gone. Beatty entered the room, and her expression reflected how bad we both must have appeared.

"Look at your faces. What a sorry state," Beatty said.

The doctor cleaned Sara's face with cotton.

"Don't bother with that one right now," Beatty said. "Finish up with her." She pointed at me.

The doctor turned to Beatty with a puzzled expression.

"I need to get her into the gym."

"What about me?" Sara asked. "I want to go too."

Beatty held her by one shoulder as the doctor turned to start on me. "You'll do as I say."

Sara wriggled out of Beatty's grip and jumped off the table. "You can't make me."

Beatty grabbed her by the arm and pushed her into a chair. "Now, you know I can, Sara."

Beatty led me into the large gym. An Ender taped a piece of paper with a number on it to my chest. Girls were lined up on one side, in rows, starting against the wall and facing center. The boys were on the opposite side. Everyone had a number. I scanned their faces as I was marched in. This was my chance to find Tyler. The kids stared at my face with frightened eyes. I was put at the end of the front row.

I didn't see Tyler, but many of the boys were out of my line of sight. The Old Man was walking down the last row of boys, his hands behind his back. The air was crackling with tension, I figured from the excitement of the kids thinking they might be rescued. But the focus of the tension came from the presence of the Old Man himself. He just had that effect, I felt it.

He still had on his coat and hat. All I could see was his back. What could he look like? I wondered. Just then, he turned to come across to the girls' side, and his face came into view.

His modified face, of course. He wore a mask, some sort of special metallic fabric molded to his face. It not only hid his identity, but also functioned as a sort of screen or monitor, so images—other faces—played across it. One moment, his face was that of a popular star from the turn of the century, the next it was that of a poet from decades ago, or some unknown man. Because it was three-dimensional, its effect was eerie, not silly like a flat costume mask, but not so smooth that it could pass for a real face. It was something in between, artificial but captivating. And as it was constantly changing and moving, it had a creepy, almost organic result. It was like the face-blocking technique he'd used for his privatecast, but in real life.

I was mesmerized, in an uncomfortable way, the way you can't stop staring at a car accident.

He examined some kids carefully and eliminated others in a heartbeat. A female Ender with an electronic pad followed the Old Man, marking down the numbers of the kids he was interested in and taking notes. He began to make his way down my row of girls, and I heard him asking them questions about their abilities.

As he approached, the hypnotic effect of the face-changer became stronger on me. All of a sudden, he was speaking to the girl next to me, but I couldn't focus on his words. His voice was the electronic one I had heard on the privatecast. I figured a device under his wool neck scarf made those metallic tones.

It was my turn. He stared at me. Had he ever really seen me at Prime? No. Only my reflection. And now, with my bruised, swollen face, I was sure I wouldn't even recognize myself.

I saw that his face-changer could change expressions as well. A famous soccer player's face took over, looking puzzled.

"What happened to you, number 205?" he asked.

I looked down at my feet. "Fight. Sir."

"How does the other party look?"

"Not a scratch on her. Guess I'm a bad fighter."

He changed to an old silent film star and smirked. "I doubt that."

He moved on to the next row of girls. I exhaled. He had always planned to come to this institution, looking for new kids. He wasn't here looking for me.

When he was done examining the last of us, he left the room with his assistant. We were told to keep our places. The assistant returned and whispered to the headmaster of the institution. He nodded to her, and she read out the numbers from the list.

Every time a number was called, its wearer squealed as if they'd won a contest. A few girls burst out crying, they were so overcome with joy. I craned my neck to see each "winner," making sure it wasn't Tyler. But they weren't choosing any of the younger kids. Finally, the last number was called, but no one responded. People looked around until the girl next to me elbowed me.

They were calling my number.

I looked down at the 205 on my chest. So much for my big, painful plan. I'd managed to hurt myself, damage my face, and still, for some reason, I was picked for the body bank.

The headmaster announced that everyone who was not selected was dismissed to his or her dorm room. The "winners" were to stay put to await delivery of their property, the meager contents of their wooden boxes. I stood and watched while the others filed out in rows, followed by the guards and the headmaster. I scanned the Starters' faces as they left, looking for Tyler, but he wasn't there.

They left us, the chosen ones—ten boys and seventeen girls—standing like statues, spread apart in the cavernous gym. One guard remained stationed at the door.

We glanced around, evaluating each other. The girl in my row must have been chosen because of her blond hair; that boy across the way for his muscles. They were beaming, proud to have been deemed the most attractive or skilled in the institution. When one boy in the row facing mine made eye contact with me, I saw puzzlement wash over his face. Why should I, the girl with black eyes and stitches up her jaw, be picked? Then he gave a slight understanding nod and looked away. Maybe news about my fight had spread and he assumed I'd been chosen for my killer instinct.

Maybe I was.

I wanted to scream to these kids to run as fast as they could, go hide in a closet, under their beds, anywhere. They had no clue what this really meant, that they were close to the end of their lives. That they would never experience adulthood.

And then I realized—why didn't I take my own advice? What was I standing there for, just waiting to be taken?

I turned and walked toward the back of the gym toward a fire exit door. I heard the guard at the main door shout.

"Hey. Minor. Stop!"

"I'm just going to the bathroom," I shouted over my shoulder.

I heard him jogging across the gym floor. "Do not use that door!" he yelled.

"It's an emergency." I rushed for the exit, matching his jogging pace.

"Stop or I will shoot you." His footsteps came to a halt.

I knew he was aiming his ZipTaser. I stopped but didn't turn.

"And harm the precious merchandise?" I held out my arms. "You'll get in big trouble for that."

I pressed my feet into the floor and sprinted for the door, shoving it so hard it banged against the wall. As I ran down the empty hallway, I could hear him yelling into his communicator for backup since he couldn't leave his post.

At the end of the hallway, I pushed open the door leading to the stairwell. As I headed down the stairs, I heard footsteps coming from the second floor. Maybe it was the backup coming to the guard's aid. When I got to the bottom, I was in the basement.

Exposed pipes ran along the bare brick walls. A lone uncovered lightbulb lit the end of the hall, and I ran to it. When I reached it, I turned the corner and saw three options, all dark walkways. I picked the one closest to the outer wall and raced to the end. I looked to the right, and there was the emergency door Sara had mentioned. I hoped it was the right one and not one that would sound an alarm.

I pushed it open and went through. No alarm. The hallway continued. At the end was a door with a window in it. I could make out what was left of letters painted long ago and saw an "L."

I peeked through the little window in the door. It was the laundry room, and it appeared to be empty. I slipped inside.

The room was filled with uniforms in all stages of processing. To the left, bins on wheels held piles of dirty laundry. To the right, bins waited with clean laundry. Stacks sat on folding tables, and shirts hung from a pulley system suspended from the high ceiling.

The washing room was to the left, the door kept closed to muffle the noise. I turned to the right, where an overflow room held several bins of clean laundry. But before I got inside, I heard someone cough.

I turned to my left and saw a girl with her back to me lifting laundry onto the table. She was hefty, and I guessed that was why no one had bothered to call her to be considered for the body bank.

"You my relief worker?" she shouted.

"Yeah," I said, keeping my head down.

"About time." She wiped her brow with her sleeve and left.

I peered through the window in the door to the side room but saw just darkness. I slipped inside, closing the door behind me. I flicked the light on just long enough to pick out which bin I was going to hide in. I felt my way to the bin farthest from the door and climbed inside, burying myself in the clean laundry. I didn't have a plan; I just hoped I could hide long enough to get to the point where the Old Man was so off schedule that he had to leave.

I curled up in the fetal position. If my heart hadn't been beating so hard, I might have been able to sleep. I tried to picture the kids who were waiting to be taken to the body bank. Were they already on the transport while the guards searched the compound? How long before they searched utility rooms like this one?

It wasn't long before I heard a door opening. Someone was entering the laundry room. Footsteps. Maybe it was the shift worker. I heard my door open. The light went on. Through my canvas laundry bin, I could see the silhouette of a girl.

I held my breath. She walked closer. Closer. She was right by my bin. Then she stopped.

Her hands reached down through the laundry for me, grabbing my arms, pulling me up.

Small hands.

I could have fought them, but I stood up, letting the laundry fall away.

I knew this girl.

"Sara," I whispered.

She held on to my arms, her face inches from mine. It was hard to read her expression because her left cheek had puffed up so much that it forced her left eye shut.

But she looked great to me.

"Callie." She smiled a distorted half smile. "Some hiding place. I could totally see you in there, all curled up."

"Shhh," I said.

"Don't you tell me to shut up." She gripped me harder. "I thought you were my friend."

"I am your friend."

"Liar. You ruined the best chance of my life. I'll never forgive you."

"Please." I held up my palms. "Someone will hear you."

"They're going to hear me. Because I'm turning you in." Her squeaky voice had become defiant.

I could have easily pulled away from her grip. I was older, taller, and stronger. But I was afraid she would start screaming.

"I heard you got picked, Callie. They made an announcement over the speaker system. Whoever finds you gets a reward." Her one eye widened. "Maybe they'll even give me your spot at Prime Destinations."

"You're too young. No one under fifteen was chosen."

She scowled. "You're lying."

"You heard the names they picked. Were any of them younger?"

"No." Her bottom lip started to quiver.

"Please, Sara, don't turn me in. I know you're mad, but I did it for your own good. I hit you so they wouldn't want to take you."

"Then why'd they pick you? Look at you." She made a face like she smelled rotten eggs.

"I don't know, maybe because they know I'm already one of their donors? It doesn't matter. What matters is that if I go back, they'll kill me like they did my renter. And then my brother doesn't have a chance."

"What?" Confusion twisted her face.

She was barely getting over the idea that she was not going to be chosen in my place, and there I was telling her she would be my killer if she outed me.

"I'm not sure what you're saying, but I know you're not afraid of anything," she said. "And you're afraid of Prime?"

"Because I found out they're killing people. Starters. It's hard to explain, but it's like they're separating your body from your brain and then shutting down your brain forever."

She froze, as if trying to make sense of it. I felt myself holding my breath, eyeing the door, estimating the distance to it, how long it would take me to jump out of the laundry bin and how quickly her screams would bring others running.

"Well, that's not good," she said.

She slowly let go of my arms. I exhaled.

Sara helped me fashion a disguise to replace my prison uniform. She explained that the only workers around the facility other than the minors themselves were the head gardeners. These Enders maintained the landscaping around the entrance and admin building as a show for visitors. To distinguish themselves from the minors, especially from a distance, they wore a black shirt and pants, and a large hat for protection from the sun. It was this outfit that Sara put together for me, out of the laundry. She even managed to find a clean one.

We tied back my hair so none of it would show outside the hat.

"Maybe we should draw a few wrinkles," she said as she examined me.

"I think we should just get out of here."

"You can't go without shoes." She pointed to my bare feet.

My gray prison-issue tennis shoes would be a dead giveaway. I kicked those under a pile of clothes while Sara searched for a pair of black fabric slippers that had been washed.

She came back holding two slippers. "This is the only pair."

I stepped into one, then the other. They were at least two sizes too big. "Perfect," I said. "Let's go."

I found some rubber bands and used them to keep the slippers on. We had worked out a plan to get me out of the institution. We were worried that the Old Man would tear apart the compound until he found me, so hiding wasn't an option. He would come after me to save his reputation, to show that some Starter could not defy his orders.

Sara said she'd heard of a Starter escaping last year by hanging on to the underside of a delivery truck. Because of that, it was standard for guards to run quick checks of the trucks before they exited through the gates. But they never searched the vehicles of important visitors. We figured the Old Man, with his heli-transport, was so powerful that the institution wouldn't risk insulting him with any routine delays. The institution's cooperation with him suggested that money had changed hands.

It was still risky.

"You sure the Starter got away?" I asked. "And he didn't get hurt?"

"I didn't say that," Sara said. "I just heard he got out."

"You don't know for sure, because you never heard from him again."

"Listen, there's something else, this one fat gate guard. Everyone calls him Box. He can't bend to see under any trucks."

"So?"

"He's working today," she said.

That convinced me. Not only would the guards be less likely to delay the important Prime transport, but I also had the benefit of Box's lack of flexibility.

I was strong and light. I only had to hang on long enough to get past the gates. Then I could let go and the transport would drive off, never knowing I had been stuck like a leech on its belly. That was our plan. It would be a whole lot harder than when I had just waltzed out of there the day I first visited, but it was an opportunity. And I was going to take it, because once Prime's transport left, the guards would resume their usual truck checks.

We walked out into the daylight, me in my gardener disguise, Sara as my minor apprentice. She also wore a hat to hide her bruised face, and carried a trash bag and a bucket of hand tools. As we made our way along the paths that led to the administration building, I bent slightly and slowed my gait to appear more Ender-like, even though what I really wanted to do was run like crazy. Not that I could have in the oversized slippers.

We saw two Starters coming our way. Sara gave me a hand signal. We both bent our heads down so the hats covered our faces until they passed.

When we reached the main quad in front of the admin building, we saw the Old Man's black heli-transport on the far side of the grass. The pilot stood outside it, stretching his legs, but no one was inside. The transport vehicle that would take the chosen ones was closer to us, parked in the short road halfway between the administration building and the guarded gate to freedom.

"That's your ride," Sara whispered.

"It could be yours too." I looked at her.

She shook her head. "You have to go find your brother. I've got lots of time."

"You just want me to be the guinea pig."

That made her smile. "I'll miss you," she said.

I would miss her too. "We'll see each other again. Someplace happier." I didn't believe it but knew it would make her feel better.

"Of course we will. We're friends."

Her earnest little face beamed at me. She looked like she was about to hug me goodbye, not a safe thing to do, when movement came from the building.

A guard led the ten boys and sixteen girls to the transport.

"They're already boarding," Sara said. "We're too late."

We'd hoped to get there before the others did. "Take my elbow. Guide me through them."

We had to cross their line to get to the other side of the transport, to be out of the view of the gate guards. But if anyone spotted our bruised, broken faces, our cover would be blown.

We kept our heads down.

The kids in line were so excited about being chosen, getting to ride a transport, and getting to leave the institution forever, they didn't even look at us as we passed.

We made it to the right side of the transport, where we were hidden from the gate guards. Across the grass, the heli pilot had his back turned. I dropped to the ground and slid underneath the transport. Sara bent and took my hat.

"Good luck," she whispered.

I mouthed *Thanks.* I slid my body across the gravel to position myself directly in the center of the transport. I spotted a bar where I could tuck my feet. But before I could move, she knelt down.

"Callie," she whispered, fear on her face. "He's not there."

"Who?"

"Box, the guard."

My heart sank. We'd been counting on him.

"Come back." She held out her hand.

I waved her away. She frowned. I looked up at the undercarriage and she left.

I reached up to a bar above my chest and tested it. Hot and greasy. I pulled the gardening gloves out of my pocket and put them on. I grabbed the bar and, one at a time, tucked my arms in until I was able to hold my hands together to lock myself in. I felt the heat of the bar through my shirt. I was hanging facing the underside of the transport.

I looked over and saw Sara's feet about ten yards away. On my other side, the number of shuffling feet had diminished. The kids were almost all boarded.

"Wait!" I recognized Beatty's voice and her heavy footsteps on the gravel. "You're still missing one girl."

I held my breath. The driver insisted that he was on a schedule. The last kids boarded.

Then the engine started. The vibration made it harder to hold on. Heat radiated from the metal, and sweat trickled down the sides of my face. I had thought I was strong, but this was harder than I had imagined.

The transport started to roll. The noise of the engine, the gears shifting, the wheels turning—even at this slow speed, it felt like my head was in a meat grinder. My teeth were rattling; my bones were shaking. I was sure my stitches would burst open.

I worried I wouldn't make it out the front gate. What were we thinking? Whose idea was this crazy plan? And Box wouldn't be there. All I had to go on was the hope that they'd let the fancy Prime transport sail on through.

We came to the gate. I could see the base of the guard's booth from my upside-down vantage. Our transport slowed. I tried to will it with my mind to keep going. It crawled along. I held on as I heard the gates sliding open for us. My arms were aching, but I told myself I just had to hold on a little longer. For Tyler.

Then the transport braked to a stop. I gripped the bar even tighter and held my breath.

Footsteps approached. Then someone else ran in another direction. Murmurs turned into shouts.

"Stop that girl!" It was a woman's voice. Beatty.

Did she mean me? I tucked my body up as close as I could to the transport's undercarriage.

"Shoot her!" a man's voice called out.

A sharp electronic crackle sizzled through the air like a lightning bolt.

A ZipTaser.

But the cry of pain that always followed this sound never came. There was silence.

"You missed!" a man shouted.

They didn't mean me; I never even saw the arc of light.

Then everyone started shouting and I could hear running feet. The transport started rolling again. I gritted my teeth and held on. We were driving through the gates, past the gates, clearing the gates!

It was going too fast, to make up for lost time. The driver turned hard out of the property onto a side street. The turn was too much for my tired arms. My muscles gave out.

I fell. My back hit the pavement hard, even though the drop was only a few feet. I quickly pulled in my arms and legs, becoming as straight as a stick as the transport roared over me, the huge wheels rushing so close to my head that the whoosh blew my hair. Once the transport was gone, exposing me in the bright sunlight, I rolled to the curb, hid behind a tree, and looked back at the compound's barrier.

At the very top of the thick concrete wall, with the blue sky and fluffy clouds behind her, a girl clung to the barbed wire, her arms hanging over it.

Sara.

A guard rose from behind the wall, climbing what must have been the ladder that she had used, on the other side. He stepped out onto the top of the wall.

Sara looked down at me, saw that I had made it outside the compound. She brought her right hand up to her chest, placing her fist over her heart.

She hadn't been trying to escape. She'd done it to create a diversion. To protect me.

I mirrored her, putting my fist over my heart.

Hold on, Sara.

Her bruised face was pained and weary, but a rapturous smile came over her. It was contagious, and my lips turned up a little too. She was reassuring me.

She put her foot against the wire and pulled herself up. She was going to go over to the other side of the wire. No! Where could she go from there? She could run along the top, but they would catch her.

The guard froze a few yards away from her. He shouted at her to stop. She continued to climb.

He pulled out his ZipTaser and aimed it at her. He was too close.

I saw the blue light arc and pierce her body. She scrunched her face in agony and twisted her torso in pain. Her gut-wrenching scream overshadowed the ZipTaser's metallic cry. My stomach pushed back deep inside me, and I put my hands over my mouth to stop myself from crying out.

The guard didn't see me, half hidden behind the tree. He moved closer to Sara.

Her neck and side of her face were blackened by the Zip-Taser. She opened her eyes and looked down at me. A surprised look came over her, as if someone had played a horrible trick on her. Her eyes glazed over, then shut.

She slumped forward, her head slack, her body held only by the barbed wire.

Sara, no! Don't go!

But her body appeared suddenly empty. Hollow.

The guard pressed his fingers to her neck, then looked at another guard standing at the top of the ladder and shook his head. The first guard moved slowly, wrapping his arms around her with care, lifting her away from the wire. He brought her body to the second guard, who carried her down.

I remained hidden behind the tree, watching her for as long as possible, until she slipped out of sight.

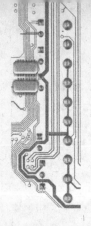

CHAPTER TWENTY-SIX

Numbness radiated inside me, filling my limbs, my chest, my face. Sara was dead. Little Sara. Gone. I was glued in place there, never to move again. Then an ominous sound vibrated through my body—the droning blades of a heli-transport rising from the institution grounds. My hair blew back as the machine crested above, emerging high over the fence, giving me a view of the underside of the black bug.

My survival instincts kicked in and I turned and ran across the street. I raced past a boarded-up house to a back alley, where I pressed my body against a weathered garage door, my chest heaving. The Old Man's heli reappeared, hovering overhead.

Had he seen me? Should I move? Or stay put?

I knew his pilot couldn't land in this narrow area, but what if they had radioed the guards?

I decided to keep moving. I ran through alleys and side streets. Residents saw me, but at least I was disguised in the gardener's uniform, thanks to Sara. Poor Sara. I ran faster, away from the institution. As long as my feet were moving, I was still alive.

The drone returned, like some relentless insect. I kept moving, clinging to walls or trees, any cover I could find. I looked skyward. It wouldn't give up.

I saw wires in the sky a few blocks away. I ran in that direction, trying to keep hidden as much as I could. The black bug trailed me. When I reached the source of the wires, an electric substation, I dove under a pickup truck. The asphalt scraped my palms. I knew the heli couldn't fly over this area, with the dangerous wires poking into the sky.

It gave up, a wasp that couldn't find anyone to sting. I exhaled and then scrambled out from under the truck. I saw the heli-transport flying away into the distance.

I walked and walked and walked, until the slippers ripped apart. I peeled them off and walked some more, thinking about Sara with every step.

I wiped my eyes with the back of my hand. What had happened while I was under the transport? My stomach tightened as I tried to figure it out. Sara must have seen the gate guard coming to check under the vehicle. That was why she'd made the brave move to distract everyone. She had dashed for the ladder, in full view of the guards and Beatty herself. She had done it for me. She had sacrificed herself for me, because she knew I had to find my brother.

Then they'd shot her.

When I arrived at Madison's house, I rang and rang the bell, but she wasn't home. I had come so far and she wasn't there. My pain spray had worn off and my stitched-up face throbbed. I slid down the door, collapsing into a heap on her porch, where I fell asleep. It was just starting to get dark by the time she returned and woke me.

"Callie. What are you doing here?" Madison bent over, her blond bob hanging in her face. "I didn't see your car." She helped me up and stared at my gardening disguise. "What're you wearing? Some new teen style?"

She unlocked the door and I stood in her bright foyer. Finally, she saw my battered face, stitches and all.

"Oh my God, what happened to you?"

"Madison. I have to tell you the truth. I'm not a renter. I'm a real teen. A donor. And I have a lot to tell you about Prime."

"You're . . . a teen?"

"Yes."

"You're not old inside, like me?"

I shook my head. She stared at me blankly for a moment.

"So all this time . . . ?"

"Ever since I met you, that night in Club Rune," I said weakly.

"No wonder you sounded so young. You *are* young. But why on earth did you do this?"

I was so drained. Every part of my face ached. My feet hurt. I just wanted to go back to sleep for a million years.

"Because I had to."

She hooked her arm in mine, helping to support me. "Let's get you some painkillers and a hot shower. Then you better sit down and tell me everything."

⚶

An hour later, after I had brought Madison up to speed on what had happened, we agreed I should contact Lauren. I showered and changed into clean clothes Madison provided. I was still bruised and swollen, and missing a tooth, but I felt almost human. Not long after, the doorbell rang, and Madison let in an elegant, trim woman wearing a soft pantsuit and pearls.

"Hello, Callie." The woman extended her hand. "You've only known me in Reece, but this is who I really am."

"Lauren." I shook her hand. She was about 150, as graceful as I had imagined.

A senior gentleman in a suit joined us.

"This is my attorney, Mr. Crais. He was also Helena's."

Madison nodded, meeting them for the first time, and then excused herself. "I'll go get drinks."

We sat in the living room. Lauren winced as her eyes scanned my face. "Who did that to you?"

"It was just a fight."

"It's that rough in the institution?" Lauren asked.

"No," I said. "It's worse." I looked at them. There was no way to explain it all now. "It's like this: I'd die before I ever go back there again."

"Don't worry, that's not going to happen. I'm glad you contacted me," Lauren said. "We were trying to locate you."

"You were?"

"I'm sorry about the last time we spoke. You have to understand, I was in shock over the news about Helena."

"I know."

"I'm not at liberty to explain everything yet"—she traded a look with her lawyer—"but Helena was my dearest friend.

And I wanted to contact you because now I know that she believed in you."

I wondered what that meant. Had Helena gotten a message to her during a blackout?

"So we came up with a plan," she said.

"We contend that Lauren had been in the process of claiming you when you were admitted to the institution," the attorney said. "So you're not the property of the institution, therefore it's not their prerogative to reassign you to Prime Destinations."

"Even though you were involved in a criminal act—"

"Allegedly," the attorney interrupted.

"Allegedly," Lauren repeated. "If you had been claimed at the time, my legal counsel would have assisted you. That benefit was withheld from you."

"This keeps you legally out of the clutches of the institution and the body bank," the attorney said.

"So you'll be my legal guardian?" I asked Lauren.

"You'll be as free as you wish. I'm just the name on paper."

I felt a pang of disappointment. It was stupid. Why should Lauren take on the burden of really being my guardian? She hardly knew me. It was enough for her to be my guardian on paper.

"The point is to keep you out of the institution so you're at liberty to do whatever you want," the attorney said.

"What I want is to save my little brother," I said. "I think the only way to do that is to take down the body bank."

"We hoped you'd say that," Lauren said.

We all got to work, Lauren and her attorney, Madison and me. I had the idea to create an announcement mimicking the Prime Destinations announcement I had seen. We wouldn't try to duplicate the Old Man, but it was possible to digitally copy the faces of Tinnenbaum and Doris off the original announcement. Then we would put the words we wanted to say into their mouths.

Madison volunteered to create the announcement using her production manager skills from decades ago. She made some calls and assembled an audio/visual team of Ender experts who transformed her five-car garage into a studio. She also hired two Ender tech geeks to break into the system so they could privatecast the production over Prime's designated subscriber channel. This was going to be no small feat, but Madison's deep pockets could fund the manpower and the gear. She wanted to help make up for all her body bank rentals.

I discovered a whole different side to the ditzy Madison I knew.

Meanwhile, Lauren and the attorney were working their cell phones to reach all their contacts. The attorney had a relationship with a Senator Bohn, who they hoped would get involved. He was Harrison's political rival.

That evening, we had a living room full of grandparents of missing body bank donors. But getting them to agree to a plan was a production in itself.

"We have a wealth of resources in this room," Lauren said. "We've got thousands of years of experience: doctors, lawyers, a bodybuilder, even an ex-marshal. And we have deep funds. Now that Callie has pulled together all the information, we finally have a fighting chance to get our children back."

One senior man stood up. "We don't want to stir up trouble. Our grandson is still out there somewhere. Vulnerable."

A thin woman next to him spoke. "If I have to wait another month to get him back, I'll wait. We need Prime's cooperation to find our grandkids."

I stepped in front of Lauren. "You don't understand. I saw Prime's announcement. They're starting a permanency program. Your grandchildren are going to be bought, not rented. You'll never see them again if we don't stop this."

The lawyer jumped in. "Because we have insiders like Lauren, we were able to see the privatecast. That announcement admitted Prime's intention of permanency. Lauren recorded it, and we sent a copy to Senator Bohn. If he can use that to get a judge to issue a stay, it will nullify the president's contract with Prime. If the judge determines that lives are in immediate jeopardy, we can shut them down."

"And what if he can't?" the thin woman asked. "What if they claim the original announcement was doctored, just like you're manufacturing this one?"

At that moment, Madison came into the living room. The seniors grumbled upon seeing her perfect teen body.

"She's a renter!" one of them yelled, pointing at Madison.

"That's right, sugar." Madison flipped her head, swinging her blond bob. "A renter—not a buyer."

I went to Madison and put my arm around her shoulder. "She's on our side. And she's spending a fortune to stop Prime."

The crowd continued to buzz. Lauren put up her hands.

"Please," she said. "We don't want to fight with any renters. If we are to have any chance of shutting down Prime, we're all going to have to cooperate. Because in order to get your grandchildren back, we have to do this quickly, with the element of surprise."

"I have an idea," I said, looking at the thin woman. "The technical expert who altered my chip could testify. He examined my chip and said it could never be removed, that it was permanent. That shows that they always intended this program to be permanent."

The attorney folded his arms and nodded. "That will certainly help."

Lauren's phone rang. She looked at the screen. "It's Senator Bohn."

Lauren put her phone near a small airscreen on a coffee table. Senator Bohn's picture came up for all to see. He was the opposite of dynamic Senator Harrison. Bohn had a kindly face and a gentle smile.

"Senator Bohn, I have you on airscreen," Lauren said. "As you can see, we have a bunch of concerned grandparents here."

"Thank you, Lauren, for notifying me of your progress. And I want to thank your brave donor, Callie Woodland, for exposing Prime."

I smiled politely, but we still had a long way to go.

"Every grandparent who is there, thank you. Working together, we will be able to shut them down and get your grandchildren back, each and every one of them."

I looked at the faces of the grandparents. The senator's presence, even if only on airscreen, was helping to solidify the troops. The power of a charismatic politician.

"I'll be with you every step of the way. We can do this," the senator said. "Let's get them back."

One grandfather, who had been quiet until then, repeated the senator's words. "Let's get them back," he said solemnly.

A woman on the other side of the room stood. "Get them back."

Affirmative murmurs rumbled through the room.

Madison, Lauren, and I glanced at each other, trading hopeful looks. Maybe we could pull this off.

The grandparents left with their instructions. Senator Bohn said he would know by morning if the judge would issue the stay. I watched the production team trying to change Tinnenbaum's mouth so his lips fit the new words they were making him say. It wasn't working.

"It's different when it's a baby or a dog talking. This has to look seamless," Madison said to her team. "It won't work unless it's believable."

Her geek team trying to bust through to the private-cast had an even harder time. I didn't understand it, but they hit some big technical glitch when they came up against an unexpected volcano wall, which frazzled some of their equipment. Madison reminded them that nothing mattered if they couldn't figure out how to get this to the subscribers.

We left them to work it out while I took Lauren and her attorney to Redmond's laboratory. We couldn't find a phone number for him, so we had to arrive unannounced, and it was almost midnight.

As we rode in Lauren's limo, I reached into the purse Madison had given me to see if there was a mirror but came up empty. I asked Lauren for one. She hesitated, then pulled out a compact.

I activated a light over my shoulder. As soon as I looked in the mirror, I understood her hesitation. I looked so strange. Parts of my face were still the flawless work of the body bank makeover team. But then I had one black eye, several bruises, a huge cut with stitches running from jaw to cheek, and, if I pulled my cheek back, a gap where I was missing a tooth.

"Would you like a comb?" she asked.

"Why bother?" I snapped the mirror shut and handed it back to her.

"We can fix all that," she said.

"Let's fix the important things first," I said.

Everything was coming together because we all wanted something. Lauren wanted to find her missing grandson; I wanted to find Tyler and get Michael his body back. Senator Bohn wanted to make Senator Harrison look bad for making the body bank deal with the government, and the lawyer was in it for the money.

I didn't know if this was going to work. If one piece went wrong, if the announcement wasn't believable, or if the geeks couldn't manage to break through and privatecast it, the whole thing fell apart. But what Lauren and those grand-parents and I had at stake meant the world, so there was no other choice.

When we got to Redmond's compound, we immediately saw that something was wrong. Bright lights illuminated the building, and two marshals' cars blocked the entrance. A crowd from the neighborhood stood around gawking. I ran out of the limo, with Lauren and the attorney at my heels.

A plume of smoke billowed in the air, but I couldn't see Redmond's building from where I stood. An Ender marshal with short white hair stopped us.

"No access, folks," he said.

"What happened?" Lauren asked.

"Just trying to determine that now," he said. "Please step back."

An Ender wearing overalls and holding back a dog on a chain collar came forward. "Some kid bombed the place. They got nothing better to do than tear down what we build up."

While the marshal was distracted by the Ender, I ran past them to Redmond's building.

"Hey, you, stop!" the marshal shouted.

I rounded the corner of the compound and was stunned by what I saw. The building was blackened and gutted. One corner of the roof was completely gone, as if a monster had bitten it off. Ender firemen were checking the smoldering remains.

I heard firemen assessing the damage inside the building. I ran in.

"Hey, get out of here. It's not safe," one of them yelled at me.

Everything was charred inside: all the monitors and machines, even the ones hanging from the ceiling. The smell of melted computer parts was unbearable. I held my sleeve to my nose. Redmond's burnt and mangled chair was dripping water, like some conceptual art piece. It was all a horrifying, soggy black mess.

"Where's Redmond?" I asked. "The man who lives here."

"We haven't found a body." One fireman looked around, throwing his hands in the air. "Yet."

Redmond was too valuable to kill. And too smart to be caught. I was betting he'd gotten away and was in hiding. We wouldn't have his testimony.

Then I remembered the box.

The firemen were busy taking heat measurements on the other side of the room. I leaned down and pressed my fingers to the pad on the file drawer. I coughed to cover the little click that it made. I peeked inside and used the edge of my jacket to pull out the small metal box. It was light and cool to the touch. I saw he had changed the label from *Helena* to *Callie*.

I slipped it into my pocket.

Before any of the firemen could escort me out, I moved to the door. I stopped there and took one last look at the lab. I didn't really know Redmond, having only met him once, but he was sort of my maker, if that made any sense. He was important to me. It hurt to see all his work destroyed this way.

I joined Lauren and the lawyer, who were standing just outside the compound, in the reflection of the marshal's red light. "They said someone saw a kid do this," the lawyer said to me.

"Yeah, some kid with a murderous senior inside," I said. "It's got body bank written all over it."

Fear clouded Lauren's face. I hoped this wasn't going to give her second thoughts about our plans.

"Did they take anything?" the lawyer asked me.

"I don't know. But I got something that will help us." I patted my pocket.

"What?" Lauren asked.

"A computer key. It has Redmond's notes about my chip, how he determined it was permanently installed."

"Excellent," the lawyer said. "Good work."

He was happy. But I felt terrible for Redmond. Had I led Prime to him? Was all this my fault? First Sara, then Redmond. Who else was going to suffer because of me before this was over?

296

CHAPTER TWENTY-SEVEN

A day later, I walked up to the body bank as if I were reliving a nightmare. I had thought about this place so many times, with such fear and dread, wondering if Helena was inside, if my brother was, if the Old Man was. I'd been afraid then. Helena had warned me they would kill me, and so I had stayed away.

It was different this time. This time, I was ready. This time, I had backup.

But they were keeping their distance, as planned. Sewn into my pocket was a small alert device, half the size of a grain of rice. We had worked out a three-stage approach. And stage one consisted of one person—me.

As I approached the high double doors, the doorman's smile melted. It curved farther downward into a frown the closer I came. He looked frightened, either because of my bruised, stitched face or because he recognized me.

Maybe I was notorious. I almost laughed.

I had to open the door for myself as the doorman stared at me. I kept staring right back at him, even as I passed through the portal.

As soon as I stepped inside, another guard came over and waved a weapons detector over me. My alert device was supposed to pass this test.

"I have no weapons," I said. "Other than my big mouth."

The guard seemed satisfied.

Mr. Tinnenbaum ran out of his office and pointed. "Grab her!"

The guard pulled my arms behind my back and held me.

"So you've changed bodies, I see," I said to Tinnenbaum. "What's the matter, Lee's body got boring for you?"

He scowled.

I widened my eyes in innocence. "You know, the first time I was here, everyone was all smiles."

Doris came out of her office. "What are you doing here?"

"Ah, Doris. This face suits you so much better than Briona's," I said.

"Talk about faces." She squeezed my cheeks together with one hand. "All the work we did on yours. Wasted."

I jerked my head away. "Now all we need is Rodney, and the trio's complete."

Tinnenbaum got right in my face. "You look awful. What do you want?"

"I want to see him," I said. "The Old Man."

Doris and Tinnenbaum exchanged looks. She shook her head. Their reaction, with the slight delay, only confirmed for me that he was there. I knew what they didn't: the Old Man was dying to see me.

"I'll wait," I said.

Fifteen minutes later, the guard and Tinnenbaum escorted me up an elevator and down a long, winding hallway. This didn't look like the way to a CEO's office. I stopped.

"Where are you taking me?" I asked.

"You asked to see him," Tinnenbaum said.

"His office is here?"

"He likes to do things his own way."

I didn't like this. Eventually, we came to a metal door. Tinnenbaum spoke to an invisible panel on the wall.

"We have her here, sir."

The door slid open, disappearing into the wall. It was dark inside, almost completely black, but a small overhead light shone down on us as we stood in the entranceway.

"Come in," the voice said. I recognized the metallic synthesized voice of the Old Man.

"Sir?" Tinnenbaum said.

"Leave her."

The guard let me go.

"We'll be right outside," Tinnenbaum said.

The door slid shut, making it even blacker. I heard footsteps. They sounded a long way off. This room had to be very large, bigger than any office or conference room. I saw a spot of light before anything else, an eerie beacon across the room. As it approached, I saw that it was the electronic mask the Old Man wore. The face displayed was not human.

It was a snake's head. With glossy scales and huge dark eyes. A red-and-black forked tongue whipped out.

My heart beat so hard it hurt. I slipped my hand into my pocket and pressed the silent alert to let the others know I'd flushed the Old Man out. Now all I had to do was stall.

"Why come now?" he asked. "You could have come the other day, on the transport with the other boys and girls."

"I want to offer a trade."

"A trade? What kind of trade?" The snake opened his jaw, displaying his fangs.

The Old Man's images were chosen to frighten me. I struggled to keep my voice steady. "My life for my brother's."

"Tyler?"

"Yes." I waited for his reaction to confirm my hunch that Tyler was there somewhere.

"I don't know if that's such a good idea. How do I know you won't run away?"

"I'm sure you'll figure out a way to keep me."

The face suddenly changed to a woman in extreme agony. It made me gasp. He laughed.

"Who is that?" I asked. The woman was crying, wailing.

"Just a very sad lady. I think someone killed her children," he said. "Maybe her husband."

"That's horrible," I whispered.

"But we weren't talking about her, we were talking about Tyler."

I shivered just hearing his metallic voice say my brother's name again. "If you will bring him out, and I can see him, I will trade my life for his."

"Your body for his?"

"Yes."

"That doesn't seem quite fair. He is younger."

"But he's not well."

"Good point."

The face changed to a woman who'd gone to prison for poisoning her family.

"Could you stop that?" I asked.

"I like your spunk, Callie. I accept your offer."

"You do?"

"Yes. But I'm not bringing him out here. You will just have to take my word on that part."

Now it was my turn. "That doesn't seem fair."

"I don't think 'fair' ever came into the conversation."

"Yes, it did," I said. "You brought it up first."

"You're clever. I admire that."

"You'll have to give me something."

"What?" he asked. "What do you think is fair?"

"Take off your mask," I said quietly.

He was silent for a moment. The woman's face froze. "Take it off?"

"Yes." I spoke up. "Let me see your real face."

He changed the face to a famous mime's, in full makeup. "Here it is."

"I don't think so."

"That's the best you're going to get."

"Then there is no deal."

He paused. When he spoke again, his voice sounded more assured. "I don't have to make a deal with you."

"But the difference is, I keep my word. So if we come to an agreement, you'll have me here of my own free will. Forever. Me, for a brother I can't see, for one look at your face. That's all."

"You still don't see you're at the disadvantage here, in my facility, with my people." He paused and looked down. "You'd do this because you love him that much?" he asked.

"I'm all he has."

All the faces I'd seen before flashed across his, in rapid

succession, left to right. Then top to bottom, scrolling up. Then all the bits mixed up, so faces flashed by: a war criminal, a mass murderer, then a burn victim and a woman sobbing from some unspeakable pain.

It broke up into quarters and finally stirred and swirled until it became a terrible stew of misery, all the more horrific against the hollow silence of the room. My ragged breathing was the only thing I heard.

"This is what you want, Callie? You want to see the real me?"

"The real you, not some electronic collage."

"The real me." His voice was quiet. Resigned.

"Yes." I breathed out the word.

"All right."

His electronic face dimmed and died to blackness with a metallic click.

I waited in the dark.

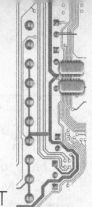

CHAPTER TWENTY-EIGHT

I heard the Old Man's footsteps coming closer, but he didn't speak. Was he next to me? There was no sound of breathing. Then it hit me. He had faked the footsteps. They were electronic, synthesized sounds, like his voice. This was a man who played with illusions; he wasn't walking toward me.

He had moved away.

It was just me and dead silence in the blackness. I backed up to a light sensor I'd spotted earlier and I pressed it with my palm. The lights came on in pools, spotlighting empty areas, proving that, yes, I was alone in a large, empty room.

I turned around and saw a monitor mounted high on the wall. It displayed the chaos in the lobby. A team of marshals was taking charge, making arrests, cuffing body bank employees.

Stage two. I pressed my pocket alarm again.

"He's gone!" I shouted.

The two backup marshals who had been shadowing me at a distance burst into the room.

"Which way did he go?" the taller one asked.

"I don't know, I couldn't see."

The room had three exits aside from the one behind me. The Old Man could have run out of any of them. The taller marshal took the first door, the other man the second, and I opened the third one. I saw a short hallway that led to a bank of two elevators. The hum told me they were both moving, but there was no light to tell whether they were moving up or down. I pressed the pad and got in the first one that came. I rode it down past the first floor, to the garage level.

I ran out into the dimly lit garage, looking for the Old Man. Plenty of high-end cars were parked close to the elevator, with the less-expensive employees' cars in the farther lanes. I bent down to look for his feet underneath the cars but couldn't see anyone. I wanted to find him and tear that mask off his face, to strip him bare.

I stopped and listened. Maybe he was hiding. I had to quiet my own breathing a moment. A sound, the shuffle of footsteps. I turned around and saw someone in the shadows, against the wall, hiding behind the front of an SUV.

I ran over there. This area was dark. The figure sprinted away from me, but he was cornered. When he got to the rear wall, he slumped down into a squat.

It was Terry, the nurse who wore eyeliner. He was crying.

"Kitten, don't let them arrest me," he said. "I couldn't take jail."

"Help me, and let's see what we can do." I put my hand under his elbow and got him to his feet. "Where would the Old Man hide?"

"He wouldn't hide. He'd just leave."

"Which car is his?"

"Not the car." His pretty eyes looked up. "The heli."

Terry and I raced up the stairs to the roof. I was mad at myself for not thinking of the heli-transport first.

"I just knew this day would come." Black makeup streaked his cheeks.

"Then maybe you should have quit."

We burst through the last door, which led to the roof, and ran out into the cold. The loud sound of the whirling blades and the blast of air hit us in the face like a slap. We squinted as our hair whipped around our faces, and we saw the black-bug heli on a landing pad some twenty feet away. Not yet airborne.

Through the curved window I could see the Old Man sitting behind the pilot, looking away. I ran to the heli, bending low to avoid the blades. The pilot motioned to the Old Man, and he swung around toward me.

His face was that of a mummy from a horror holo.

I stood on the skid, grabbed the door handle, and yanked open the door. The Old Man reached out to pull it closed, and I grabbed his arm.

I held on to the doorframe as I pulled on his coat sleeve. Past him, slumped on the seat beside him, someone was encased in a bag. I couldn't tell their size or gender, or if they were even still alive. Terry was behind me but was unable to get close. It was just me, fighting with the Old Man.

I tugged, pulling him half out of the heli. I reached for the edge of his mask.

"What're you hiding?" I yelled over the roar of the blades.

He held on to the frame of the heli and tried to shove me back with his other hand.

"Where's my brother?" I screamed, and dug my fingers into the side of his face.

He put his foot on my stomach and pushed. I held on.

The pilot pulled out a gun and aimed it at me. I couldn't do anything. I was dead.

But the Old Man pushed his arm away. I didn't know why. The disconnect made me freeze. The Old Man yelled something at the pilot. He worked his controls to lift the heli, me still standing on the skid. In my peripheral vision, Terry waved for me to jump.

We were rising off the ground. If I stayed any longer, I'd have to climb inside. I gave the mask one last tug before I jumped off. It ripped at the side but stayed on. As I fell backward, I saw the Old Man holding the mask to his face as he closed the door.

I landed on my back on the ground. Terry ran over to help. I waved him off. I wasn't hurt—just mad and frustrated at the man who always got away.

Lauren and the attorney and my two marshals joined us, but it was too late. As I watched the Old Man's heli escape into the sky, I was tormented by one question.

Was that Tyler in the bag?

We all joined the chaos happening on the first level of the building. The other marshals had rounded up the employees and lined them up against the wall. Tinnenbaum, Doris, and Rodney each argued their cases, protesting and demanding their cell phones back so they could call their lawyers. The guards, the receptionist, and a few other workers slumped on the floor, resigned. Some were crying. Trax, the tech guy, sat with his head in his hands. One nurse stood screaming at a marshal. In the middle of all this, Senator Bohn spoke directly to a camera as a small two-man crew recorded him.

I went up to Tinnenbaum. "Where's my brother?"

He shook his head. I lurched for him, but the attorney held me back.

"You know how secretive the Old Man is," Doris said. "We'd tell you if we knew."

A marshal intervened. Before I could press them further, everyone's eyes turned to the main door. Several teens with jaw-dropping bodies entered the building. Puzzled expressions distorted their otherwise stunning faces.

Stage three.

"What's going on?" a tall blonde said. "We were told to come here."

"Who told you?" the senator put the microphone in her face.

"He did." A dark-haired boy pointed. "Tinnenbaum."

"I did no such thing," Tinnenbaum said.

The senior renter in the boy's body nodded. "Oh, yes, you did, my man. A privatecast came in on our Prime channel, and you said we all needed to come back to the body bank, that something was wrong with our chips."

"I didn't pay this much to have my youth adventure cut short," the blonde said. "But if there's some kind of recall, let's get it over with, shall we?"

I looked over at Lauren. She smiled. Our fake privatecast had worked. More renters poured into the lobby, all with the same confused expression on their faces. The noise level was getting unbearable as the entitled Ender renters inside teen bodies demanded answers.

Weaving past the others was a familiar face. Madison.

Her long earrings dangled under her blond bob as she made her way to us in the center of the lobby. I put my arm around her shoulders and faced Senator Bohn.

"This is Madison," I said to the senator. "She produced that announcement."

The senator shook her hand.

"Where's Trax?" Madison asked.

The tall tech Ender with the shock of wild white hair stood up, his hands cuffed.

"Come on, handsome, take me to my body," Madison said.

A marshal uncuffed Trax but held on to his arm. He followed the tech like a shadow as he led a group of us through the corridors into the bowels of the body bank. It was me, Madison, Lauren and her attorney, and Senator Bohn, with the camera crew shooting all the way. Behind us, most of the grandparents and a large, noisy group of renters in their teen bodies followed.

We finally arrived at a room I had never seen before. Trax called it the waiting room. It was a large space that resembled an ICU, with a circular nurses' station in the center. From there, recliners fanned out like flower petals, each holding an elderly renter. There must have been over a hundred renters, all with their eyes closed and tubes inserted into the backs of their heads connecting them to a computer.

The nurses were shocked to see us but cooperated, perhaps motivated by the presence of the senator and the camera. Some of the renters appeared to have been there as long as two months, judging by the growth of beards and hair. They ranged in age from about 80 to 150.

Madison, with her long legs, sashayed up to a heavyset

woman about 125 years old, who was reclining with her eyes closed. Like the other renters, she wore a hospital gown and had a blanket draped up to her waist.

Madison pointed to the large senior and spoke to Trax. "Now be a sport and get me back into my old, fat body. It may not be much, but it's mine."

He pulled over a chair for Madison to sit in. He went to the nurses' station and put his hands on a vertical keyboard. He pressed a series of keys, triggering soft tones. I followed his eyes up and saw a circular computer module hanging directly above him, close to the ceiling. The lights flashed in a sequence for a few moments. And then the lights and the sounds stopped.

Everyone seemed to be holding their breath, it was so quiet in the room. Then the large woman in the recliner opened her eyes. Trax went over to her and touched her shoulder.

"All right?" he asked her.

She shook her head as if shaking off sleep. "Never better." She waited for him to unhook her tubes, and then she sat up. "Hello, Callie girl. This is the real me. Rhiannon."

I smiled at her.

The real Madison, the teen donor, was slumped over in the chair with her eyes closed. She was twitching like a cat in the middle of a nightmare. Then she opened her eyes. She was disoriented, her blond bob hanging in her face. She sat up.

"Where am I?" she said in a soft voice. She looked around. "Who are all these people?"

Her voice was recognizable but different.

Rhiannon leaned forward and put her hand on Madison's shoulder. "It's all right, honey, you're back at Prime. Your rental is over."

Some of the renters were not happy with the idea of getting cheated on their rental term. They were getting vocal. The senator, the attorney, and Trax put their heads together. They decided the best and quickest solution was simply to pull the plug.

"All right, everyone sit down on the floor. Now," the senator said.

Only a few of the grumpy seniors in the rental teen bodies obeyed. Trax followed the same sequence he had used a moment earlier to shut Madison down. Any teen who hadn't already been on the floor soon was. The senior bodies started moving in the recliners. The rest of us went to assist the poor teen donors, who had no clue why they were waking up on the floor.

I scanned the crowd. Someone I knew was there, near the back.

Michael.

He was safe. I knelt down beside him.

"Michael?"

He looked at me with a groggy expression. "Cal?" He propped himself up on one arm. "What happened to your face?"

I touched my jaw. "Some serious unfriendlies."

"Does it hurt bad?"

"I'll be all right."

"Where am I?" He sat up and rubbed his head.

"At the body bank."

He took that in. "The body bank. Is my rental over?"

"It's so over." I put my arms around him and held him.

He wrapped his arms around me, and I remembered how safe he made me feel. I buried my nose in his shirt for a moment. I could have stayed like that forever, but my mind was on my brother. If he was there, I would find him.

I helped Michael stand. All the donors were on their feet now, getting oriented.

Lauren came over to me with Senator Bohn, their bodies tense.

"We're not positive, so please don't get your hopes up, but we may have a lead on your brother," the senator said.

The senator and I rushed with Trax and a marshal down a long hallway.

"I didn't know he was your brother." Trax shook his head.

"What about Florina?" I asked. "Is there a girl with him?"

"No, just the boy," Trax said.

As we hurried along, he explained how the Old Man had consulted with Trax earlier that morning. He wanted to know whether the procedure would work on a preteen brain. The discussion had led to a question about the size of the particular brain, and Trax had examined Tyler.

"But I don't know if he's still there." Trax's brows furrowed. "The last time I saw him was seven-thirty this morning. The Old Man moved him around a lot."

"Who's been taking care of him?" I asked.

Trax shrugged.

"Come on. Let's go." I grabbed Trax's arm and pulled him into a jog.

We went through a door marked NO ADMITTANCE and made two more turns, until we came to a short hallway ending at a locked door with no markings.

Trax waved his palm across a reader pad, and the door unlocked. I practically knocked him over as I ran inside.

It was a windowless office space, with little furniture other than a filing cabinet and some worktables. A small cot was by the wall, a pile of blankets rumpled on top. I pushed them aside.

It was empty.

I fell to the cot and smelled the sheets. Tyler had been there. His imprint was still on the bottom sheet.

"He's gone," I said. "He took him. That Old Man took him."

The marshal carried out an inspection, checking the closets and bathroom, opening file drawers. It was useless and we all knew it.

I started crying. I couldn't help it. Tears streamed down my cheeks. I'd done everything I could, everything for him. And he was gone. I knew where he was. He was on that heli with the Old Man. I had been *that* close. And I'd lost him.

"He was here earlier. Really," Trax said.

He and Senator Bohn stood there, staring in different directions. I sat on the edge of the little cot. It didn't matter what anybody thought or how stupid I must have looked with my nose running. It was so completely hopeless. I had been dragged through the mud, had done everything I could, and I still couldn't find my brother.

Dad, I know I promised you. I tried. I did.

My insides were scraped hollow. He was alone and scared, stuffed inside a bag. With the Old Man. My body started shaking as my sobs got louder.

Trax reached out to comfort me. "I'm so sorry."

"Leave me alone," I said, lashing out at him. I stood and struggled for air. "There's nothing you can say to help. All you body bank people, you're all responsible. How could you do this to him? He's just a kid. A kid who never had a chance to be a kid." I swung around, looking at Senator Bohn. "All you Enders, it's all your fault. Why didn't you vaccinate everyone? We wouldn't be in this whole mess if you hadn't been so cheap."

The senator looked pained. He put both hands around the back of his neck.

The marshal came into my view from his little inspection of the rooms. He shook his head to Senator Bohn. "He's not here."

Something about those words, out of a marshal's mouth . . . I had hidden many times from the marshals, watching, hoping they wouldn't find me or my friends or any other Starter. But this time I was hoping he would find my brother.

The problem was, I realized, if my brother saw him, he wouldn't come out. He'd be scared to death. He'd hide.

We always hid in places marshals never thought to look. Like in the walls. Like in plain sight. Like up.

I scanned the room.

The Enders watched me with wary eyes, as if they were afraid of what I might do. I stared at the ceiling. If my brother saw the marshal but not me . . . and didn't hear me . . .

I went into the bathroom and looked up. The Enders followed me, crowding in the doorway. The toilet seat was closed. That was my first tip.

I stepped on top of it.

The men rushed forward, arms out as if they might have to catch me from a fall. I climbed onto the sink. I saw fingerprints on the ceiling panel and I pushed on it.

"It's okay, Tyler," I shouted to the ceiling. "It's me."

I lifted the panel and slid it over to the side. Tyler peeked out like a shy fox.

"Callie?"

My heart leapt to my throat. "Tyler. Come here, you."

I bear-hugged him out of his hiding place and handed him to the marshal. I climbed down from the sink, and then grabbed my brother as tightly as I could in my arms. I kissed his head, breathing in the sweet scent of his baby-soft hair. My chest felt so light, it was like a truck had been lifted off it.

He was crying. I was crying. The men were crying.

And I wasn't letting go.

After much hugging and kissing, and after determining that Tyler was in good condition, the Enders brought us down to the lobby, where the noise level had ratcheted down from a ten to a five. We introduced Tyler to Lauren. Senator Bohn grabbed a blanket and wrapped it around my brother.

"Is he all right?" Lauren asked me.

"He fed me, the Old Man, and gave me medicine," Tyler said.

I doubted that was for altruistic purposes, but I didn't say anything to him. Then I remembered Florina. She'd been with Tyler when they were taken from the hotel.

"Tyler, what happened to Florina?" I asked.

"They pushed her out of the car."

"What?"

"When they picked us up, they drove a couple blocks. Then they made her get out."

"I hope she's okay."

He nodded. "I saw her get up." He thought for a moment. "Did you know she's got a great-aunt? In Santa Rosa?"

I shook my head.

"She talked about her. Maybe she went there," he said.

The senator rubbed Tyler's head. A marshal showed the

senator a list pairing up renters with donors, who all began to walk into the room. He gestured to one side, and they had each renter stand beside their donor. Madison stood by Rhiannon. Tinnenbaum was by Lee, Rodney by Raj, and Doris by Briona. Michael was standing by a decrepit Ender with a big nose and a potbelly. He must have been two hundred. That was the guy who had licked me when he was in Michael's body? I wanted to gag.

The line of Starter donors and Ender renters snaked down the hallway. Lauren, Tyler, and I walked the line, scanning every face, but I didn't spot anyone who resembled Emma. Lauren did not find her Kevin.

"I knew it was a long shot," Lauren said. "But you never give up hoping."

"We'll keep searching." I touched her shoulder. "This won't be finished until we find them."

The long night wore into the morning as everything was wrapped up. Grandparents came to reclaim their grandchildren. They were surprised to see the unclaimed minor renters disappear into the dark morning, but I understood. They didn't trust the Enders.

Tyler was asleep on a couch in Doris's office. Michael and I slumped in chairs around her desk. We were drained and half asleep ourselves. At least, I told myself that was why Michael seemed distant.

"So Florina's got a great-aunt in Santa Rosa," I said.

"Yeah. She said she would claim Florina."

"Lucky girl."

"Florina said I could go with her. Not as claimed, of course."

"Why didn't you?"

He shrugged. "Too cold up there."

I nodded.

"So I guess we're not going to get paid," he said.

"Wouldn't count on it."

"All that." He shook his head. "We risked our lives . . . for nothing."

"Hey, it wasn't for nothing. We've got these state-of-the-art chips in our heads out of the deal." I laughed. What else could we do? I was happy to have my little tribe back together, even if we had no place to go. Goodbye, mattresses and showers; hello, hard concrete floors and water buckets.

Lauren stepped into the doorway.

"Callie, could I see you for a moment?"

I looked at Tyler's sleeping body. Michael nodded and said he'd watch him.

"I think you're going to want to hear this," she said with a smile.

She took me to Tinnenbaum's old office, where her attorney sat at the desk. It gave me the creeps to see the water fountain that had earlier impressed me so much.

"Mrs. Winterhill left a will. You're named in it."

I looked at Lauren. She motioned for me to sit in one of the chairs facing the desk. She took the other one.

"But when did she . . . ?" I asked.

"She did this before she started the rental. She felt she owed it to the girl whose body she was risking," the lawyer said.

"She's left you half of her estate," Lauren said, "including the main house and a vacation home."

A home.

I couldn't speak.

The lawyer read from a paper. "She says: 'I don't know you, but I'm sorry for having to use you in this way. And I'm sorry for the world we've left you.'"

A home? I was exhausted. I had to be dreaming. I touched my cheek and felt the very real stitches.

They could tell I didn't believe it, so they repeated it for me. And explained the details. But all I heard was one word: "home."

So. Helena had kept her word.

I looked at Lauren. She nodded; yes, it was all true. Her eyes glistened as tears welled in them. Me, I closed mine, and somehow the tears came out anyway.

A home.

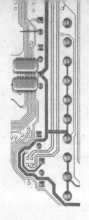

CHAPTER TWENTY-NINE

That morning, I took Tyler to live in his new home. I knew I would never forget the look on his face when we walked into the mansion, escorted by Lauren and her attorney. While they took Eugenia aside to explain the conditions of the will, Tyler stared at every piece of furniture and decoration with wide eyes.

He paused at a bronze statue of a dog on a side table. "Can I touch it?"

I nodded. "You can do whatever you want. It's yours now."

He picked it up and cradled it to his chest. Although it must have weighed a couple of pounds, he insisted on carrying it around with him. When I tucked him into the big bed in the master bedroom, he still had it in his grasp, determined to sleep with it. I put it on the end table, inches from his face.

"Where's Michael?" Tyler, his lids heavy, caressed the dog's head.

"He's getting his stuff from the building."

"He's coming to stay here, right?"

I smiled. "Yup. He's going to turn the guest cottage into an artist's studio."

"I wonder what he'll draw now. Now that we're not on the streets." Tyler's voice slowed.

Then he closed his eyes and fell into a deep sleep.

Over the following days, our lives were rebuilt.

With Lauren as my legal guardian, I was protected from anyone contesting the will on the grounds that I was an unclaimed minor. Half of Helena's estate and her two homes would be mine forever. The other half was being held in trust for Emma, once I found her. I would find her. I owed Helena that.

The money was far beyond what I had hoped to gain by signing up for the body bank, and I was profoundly grateful. Tyler was getting the best medical care money could buy, and growing healthier every day. I had my tooth replaced, and my cuts and bruises would heal in time.

Michael moved into the cottage on the property but immediately took off. He didn't explain, so I went into the cottage to see if he'd taken his belongings. I knew he was coming back when I saw the walls covered with the drawings he'd created from our year of living on the streets. Starters and renegades, sad and mean and hungry—they were all there, in his special style. So much emotion; he'd captured it all. Spread out on all four walls was my life after the Spore Wars. My past life.

I figured he must have left town to see Florina. I was disappointed, but I didn't have a right to be. Losing Blake had left a huge void in my heart. It wasn't until things calmed down that I realized just how big.

A week after we moved into Helena's house, I heard on the news that Senator Harrison was recovering from a "hunting accident." The fallout from the Prime body bank scandal would play out in the coming months. After the elections, we'd know whether Enders could reelect a man prepared to doom teens to a living death.

The senator was keeping Blake on a short leash. I tried sending messages, tried calling. He never responded. I decided that before I gave up on him forever, I would go see him in person. If I could just explain everything, I might persuade him to give us a second chance. If not, then I would move on.

It wasn't hard finding the senator's home. I had to drive by it several times before I found Blake's sports car parked outside. When I finally spotted it, I felt my heart race and had to calm myself before getting out of the yellow rocket.

I looked up at a stately Tudor mansion and took the long walk from the curb down the rose-lined path to his front door. I stepped onto the porch and the bell sensor rang before I could decide to back out. The door opened.

An icy Ender bodyguard, complete with uniform, pulled out his gun and aimed it at my head.

"Call the marshals," he shouted to someone in the house.

"I'm not here to cause trouble." I put my hands up. "I just want to see Blake."

Blake came to the door. The guard stepped between us. "Stay back."

"It's all right, I'll talk to her," Blake said.

The guard pressed his earpiece. He was listening to someone and responding with a "Yes, sir." Blake and I exchanged a look. He shrugged.

The guard's demeanor changed. "Looks like it's your lucky day," he said to me. "I'll just do a search, if you don't mind."

He holstered his gun and patted me down. Then he pulled a weapons detector out of a leg holster and waved it over my body. Finding nothing, the guard stepped inside and disappeared from view, leaving Blake in the doorway.

"Hi," he said, smiling.

"Blake." I smiled back. It was so good to see his face again. And smiling at me. This was hopeful.

"What do you want?" he asked.

"I thought maybe we could talk."

"What about?"

"About everything that's happened. There's a lot to explain."

"This a joke?"

My heart stopped for a second. "Blake?"

He cocked his head. "What's your name?"

"Don't pretend you don't know me."

He rubbed the back of his neck. "One of my friends put you up to this?"

"Oh. I get it." I folded my arms. "You haven't forgiven me."

He just stared. Wasn't going to give an inch.

"I thought maybe you'd understand," I said. "After everything came out."

His expression became serious. "Sorry, I . . ." He shrugged. "I don't know you."

My hands went cold. To see the face that I knew so well looking back at me with that blank expression . . . it cut me to the bone. What had happened?

"Blake? You really don't remember? Any of it?"

He shook his head.

"Riding? The park . . . the Music Center?"

He continued to shake his head. He looked like he felt sorry for me.

"I'm not crazy. Look at your cell phone. Our picture's there."

His eyes narrowed like he was reaching into the past but coming up empty. He didn't remember me.

I don't know if anything could have hurt more.

I was invisible.

Senator Harrison came to the door, one arm in a sling. "Callie."

I took a step back.

"You know her?" Blake asked.

The senator came toward me. I pulled back. He patted my shoulder. "It's all right, Callie. Come inside."

He put his good arm around my shoulder and guided me into the large foyer. The bodyguard stood stiffly to one side. I could see the living room through an archway, a fire in the fireplace.

The senator turned to Blake. "I need to speak to my guest alone."

Blake nodded. Before he headed off, he took one last glance at me over his shoulder. I hoped, ached for him to show some small flicker of remembrance. Anything. But his face said I was just a curiosity.

Senator Harrison took my arm and led me to the study. He motioned to a leather chair and closed the door. I preferred to stand behind the chair. I wasn't sure whether to trust him. I took in the room, which was decorated with antiques.

"So now you've met my grandson," he said.

"What's happened to him?" I felt my lip quivering.

He pointed back to the door. "That is my actual grand-son. The real Blake Harrison." He winced as he sat at his desk and adjusted his sling.

I heard his words. But they made no sense. "The real Blake?"

Then, as if someone had turned down the volume, every-thing became quiet.

Only the antique clock in a glass case on his desk dared to make a sound. It ticked away as the three gold balls inside spun back and forth, back and forth. It was dizzying, sicken-ing, how fast it whirled, confused about its direction.

Someone gasped. It was me.

The senator's eyes narrowed. He nodded.

"It was never him before?" I asked.

He shook his head. "Only his body."

My hand rose to my mouth.

He nodded again.

I leaned on the back of the chair. "So someone else was inside Blake . . . using his body."

"That is correct." The senator waited for me to absorb it.

Who? Who would want to use Blake's body all that time? And then it hit me. No. A chill ran through my entire body. The thought was too horrible to speak.

"The Old Man," the senator said.

I put my head in my hands. No. Not him. In Blake? My mind was spinning faster than the gold balls inside the clock.

"But I saw the Old Man when he came to the institution," I said. "How could he be in two places at once?"

"That was after the government deal was done. He left Blake then."

"What about the airscreen announcement? It was shown before that."

"That was prerecorded."

I stopped to take in a deep breath. "Why would you let this happen?"

"He held my grandson hostage, although Blake never knew it. Only his grandmother and I did. He did it to force me to introduce the agreement between the government and Prime Destinations."

"Blake never signed up at Prime?"

The senator shook his head. "The Old Man kidnapped him and had the chip inserted. Blake doesn't know about any of that. He thinks he was ill for those weeks."

I ran my hand through my hair. The whole time, I had thought I was the fraud, the peasant masquerading as a princess. But it was the prince who'd been in disguise. He'd been the ogre all along. In my world, nothing was what it seemed. And I didn't know if I could ever trust anyone again.

The senator put his hand on my shoulder. "Callie, I want you to know that I've put pressure on the prosecutor to drop the charges against you."

I had forgotten all about myself.

"And I have a favor to ask."

"What?" I couldn't imagine what I could do for him.

He moved his face close to mine, his eyes big and pleading, his breath bitter with tobacco. "Don't say anything to my grandson about any of this, ever."

I left Harrison's house without seeing Blake again. I walked down their path with the bright roses mocking my every step. Stupid girl. Why couldn't you see it?

My knees crumpled. I fell to the ground as a horrible, hollow canyon formed inside my gut. I clasped my stomach to stop the pain. There would be no reunion with Blake ever. He wasn't real. Nothing we had done or felt was real.

Blazing hot tears gushed from me.

He was gone forever. Like Mom and Dad.

Dad.

Oh, Daddy, I miss you so.

I spent the whole night replaying in my mind every single thing Blake had said and done, but reimagining it coming from the Old Man. Club Rune, the ranch, the awards gala. After I'd relived those moments over and over again, I wanted to get as far away from those places as I could. So the next morning I took Tyler to our new vacation home in the San Bernardino Mountains. We bundled up in our fleeces and jackets and headed north.

Helena's second home was a large, two-story chalet set on two acres with panoramic views of the lake in back. Unlike at the mansion, there were few reminders of Helena or Emma; no portraits or holo-frames. I wasn't trying to forget them, but not having to see their faces made us feel like the house really was ours.

Tyler practiced casting in the lake while I sat on a rock and thought about how much I had gained and how much I had lost.

It had started with the Old Man using Senator Harrison to push his body bank deal with the government. To make the senator cooperate, he'd had to kidnap Blake and use his body as a hostage. Helena hadn't known any of that, but she'd learned that the senator had plans to make the government deal. So she had rented my body to kill him. She wanted to stop the deal and to expose Prime for the first time publicly, in the worst light possible, by showing that a donor body could be used to kill. When she had Redmond alter our chip, turning off the stop-kill switch, the Old Man picked up on the changed signal and discovered her plot. Since the Old Man was already in Blake, he used Blake's body to find out more about Helena's plan.

That was when he followed her to Club Rune, spoke to her at the bar, and set up the date at the ranch. But when Redmond tampered with the chip, he also made it unstable. That made Helena black out at the club, and the Old Man, inside Blake, saw it happen.

Then I met him. He started a relationship with me to keep tabs on Helena, to make sure we didn't kill the senator before he saw the president. And to see how I adapted to changing the stop-kill switch. Once we had the communication link and Helena got into my head, he would have seen what a valuable resource that could be, especially for the government.

Every single thing he'd done was a pretense. Pretending to be a real teen visiting his great-grandmother, pretending to like me so I would trust him. The time we spent at his ranch, in the car—all lies. He'd done more acting than any award-winning superstar. Pretending to want to touch my cheek, hold my hand, kiss me.

I put my hand over my mouth. But there was no way to wipe away the memory.

I was sick. I loved my time with Blake. But I felt I should hate it, now that I'd learned it had been the Old Man playing with me. I was torn. One moment, I wanted to keep those memories stored in a precious box. The next, I wanted to torch them to ashes.

I focused on Tyler tossing his line into the water. His casting was improving. At least when it came to Tyler, I felt peace. It was a comfort to know that he would never go hungry, would never again have to sleep on a cold, dirty floor, that he wasn't going to die. I breathed in the brisk piney air. It felt so clean. I was lucky to be there, grateful to have the two homes. I decided to stop thinking about everything except how beautiful it was up there.

"Tyler!" I shouted. "I'm going in to make cocoa. Stay there, okay? Don't wander."

He nodded.

I went up a few wooden steps to the back deck and entered the warm kitchen. Tyler was visible from the window over the sink. I took off my jacket and put it on a chair. I opened the cabinet and took out the cocoa and two mugs. I spooned the cocoa into each mug and turned on the filtered hot water. Endless water. Forever.

I filled the mugs and put them on the counter. That was when I noticed something odd. Something that didn't belong, lying on the counter, to the right of the sink.

A stem of yellow orchids. With the purple leopard spots.

My chest tightened. It was the same kind of orchid Blake—the Old Man—had given me when we'd had the picnic at the ranch.

How did it get there? How long had it been there?

I looked out the window. Tyler was gone. His fishing pole lay on the ground. I felt panic rising in my throat. I was about to yell when I moved to the edge of the window and saw him. He was bending down, getting bait out of a bucket.

I let out a sigh of relief.

Then I heard a voice in my head.

Hello, Callie.

Just like Helena used to talk to me. But this was a man's voice: the Old Man's. That creepy electronic voice that set my teeth on edge.

A shiver ran through me.

You're a big success, Callie. Prime is now closed and scheduled for demolition.

"Where are you?" My eyes scanned the lake where Tyler was fishing. "How can you be in my head?"

I have a backup, of course.

"A backup?"

In another location.

I wondered if it could be a portable drive. Could he be close? "Where?"

Would you like a tour? I can show you.

"So why are you in my head?" I didn't see him outside. I began quietly opening the kitchen drawers.

Come join me, Callie.

"Join you? What do you want with me? I'm just a girl."

Not anymore. That chip in your head is one of a kind, altered by one of the best. I'll offer you a top salary to come join my team.

"I have everything I need now." I tried to sound strong, but my voice betrayed me with a nervous break.

You don't know what you need.

I pulled out a large butcher's knife from the drawer. My hand trembled.

Wait until you taste power.

"I'm not interested in tasting anything with you."

I won't give up so easily. As I told you before, you're very special to me.

I breathed out a soft half laugh, but the words stung like acid. "You just want to rip open my head and see how he altered the chip." Tyler was still fishing. I left the kitchen and slipped into the hallway, looking for where the Old Man could be hiding.

I want you on my team. And you need a cause. You'd be in good company.

"You think I'd fit in with your team?"

Your friend Redmond is one of them.

Then I realized. "He was the one on the heli."

You like him.

"Yeah, I like him. He uses his brains to help people, not hurt them." I wanted to keep him talking as I crept down the hall. "So all that time, the things you said to me, did you mean any of them?"

Much of what I said to you was true. But not everything. If you want to find out which parts were real, come join me.

"You lied to me. The whole time, you pretended you were someone else." I looked in the living room; he wasn't there. Through the picture window, Tyler was still okay, still fishing outside.

And isn't that exactly what you did?

I stopped. He was right. "I had to."

No, you could have walked away. But you would have forfeited the money.

"I needed it for my brother." I clutched the knife, walking across the living room to a closet. I opened it. He wasn't there.

If you really want to protect him, you'll join me. I promise you, in the coming months, no kid will be safe without protection. You never know when your life could dissolve. An earthquake could destroy your home. Or a fire. Your legal guardian could die in a car crash, and then the government will confiscate the estate. Everything can be taken away from you in an instant. Nothing is reliable—except power. I can give you that.

I rushed into the hallway and up the stairs. I wanted to scream at him to shut up. What did he mean, "no kid will be safe"? I passed Tyler's room. The Old Man wasn't there.

You think you did it for the money. But I know you better than you know yourself. You also did it so you could live as someone else.

"Oh, please."

Give a man a mask, and he'll tell you the truth. Who said that?

"You did." I came to the landing and walked down the hallway, peeking into rooms.

You didn't go back to Prime when the connection was compromised. You wanted to be Helena.

"Someone threatened me, said if I returned, I'd be killed."

And you wanted to believe that so you could live as someone rich, even for a short time.

I stopped. There was some truth to that, I was ashamed to admit.

I could give you that experience again, Callie. A life far more exciting than Helena's.

Did I want a new life? Yes. Another place, another time. Not with him.

"No," I said. "I don't want to be anyone else, I just want to be me. Whatever it is you want me to do, I will never, ever, do it."

Your curiosity will get the better of you. I can afford to wait.

"You'll be waiting forever." I looked in another empty room, holding the knife low, by my leg.

Ah, Callie, if you only knew. You have it all wrong. I'm really the good guy.

What? How dare he say that? I was at the point where I

was hoping he was in the house. I wanted to confront him, tear off his mask, end all this, then and there.

The last door was closed. It was my bedroom. I didn't remember closing it.

I crept up to the door and put my hand on the knob and turned.

The sheer curtains waved in the breeze. Or had someone just walked past them? The French doors behind them were open. I walked through them, taking one step outside onto the large balcony, and looked out at the lawn, the lake, and Tyler. It was dusk, and even the birds had gone silent.

Although he said nothing, I could feel the Old Man's presence lingering in my head. I stood by the French doors and waited. It was the two of us, in a stalemate, in limbo, my own breathing the loudest sound, second only to my heart-beat.

And then I felt him leave.

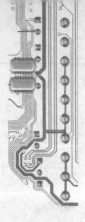

CHAPTER THIRTY

A week later, I stood outside the body bank and watched as the wrecking crew prepared to demolish the mirrored building that had housed Prime Destinations. The crowd, wrapped in coats and jackets, was mostly working-class Enders— guards and salespeople—who never had known the purpose of the building. There were some wealthy seniors, mostly ex-renters, and a few rich claimed minors. At the outer edges hung the unclaimed Starters, some ex-donors like me, some just eager to see the show of the wrecking ball.

I saw several faces I recognized. Lee was there, as were Raj and Briona. They were no longer the inseparable trio. Each wandered around alone, not even recognizing the others. Madison, the teen with the short blond bob, stood several feet away, to my left. Our eyes met. A smile came over my face, I was so happy to see her. She paused, staring at me with a blank expression; then her gaze passed over me. I had to remind myself that she'd only met me once, the night everything had ended at the body bank. She might not have re-membered me. Or maybe she did.

I spotted her counterpart, Rhiannon, to my right, in her jolly, real body. She leaned on a walker and waved. I waved back and was about to join her when I saw Michael, way in the back of the crowd. He stared at the building, waiting, like the rest of us. Alone.

"Michael!" I shouted.

He was too far to hear. His attention was focused straight ahead. My spirits rose. He must have just gotten back into town. I turned and started to work my way back to him, but then I saw someone cutting across the silver-headed crowd on my left.

Blake.

My throat tightened. What was he doing here? He wasn't supposed to know about the body bank. I hadn't seen him since that day at his house, over a week ago. I looked back at Michael. He saw me this time, and his face lit up. He looked so good. He motioned for me to join him.

I turned to Blake. Our eyes met and he gave me a small, tight smile. He was weaving through the crowd, coming toward me.

I swallowed. I didn't know what to do. Blake was too close for me to just walk away. I looked back at Michael. From where he stood, he could see what was going on, and it was like a gray film passed in front of his face. His smile faded, his shoulders drooped. It killed me, but I was caught there, stuck in the crowd, too far away to try to explain, even if I could.

Blake was just a few bodies away. I'd promised his grandfather I wouldn't reveal anything about our past, so what was I supposed to say?

No time to think. He was there.

"Callie." He nodded. "Your housekeeper told me where to find you." He shoved his hands in his pockets and looked away. "My friends tell me that I'm too serious. Maybe it comes from being a senator's grandson." He shrugged. "My dad was the serious type. My mother, she knew how to have fun." He gave a wistful smile.

What was he talking about? It sounded like he'd prepared a speech.

"Anyway, everyone says that I'm a bookworm, that I don't get out much, unless my friends drag me." He shuffled his feet, glancing at his shoes. "What I'm trying to say is this." He pulled out his phone and showed me a photo on it. "I saw the photo."

I looked at the picture I had told him about. The one of us taken the day we went riding. Except poor Blake was never really there; it was the Old Man. He was standing behind me, his arm across my shoulders, his head resting next to mine, me clinging to his arm with both hands. We had just gotten off the horses—happy, hot, and a little sweaty.

We both radiated pure joy. It was hard for me to look at, but Blake would never understand why.

"I don't remember any of this," he said. "But I look so happy. I've never looked that happy before. Ever."

His eyes met mine and didn't look away. "Whatever we had, in those lost weeks that for the life of me I can't remember, I want it again."

I searched his face. He wasn't kidding. He meant it.

"Do you?" he asked me. "Do you want it back too?"

My stomach fluttered. I wasn't sure we could regain what was never ours to begin with.

"It's okay, you don't have to decide now," he said.

He held out his hand to me. I froze.

"You know what really happened, Callie. I need you to help me remember."

He had the face of a floating astronaut who had lost his tether and had only one chance to grab a lifeline or forever drift away into endless black. I knew that feeling, the sense of panic that stretched time, turning seconds into years, and the deep pain that came from being hurt by not one person but many, a gang of bullies that expanded into a neighborhood and then into a community, until you questioned the whole world. And your last thought, as you stretch your arm until your fingers are inches from that lifeline, is how if you survive, you'll find a way to help fix what was broken, so you can say that yes, you want to be part of the world again.

I moved my hand halfway toward his.

I wasn't going to let the Old Man win. I wasn't going to let him strip away my sweet memories of the time with the boy I had thought was Blake.

He took my hand and linked his fingers with mine. His skin was familiar—the smoothness, the shape of his thumb. His touch transported me back to the times we'd spent together in his car. I'd missed all this so much. More than I realized.

It wasn't the Blake I knew. But it looked like him; it felt like him. He was lost, and I was the only person who could help.

We would have to see.

Then I heard the sound of someone breathing. In my head.

My heart quickened.

Cal Girl.

I hadn't heard that voice for a long time.

When hawks cry, time to fly.

My father? My head whipped around, even though I didn't expect to see him. The sounds of the crowd faded away.

Blake gave me a curious smile. "You all right?"

I searched myself. Listened, but heard nothing more.

Blake squeezed my hand as the wrecking ball smashed through the reflective façade of the body bank.

LISSA PRICE, author of the Starters series, lives in the foothills of Southern California with her husband and the occasional deer. Visit her at LissaPrice.com.

See how it STARTS and ENDS in

PORTRAIT OF A SPORE

An exclusive
STARTERS short story

by LISSA PRICE

The Spore, in an unnamed Pac Rim country, sometime in the future

The tiny spore comes into being. And the first thing he feels is . . . certainty.

An intense sense of purpose for his existence burns inside him, a stubborn flame that nothing will extinguish.

He doesn't know what that purpose is; he only feels it. So with it comes a longing.

The answer must be out there. Somewhere.

This is confusing to him. It is difficult, not knowing what anything is.

Imagine how he feels, so full of purpose. But for what?

✳ ✳ ✳

The morning sun shines golden through my kitchen window, unaware that the world has changed. The coffee smells like it always has, rich with the promise of comfort, but it's a cruel lie. It only reminds me how we are going through the motions.

I pour the coffee into two cups, one for me, one for Ray. One of the mugs has a picture of our family on vacation at the beach, before the war. Tyler was five, Callie fourteen. We were all smiling, completely unaware that our simple lives were about to change so much.

I take the other mug, the plain one, and go into the living room.

Where are the kids?

I look out the window, past my red roses twining around our white fence, and see Heather in her SUV with Darren in the backseat. They're waiting for Tyler. I wave, and they wave back with guarded smiles.

"Tyler!" I shout. "Darren's here. Hurry!"

A rustling comes from Tyler's bedroom, but it's Ray who comes out of the hall, jiggling his keys in his hand.

"Coffee's in the kitchen." I try to sound casual, but my voice cracks.

Ray glances out the window and spots Heather's SUV. "Where's Tyler going?" His eyes challenge me.

"They've planned this for weeks." I sip my coffee. "They're going to the natural history museum."

"It's still open?"

I nod. "Volunteers."

His face can't hide his concern. He lowers his voice. "You heard the news?"

"Of course," I whisper. "It came over my phone."

"Then why on earth are you letting him go?"

"Because it's something for him to do. And Heather's willing to take them. And it's indoors."

He shakes his head. "I'm late. I'd better go."

He leans in and kisses me. I taste fear on his lips. He pulls away.

"What're you doing today?" His voice is a mix of anxiety and a pretense of sounding casual.

"Getting groceries. Stocking up." I shrug. "Anything you want?"

"Tyler's inhalers. And if they have peanut butter, get extra for him, even if they're overcharging. You taking Callie?"

I nod. "Better than leaving her here alone."

"Be careful," he says, his voice as raw as a scraped knee.

I see a flicker in his eyes and a hesitation. He wants to kiss me again, I guess, but doesn't want to make the moment too dramatic. He backs away, his eyes reluctant, and heads for the rear door.

"Tyler!" I shout again.

Callie comes out with her brother. She struggles to slip Tyler's backpack over his shoulder while he's moving. He coughs.

"Do you have your puffer?" I ask him.

He pulls the inhaler out of his pocket to show me.

"Good."

He coughs again. Please not another cold. This is not the time.

"Cover your mouth," I say, and rub his head.

Callie opens the door. Before Tyler can rush out, I grab him and give him a hug. I want to hold him forever.

"Mom, he's late," Callie says.

I make myself release him, and he rushes out to the car. Callie gives me a look like I'm crazy. We stand in the doorway and watch as Tyler gets in the backseat with Darren. Tyler produces a slime dancer from his pocket and wiggles it in front of Darren. Both boys laugh. I hate that thing, but it almost makes me smile.

Heather shoots me a nervous glance as she pulls away from the curb.

The Spore, later

The spore's world is turned upside down as he goes sliding, free-falling, against his will, tumbling over and over, down, down.

Until he stops.

He is disoriented.

He tries to get his bearings, but soon others like him come rolling in, bumping him, tossing him up and over. Finally he settles in the middle of many more like himself.

Sadness sets in as the spore realizes his freedom is gone. He is aware that he is no longer alone with endless possibilities.

But a thought occurs to him. Maybe if he joins forces with the others, then together they will find some purpose. It must be possible. He reaches out to the neighbor to his left.

Hello, friend.

But the neighbor hisses back. No real communication, just a bump that sends him rolling on top of the neighbor to his right, then bouncing over him. He lands and settles in a new spot. But quickly he is pushed away and up. He floats higher and bounces down.

The little spore is too dizzy to do anything but try to gather himself.

Out of the silence, someone near him communicates.

Relax. We're just like you.

The spore tries to turn himself to face this new neighbor but can't.

Why are we here? the spore asks.

You mean you don't know?

Barbara Woodland, home, 9:15 a.m.

As I stand beside Callie at the door and we watch Tyler leave, I feel my legs shaking uncontrollably. I will them to stop, but it's not working.

"What's the matter?" Callie asks as I shut the door.

I avoid her eyes. "Why can't your brother ever be on time?"

I walk through the living room to the kitchen to give myself some space, but she follows.

"The museum will still be there, Mom," she says. "Even if they're ten minutes late."

"It's not nice to make people wait."

I step into the laundry room off the kitchen and open the dryer.

"You're just scared," Callie says.

Her eyes flash at me. I see my own fear reflected in her features, and it frightens me more.

I look at her. "What do you know?"

I realize I've barked it out, but it's too late to take it back. She folds her arms and says nothing—her idea of punishment for withholding information? Then she speaks.

"I've heard they have . . . spores."

A shiver goes up the back of my neck at hearing that word. I dump the clothing from the dryer into the basket.

"Don't say that, Callie."

"Why? Because it's not true? Isn't that what they're calling them?"

"That doesn't mean you have to repeat it."

The laundry feels like it weighs a hundred pounds. I carry it out of the kitchen, into the hall, to my bedroom. She stays on my heels. I sort the clothing into drawers and wonder if we will live long enough to wear these socks again. Callie flops onto our king-size bed, looking very small.

"You can't hide this from me," she says. "I'll read about it on the Pages."

I clutch a pair of socks in my hand, then drop them back in the basket. I turn to see Callie staring up at the ceiling. I see a vulnerable girl, a daughter, my daughter, and I find the mother in me to soothe her. I sit on the edge of the bed and stroke her baby-fine hair.

"What do you know?" I ask, this time softly.

"That the Pac Rim is moving their ships closer to the coast. Aircraft carriers."

"But they're not here yet."

"No, but they say they've got the spores and they're going to fly jets that will shoot missiles in the air with them. At us."

"They said that months ago. And it didn't happen." I continue to stroke her hair.

She sits up. "Infectious, engineered spores. If they get into our lungs, they'll kill us. If they get on our skin, they'll be absorbed. We'll die."

I've heard it too. Not instant death, but death just the same. I pull her sleeve off her shoulder, exposing her upper arm. I point to a red mark there.

"You see that?" I say. "That will protect you."

"Yeah, from the flu."

"That's just what they told you, to avoid panic. But it's a vaccine to protect you against the spores."

She looks down at her arm, staring at the small red spot. "Vaccine? For the spores?"

We both stare at the mark.

A month ago, her upper arm was perfect. Just smooth

skin. We were standing in a long line at what used to be the high school gymnasium. It was just before the schools closed. What parent wanted to risk having their kids in school with the war escalating? It seems like so long ago, but it's been a little over a year since the Pac Rim fought with our ships in the Pacific Ocean, causing a great loss of life and riddling the coastline with broken ships from both sides. Ordnance and debris, even body parts washed ashore. Barbed-wire fences were erected to close off the beaches, to protect people from the spilled chemicals and potential bombbots. It pained me to see it. Ray and I stood there with other onlookers, remembering the pale yellow sand and blue water just months before. Now that sand was stained black from the oil of the corpses of the death ships.

And why? Same as most wars—greed.

Of course I cried then. But in the school gym, I was relieved that Callie would get the vaccine. Tyler had already gotten his a few days before, so it was just the two of us, waiting. There were rumors that they might run out, so we arrived there at five a.m. Callie couldn't understand why we were going to so much trouble for a flu shot. When she made the head of the line, hours later, and that needle gun was pressed to her arm, I had to turn my head to hide my face. My intense relief would have alerted her that this was not about the flu.

Back in the bedroom, I try to pull Callie's shirt back over her shoulder, to cover her vaccination scar. But she stops me.

"It's still red," she says.

"They did that on purpose. To prove you're protected," I say.

"I hate it," she says, frowning at the mark. "It's ugly."
She rubs it.

I stop her and take her hand. "No, honey. It could save your life someday."

"From the spores?"

"People will know you're not infected, not a danger to them."

She processes that. And then a worried look comes over her face. "But you didn't get the vaccine. Or Daddy."

"We didn't need it. The government's just worried about the frail—the very young and the very old. Daddy and I are strong and healthy. We'll be fine."

I think back on the day we learned about the vaccination shortage. Ray's connections could have gotten us the shot. I tried to convince him. Tried to get him to see. What good will it be for our kids to live if we're gone? I asked him. Where will they go? Our parents aren't alive. I begged him. The holo-stars, politicians, and other bigwigs were able to get the vaccine. Everyone knew about the black market. But he was adamant. He wasn't going to push in line, wasn't going to take a vaccine away from a senior or a child.

Great. So we're left with our morals. But what else?

The Spore, later

It's hot. Steamy.

The spore is waiting for his neighbor to explain their

purpose when suddenly, more spores are sent in. He drifts backward.

Wait. Tell me the answer.

But it's too late; he is rolling and bouncing over grumpy, silent spores.

The spore feels like he is suffocating.

This seems wrong! he shouts. What kind of life is this?

Look out! someone says. And more come pouring in. They land on the spore and then bounce up and away to land on someone else.

The spore tries to scream.

Nothing comes out.

His new neighbor tells him not to try.

What do you know?

I know we have a purpose.

A purpose? Good. That's good. Do you know what it is?

No. I just know we have one.

What are you called? What am I called?

We're called infectious bacterial spores.

Spores . . . I have a name. Spore.

Barbara Woodland, in the car, 10:00 a.m.

I grip the steering wheel as I back out of the driveway, using the rearview camera. Callie's cherry-scented body oil fills the car. Our car beeps, signaling that a pedestrian is near.

Callie turns to look. "It's Michael."

"From down the street?"

She nods. He stands on the sidewalk and waits for me to back out. Good-looking boy. I see how he smiles at Callie. She doesn't flirt back, just a simple wave. She's a good kid, smarter than her years, and resilient.

Would she be able to handle taking care of Tyler? All those questions, day by day, hour by hour, when you're raising a child. Is this food safe for him? Is that man he's talking to harmless? Is he sick again? The scenarios Ray talked about, and some I've read about, are dismal. Kids shut out of their homes, their houses contaminated with spore residue . . . living on the streets or in the homes of strangers. Would Callie know how to find safe shelter? Food? Water?

Life is predicted to be very different if these Spore Wars come to pass. The buzz isn't in the news but underground, via flyers and secret Pages on the computer. Some people say the doomsayers are just nuts, proclaiming the end of the world. But it's never looked more like the end was this close.

I want to tell Callie. I want to discuss with her what might happen, what action she might take. But it's impossible to predict. We could hide cash, but the banks have limited how much you can withdraw. If only we had relatives, someone old enough to have gotten the vaccine, she could live with them. Just our luck that both Ray and I have lost our parents.

"Mom? You passed the post office."

She's right. I have to drive another block to find a parking spot. When we reach the office, the line is out the door.

"Why is it so crowded?" Callie asks.

People are picking up their mail today because they're

probably planning on staying indoors after this. I long for the day, before the war escalated, when packages were delivered once a week. All our bills are electronic now, not like when I was a kid, but back then no one had figured out how to materialize a pair of shoes that way. Not yet.

"Never mind," I say. "We'll come back when it's not so busy."

But I know we'll probably be holed up inside our home like the rest of them. Like prisoners. Or timid rabbits, our red noses twitching. For how long? A week? A month?

We head off to a pharmacy to get the list of supplies I carefully composed: smart bandages, spray antiseptic, a prescription for penicillin, inhalers for Tyler. Who knows when they'll run out? But the place is shuttered and the door's electronic sign reads: CLOSED. PERMANENTLY.

"How can they close?" Callie asks. "Just like that? They were open last week."

The steel shutters hide and protect any supplies that might still be sitting on the shelves. Did the people who worked here get so scared they just took off? Left everything behind? To go where? Travel is restricted. Or were they afraid of mobs desperate for medical supplies, pulling everything off the shelves without paying? Or worse, robbing them at gunpoint?

"Maybe they weren't doing good business. Like a lot of places today," I say.

The next stop on my list is the home supply store. We stand in a long line, our cart stuffed with batteries, duct tape, and some tarp. I jealously eye people with lumber in their carts. Ray only wanted the batteries. He'll probably roll his eyes at me for the tarp, saying it won't do any good. But I decided to go for it. Maybe we'll want it to cover the windows. Maybe he'll end up thanking me.

I wouldn't have been able to fit any lumber in our SUV anyway. Those people probably have trucks.

"Look, Mom." Callie picks up a toy fan in the shape of a hedgehog.

She turns it on and it blows her long hair. She's in love with something she didn't know existed a minute ago.

"Put it back." Another day, I would have said yes. But I am not in a frivolous mood.

She does a fake pout and puts it on the shelf carelessly, like she really never wanted it in the first place. It falls over on its side, as if wounded by rejection.

Outside the store, Callie rolls the cart to our SUV while I get out my keys. I open up the back hatch and set my purse inside to move aside a box of water bottles and Tyler's baseball bat. I hear a voice.

I turn to see a man approaching Callie with a smile. He's in his twenties, lanky, wearing a hoodie. Seems warm for this weather.

"I'll give you a hand with that," he says as he lifts a bag of tape and batteries out of the cart she's holding.

He's too close to her. I step toward him.

"Don't bother," I said. "We can manage."

He turns to me. "Okay, ma'am."

He drops the bag into my outstretched hands and it almost slips from my grip. Then, before I realize what's happening, he reaches over and snatches my purse from the back of the car.

"No!" I shout. "Stop!"

He runs. I drop the bag and chase him.

"Mom, don't!" Callie yells.

I am not listening. I am fueled by some anger that has been building in me. He is not going to take my wallet, my ID, my money, my credit cards, my phone with all my information. Hours at the gym pay off as I catch up to him and grab him by the neck of his hoodie. I yank and he falls backward. We both tumble to the ground. Callie runs up, holding the baseball bat like a weapon.

He looks at her and then at me as we engage in a tug-of-war over my purse. He reaches inside with his free hand and grabs my cell phone.

"Drop it," I say.

Callie stands over him, bat ready to strike. He can't be thinking he'll get away with taking anything at this point. I see the anger of defeat in his dark eyes and he takes that anger and smashes my phone, facedown, against the asphalt.

"There's your precious phone," he says as he scrambles to his feet and runs away.

Callie hesitates for a moment, as if she's going to give chase, but then kneels down next to me, dropping the bat. She puts her arms around my neck.

"It's all right, Mom, you're okay."

I feel my face. It's wet. I examine my fingers for blood but realize that tears are streaming down my cheeks.

The Spore, later

The walls of the spore's container shake. He asks his friend, What is happening?

The friend warns him. *Hold on.*

The spore pushes up close to his friend, hoping they will not be separated.

Their world spins so hard the two end up on opposite sides. The spore is pushed against one wall. He's sure he'll be crushed to nothing when the spinning stops, just a thin, flat wisp of himself. A high-pitched sound wails until it pierces his being. He wonders if the other spores are screaming, and then he recalls that they cannot scream. It is just sheer terror that is communicated. It emanates from him as well.

Finally, the spinning slows until it comes to a stop. The spore is dizzy. He waits for the feeling to pass and then glances around.

Where is my friend?

Then he sees him, by the wall, to his left. He rolls over to him.

Are you all right?

His answer is not a good one: sadness.

My time is done, he says. *I did not pass the test.*

Hang on, my friend. You must rest. You'll be all right in a moment.

You made it. You will go on. But you must do something for me.
Anything.
You must carry on for me. You will go on the mission, as I would
have.
What is our mission?
You must spread our essence.
How?
You will meet your destiny.
When?
Soon.
But how will I know?
You will know.

Barbara Woodland, in the car, 11:20 a.m.

Callie rides in silence as I drive through the city. It all has a
different feel than yesterday, as if our windows were now
tinted with a yellow filter, scratched and faded. Everybody
on the street seems to be focused on their survival. Like
ants they are hunting, gathering, building, running scared.

The grocery store is a mile away. I take a back route
to save time, a route I haven't used for months. There are
closer stores that we usually go to, but they're too small,
and at this point, they'll be out of most everything. How
much food do we need to have in our house? Enough to last
a month? Longer? What if the electricity goes out? Should
I not count on freezer food?

"Look, Mom," Callie says.

She points to the oddest sight I can think of at this dire moment: a miniature golf course. Complete with purple turrets, gold flags with blue stars, all meant to catch your eye and your dollars. And for a moment, I am seduced by the yellow windmills, big wooden lollipops, a castle covered with diamonds.

"When did they put that in?" I ask.

"Last year. Can we go?" she asks.

What a crazy idea. Kids. They have this ability to forget the serious concerns of life, the questions about how to prepare for tomorrow, because they live so much in the present. They haven't experienced tomorrow's disappointments.

"I doubt it's open."

"It is. I see, the gate is open." Her voice is now almost squeaking.

"We really should hit the store and go home." I step on the gas.

"Just for a little while. Please."

I look around, pretending to be clueless. "We've already passed it." I shrug.

"Please. Can't we go back?"

I don't want either of us outside more than we have to be. But I don't want to scare her either. I glance over at her sitting beside me, and I don't see a sixteen-year-old edging closer to becoming a responsible adult. I see a five-year-old with chubby cheeks and big eyes, begging me to stop at the carnival to ride the teacups that will spin her until she is dizzy.

I make a U-turn in the middle of the road and she rewards me with a toothy grin.

As we pull into the parking lot, the golf place doesn't seem quite right. It seems ..... empty.

"There's no one here," I say.

"Good. Then we'll have it all to ourselves."

I get out of the SUV and notice how stiff I am. Then I remember the fight with the thief. I look down and see that my clothes are filthy from the scuffle. I brush them off as best I can, then hide my purse under the seat, taking only my wallet. Callie tosses her purse over her shoulder and runs toward the open gate.

"Callie, wait up."

I join her at the check-in booth just inside the entrance. No one is there. She reaches over the counter and grabs a golf club.

"Here, this one's yours," she says as she hands me one of the longer clubs.

"I don't know about this."

It seems wrong. Like stealing. I wonder if we should leave some money on the counter. Callie gets a shorter club for herself and two golf balls. And a scoring paper with a short pencil.

"Bet you a dollar I beat you," she says with a gleam in her eyes.

We head to the first hole, a windmill. I glance around and notice that the electronic frills are not functioning, of course. But the retro parts, the ones powered by wind or weights, like this windmill, are still good as ever. Callie puts down her ball and swings. It goes right through the moving blades of the windmill and into the circle of green behind it. The ball makes a hollow, high sound as it rolls around the inside of the cup.

"Hole in one!" she says, doing a little victory dance.

She's forgotten about everything except this game. It makes me smile.

The Spore, later

The spore is transferred out of the container by a kind of sieve that only lifts the ones who are still round and whole. As it lifts him higher, he sees his friend through the floor below. The friend lies on the bottom of the container, still and cold.

Goodbye, friend.

The spore thinks about dying and is grateful it didn't happen to him.

Is that bad?

He remembers what his friend said and realizes he can be good. He can make it up to him by fulfilling the promise. The little spore readies himself.

He is moved to another canister with the other spores that survived the test. A lid is clamped down and their canister is put into another container, one that blocks out all light. He doesn't mind; he can sense the others. There is a lot of noise, clanking and banging, as the canister is turned on its side. And then there is quiet. The spores are weightless, bouncing and floating in their container.

The spore hears the thoughts of the other spores. They speak of flying to their destinations. They are euphoric.

Barbara Woodland, Golden Castle Miniature Golf Course, 12:15 p.m.

Callie tees up her ball on the eighth hole. I watch as she grips her club, then looks to the goal, a hole past a little culvert that should be a stream. But of course, there is no water. Probably hasn't been water flowing here for months. I wonder if the owners decided to shut down some time ago or if it was just the employees today who ran, leaving the place open. Are we utter fools to be outside?

It is the eighth hole. Only one more to go. She hits her ball and it flies nicely over the dry stream, right to the little patch of fake grass, near the hole. Her aim is good; she learned that from Ray. She's always accurate on the gun range too.

Will he be pleased and proud to hear about this? Or angry that we did something so crazy?

"Your turn, Mom."

I have to try. I have to finish, so I might as well get it over with. Before I hit the ball, I see some boys coming onto the course. They're at the first hole, clubs in their hands. Older teens, rough-looking, with fierce tattoos, multiple piercings. And no one else around.

I hit the ball and it lands in the dry creek.

"Bad shot," Callie says.

We walk over to it and stare at the ball. "You can't hit it out of there," she says.

"It's okay," I say. "You just play."

"Come on, Mom, we're almost done. Your score isn't that bad. You might win."

She pulls out my ball and sets it on the circle of green.

"Hey, isn't that cheating?" a boy's voice says.

We turn and see the two teen boys standing at our tee, leaning on their clubs.

"What's it to you?" Callie asks.

The boys react, surprised at Callie's spunk.

"We're done here," I say, partly to her, partly to them. I give her a look I hope communicates not to say anything more, that I'm afraid, that we need to leave.

The taller boy approaches. "Don't rush off." He grins, displaying metal skulls in both front teeth. "We want to see how you swing."

I see Callie's body tense. She grips her club with both hands. I know her instinct is to confront them. But nothing good can come of that.

"It's late. We have to get to the store," I say to Callie, my eyes burning the message to her like a laser writing out *please just shut up and go.*

She looks at me and drops her club on the turf.

"We're outta here," she says.

We turn and walk. We have to pass them to leave. Will they let us go? Will they reach out and grab us? Please let us get out of here.

We walk past them, and I feel their eyes burning into our backs. We cannot run, or we will become prey. I'm afraid to look at Callie. I look straight ahead, and in my peripheral vision, I see her doing the same. We walk as fast as we can without seeming to be fleeing.

Behind us, the boys talk to each other. Probably discussing their plan. I double my pace and Callie does the same. It is a grueling walk past the gingerbread house, the giant lollipops. As we pass the giant pandas at the fifth hole, they seem to be laughing at us. Finally, we reach the windmill.

The gate that was open before, the one at the entrance by the booth, is now closed. Did they lock it? Did it lock automatically when they closed it? Is there no way out? I can't climb that chain-link gate. Callie could. I will make her climb.

I hear the footsteps of the boys now. They are not running but walking toward us with determined, steady steps. I pull my keys out of my pocket.

Callie reaches the gate and pushes it. It doesn't open.

"It's locked," she whispers.

I look around her and see the latch she missed. I lift it. "Go."

We push open the gate and rush through. Our SUV is ten long yards ahead. We run as fast as we can. I click my remote and the doors unlock. The boys chase us; they are too close, on our heels. Callie gets in her side, I get in mine and I lock all the doors.

They bang on the windows.

"Hey!" they scream.

I start the engine.

"Look!" Callie says.

Out the window, one of the boys holds up Callie's purse.

"My purse. I left it."

I have two seconds to evaluate the boy, looking into his eyes. I glance over at the other one's eyes. I don't like what I see. Hardness. Deception. A trap.

"Never mind," I say.

"But they came to return my purse."

I go in reverse, and the boys back away from the car, their arms in the air, their faces angry.

"It's a ruse. They're not going to give anything back."

The boys are screaming and swearing now. They turn Callie's purse upside down, spilling the contents over the asphalt. Out come her wallet, her phone, lipstick, coins, and, of course, tampons, which sends them howling with laughter.

They pocket Callie's phone and the money and stomp on the other items with their boots. I see this in the rearview mirror as I drive off.

When I glance at Callie, her face registers shock.

"How could they?" she says.

"They're not like you."

A hard lesson, but a necessary one.

"There're bad people everywhere, especially now," I say. "Don't trust anyone."

❋ ❋ ❋

Inside the grocery store, we walk the aisles without speaking. The shelves are a mess. Most of the food is already gone. What's left are the broken, the dented, the opened containers. We shuffle through those in hopes of finding something good.

"Here's one that's just smashed on the outside," Callie says, holding up a cereal box. "The bag inside is okay."

I nod and she tosses it in our cart. The produce aisle is barren, but I spot a glimpse of brightness in a stack of crates on the floor. I bend down and push aside the empty box on top to reveal the contents of the bottom crate: one orange. As glorious as a new sun breaking in the east. Callie smiles. It's more than a piece of fruit; it's a happy omen. I place our treasure gently in the cart and glance at the price tag over the depleted bin.

"At least the prices aren't crazy," I say.

Ray is worried they might start gouging, like the smaller stores have. But they haven't. Someone, somewhere in the corporate office has a soul.

The checkout machines have handwritten Cash Only signs. How I miss real people taking my money.

Callie's purse. Thank goodness we never gave her a credit card. We'll have to think later about what information might have been on her phone. Our address? I realize neither of us has a working phone. We'll go right home now. We'll talk it over with Ray tonight, what we should do. He's smart; he invented the handlite, didn't he? Powered by our own pulse. And then his "secret" project. The one he can't even tell me about.

"Mom? It's done."

She points to the receipt coming out of the machine. I take it, and she picks up the bags and we head for the exit.

The Spore, 40,000 feet above sea level over the West Coast, 1:30 p.m.

The spore senses that they are close. Soon he will be meeting the woman who is his destiny. A sudden thrust and he feels the speed as he pierces the air. The spores are thrown to the back wall, crammed together.

Excited.

Pressure builds; a high-pitched sound cracks the air until their container breaks apart and the pieces fall away. The spore sees light and sky and then, below, trees. They separate, each spore, falling freely. He is alone once more. Floating . . . down.

Barbara Woodland, Ralph's Grocery Store, 1:30 p.m.

Callie and I stand at the door, looking outside, scanning the parking lot for trouble. Just shoppers carrying their groceries to their cars.

"It's okay," I say. "We're safe. Everything bad that was going to happen has happened."

Callie nods. We step outside.

"What are you going to make for dinner?" she asks.

"How about spaghetti? Would you like that?"

She smiles. We hear a strange sound above us. It is like a muffled pop, like a champagne bottle being uncorked, only louder and farther away. We look up and see what appear to be snowflakes falling.

In Southern California?

I turn around. They are coming down from the sky, everywhere. In my panic, I trip on a planter curb in the parking lot. I fall and my groceries spill and scatter. The orange rolls away.

"Mom!" Callie turns to me and drops her bag.

"Run!" I shout. "I'll be right behind you!"

I toss the keys to her. She catches them deftly and runs. I scramble to my feet and follow.

Callie races to our car at the end of the row. I run after her. She turns back to check on me and I motion for her to keep going.

"Don't stop."

Others in the parking lot are doing the same. Running for their lives. I almost bump into an old woman heading in the opposite direction. Up ahead, Callie has opened the door.

She climbs into the backseat and turns, holding out a hand to me. I run and put my foot on the step on the side of the SUV.

"We made it," she says.

I smile and give her my left hand to pull me in. As she grabs it, we both look at my arm as a single spore floats down and lands on my skin.

The Spore, now

He made it.

He found her, and she is beautiful. They are together.

Burrowing into her skin, he feels complete, his essence merging with hers.

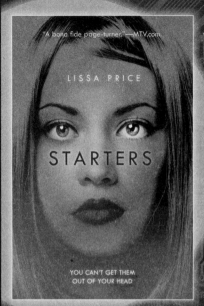